THE LIAHONA EFFECT

This novel is a work of fiction. Any references to real events, businesses, organizations, and political figures are intended to give the story a sense of reality and authenticity. Any resemblance to actual private persons, living or dead, is entirely coincidental.

The Liahona Effect

Copyright © 2017-2019 by Keith Katsikas

All rights reserved.

Published by TopShelf Publishing
An imprint of TopShelf Authors & Books, LLC
www.topshelfmagazine.net

Book design by Keith Katsikas
Cover design by Keith Katsikas

Trade Paperback Edition
September 2019

ISBN: 978-1-946865-17-5

Our books may be purchased in any quantities through
Baker & Taylor and INGRAM

THE LIAHONA EFFECT

KEITH KATSIKAS · EFFECT

www.KeithKatsikas.com
www.TopShelfPub.com

This book is dedicated to my
amazing family. I swear, I may
be the luckiest man alive.

I Love You!

ACKNOWLEDGEMENTS

There are so many people who have inspired and helped me. First and foremost, my wife, who stands behind me in all my crazy ventures; my uncle Donald, who has been excited about this story since its conception and whose help has benefitted me in ways he may never realize; my dear friend, Jon Land, who has helped my both personally and professionally over the years; Rosemary and Patrice, two delightful friends who happen to be world-class editors and whom I credit as the reason why this book has no embarrassing errors; James Rollins, Allan Leverone, Steve Berry, and Jon Land (again) for reading this book and sharing their sincere feedback and most humbling praises; and last but certainly not least, God, for giving me this wonderfully fun talent.

PROLOGUE

June 27th, 1844

There is that one moment in our lives that changes everything. For the young Joseph Smith, that moment was now, though sadly, he would not live to look back on it.

He huddled over a small desk in the corner of the warden's tiny second-floor bedroom, writing. His full concentration was fixed on the task before him. For Joseph, there was nothing in the world more important than what he was doing right here, right now.

His brother Hyrum nervously swayed in the hand-hewn oak rocking chair that occupied the far corner of the room, while two of Joseph and Hyrum's closest friends, who had stuck close by them during this difficult time, sat on the bed, feet away, attempting to lighten the mood with small talk.

But Joseph heard none of it. He just wrote, completely blocking out the world around him. He'd write a few lines, then tear it up. He'd write some more, and tear it again. He did this for what felt like an eternity before finally sitting back and taking in a deep, accomplished breath.

It's done.

The Disciples had broken contact with him years ago and for the first time in decades, Joseph genuinely feared that The Secret—a secret that The Disciples had entrusted in him to protect at any and all cost—was about to become exposed.

He could not—he *would* not—allow that to happen.

Beads of sweat gathered on his brow as the door at the bottom of the stairway crashed open.

"Where's Joe?" a man bellowed as a small army of male voices began shouting, "Give him to us!" and "Joe's a dead man!"

Joseph knew in his heart—regardless of reassurances that he and his men would be protected—that this day would come. Ever since the Governor issued Missouri Executive Order 44— known to many simply as the Mormon Extermination Order— a militia calling themselves the Carthage Greys had been calling for his death. These monsters were not about to stop until they bathed in Joseph Smith's blood.

Now, it would seem, death had caught up with him.

Without hesitation, the relentless hoof-like stampede tromped up the staircase along with what could only be described as devilish screams and howls.

Joseph gazed at the simple, yet carefully crafted message. It was exactly as The Disciples had instructed. He rolled it tightly in his hands and glanced over at his dearest friend and personal secretary, Brother Willard.

"Please," Joseph said with a calm authority that only he had. "Promise me, at all cost, you will get this to Emma."

Joseph placed the rolled parchment in his friend's sweaty palms and smiled with confidence. He wasn't stupid. He knew what was coming. However, he was prepared for it. He was willing to make the ultimate sacrifice to protect The Secret. "Remember what I told you, Willard." Tears formed in his eyes as he took his dear friend in his arms for one final embrace. "You do remember, don't you? It was prophecy."

Willard nodded. Tears marking trails down his cheeks.

"Not a hair of your head will be harmed."

The crack of gunfire seized the room, splitting the door and filling the tiny space with the pungent stench of gunpowder, as a bullet came smashing through. Hyrum stood there a moment, holding his cheek in shock as blood began pouring out of his face. "I'm a dead man," he cried, as he collapsed to the floor. The mob kicked and ripped their way through the splintered door pulling it clean off its hinges.

Joseph ran to his brother's side and fell to his knees. He grabbed Hyrum and cradled his lifeless body in his arms.

"No!" he shouted. As much as he prepared for this day, nothing could stop the pain of watching his elder brother die. But he knew this was only the beginning. Their eternity was just about to commence. He prayed at that moment that his efforts to protect The Secret would be fruitful. If not, everything he had sacrificed so much for would be lost.

In the chaos that followed, time slowed.

Then froze.

So this is it, Joseph thought. *This is how it ends. Lord, protect my dear Emma. May your Spirit keep her warm this day.*

Willard succumbed to the agonizing tears that had been swelling in his soul as he watched his dear friend and Prophet rise up from the floor and stand resolute. He could tell the Prophet's heart was broken; however, his spirit and will were as determined as he had ever seen them.

Several Carthage Greys, their faces smeared with gray paint and foul mud and their eyes ablaze with killer-lust, piled into the tiny room. Another shot rang out, smashing into the ceiling above Joseph's head, sending a plume of plaster dust raining over him. He wiped the plaster and tears from his eyes and gave Willard a solemn nod.

Without hesitation Joseph turned and ran for the window, taking the attention and gunfire away from Willard—away from the message held firmly in his grasp.

Willard watched in horror as bullets riddled Joseph's body.

The sight of The Prophet of the Restored Church being murdered before my eyes, Willard thought, *may actually be more painful than being shot and killed myself.*

The shots were relentless, striking Joseph in the back—

Bang! Bang! Bang!

—sending his body crashing out the second story window, landing with a bone-crushing thud on the packed earth below.

1

Present Day

Jonathan Batnaz was the senior apostle and first counselor to the president of The Church of Jesus Christ of Latter-day Saints, renowned around the world for his old-school charm, warm spirit, and quick-witted humor, which made everyone around him smile. Today, however, he wasn't feeling much like that man.

Batnaz somberly made his way through row after row of pristinely kept graves, each decorated with a large, yet simple monument, pausing briefly to pay his respects at each one.

The afternoon heat was scorching, the air sticky, hellishly humid, and yet the canopy of flowering trees and tall shrubberies enveloping the tranquil space made walking somewhat more tolerable.

It was a quaint cemetery if one could call such a place quaint, and yet he did. It lay nestled on a tiny island, not far from where he was raised, and no matter how difficult life became, no matter how busy he got or how far away life took him, he always returned to pay respects. It was the least he could do for family. But on this day, he was there for someone extra special. The pain was still very fresh.

As Jonathan Batnaz stumbled up a small grassy hill, towards a massive granite obelisk towering high above his head, his smartphone vibrated in his breast pocket.

Tears welled in his eyes as he gazed upon the stone.

It had been just days. Of all the losses in his life, this one was the most difficult for him. This one cut really deep.

He brought the phone to his ear, his attention still fixed on the monument. "Batnaz," he answered, wiping his eyes.

The man on the line was his dear friend and Second Counselor to the Prophet, Jacob Bethsaida. "The Prophet..." Jacob was clearly out of breath, as if he'd been running.

"What is it?" Batnaz questioned.

The line was silent.

Something was very wrong.

"Speak to me, Jacob."

"Drop everything, Jon. Come quick!"

Before Batnaz could respond, the line went dead.

He gazed up at the monument, a sudden look of certainty in his eyes, and he laid his hands upon the cool, smooth surface of the obelisk. "The time has come, my love."

He had waited decades for this day, and now it was here. He turned and stormed back toward the entrance of the cemetery, where a large helicopter sat idle, awaiting his return.

2

"And there it is," I say to myself, as I gaze out one of the suite's dozen panoramic windows, each showcasing its own once-in-a-lifetime, breathtaking view.

We had planned this trip for years—two, to be exact.

We scrimped.

We saved.

We sacrificed more than either of us may choose to admit.

Now here we are, enjoying the infant moments of a belated honeymoon, smack dab in the heart of Paris, France.

The city of love.

The sun's just beginning to set.

Drifting slowly beneath the distant horizon.

Paris's elegant, yet bold splashes of orange, green and purple, blending with that calico sky, create a brilliant masterpiece that can only be painted by the hand of God.

Crystal sets down all but one tiny bag on the sofa as we enter the room, shoots me a suggestive glare, and without a word, disappears down the hall and into the bathroom. I'm telling you, this place is fantastic; even better than it appears online. I mean, it's like a Rococo Revival palace in here. There is nothing in this place that says hotel. From the 16th-century Victorian high back upholstered sofas—that's right, there are actually two luxurious sofas—to the three 18th century Louis XV style chairs, the vaulted 30-foot-high ceilings, and the oversized mahogany cabinets arranged meticulously with an assortment of fine china and gold cutlery. This place could just possibly be *too* good.

We arrived early this morning. The sun hadn't quite crested the horizon yet. Can't tell you how the flight was; Crystal insisted that I take a double-dose of anxiety medication, so, let's say, I don't remember much. We spent the bulk of the day sightseeing, shopping, eating; my God, the food, I've never experienced anything like it. I swear, French people in America are not French. No, the *real* stuff is right out that window. Down there, on the corner of that second to last gold-lit street. One of the windows to my right is open just enough to allow the sweet scent of Café Liégeois and Spiced Crème Brûlée to bleed in. I place my hands on my belly and smile, then return my gaze upward.

Wow! From here, the Eiffel Tower is like nothing I have ever experienced. Between you and me, the greatest pictures ever taken of that thing don't come close to serving justice. Its magnificent amber glow ignites the sky like a beacon of hope and glory in a world that's getting darker by the hour.

I loosen my necktie and collar and make my way toward the bedroom—the living room lights fading to an ambient glow as I leave that room and increase slightly as I enter the hallway. The visual effect was strange at first but impressive.

This is awesome!

As I approach the bedroom, I catch my reflection in the polished white marble covering the hallway wall opposite of the bathroom. I pause for a moment to adjust my hair. It's hard to believe how far I have come in just two years. From being a 38-year-old bachelor, teaching at Harvard School of Divinity, to stopping a global terror threat that nearly destroyed the Catholic Church, to staring at my reflection in the polished stone of a palace, smack-dab at the heart of Paris, married to the most amazing woman I have ever known.

Sure, my hair may be turning somewhat gray around the edges—okay, a lot—but at least it's all still there, and those lines in my forehead and around my coffee-brown eyes, I think they may be getting lighter. It's been a really great year.

I undo my belt and start loosening my khakis when I catch something out of the corner of my eye. It's Crystal's reflection. I turn toward the bathroom and peek inside. She's standing, gazing into a massive, gold-framed mirror. Her crystal-blue eyes, sparkling in the golden sheen of the spalike space, meet with mine in the mirror. She doesn't say a word. Not even a smile. It's a look I've never seen in her before. Suddenly, her blouse slips off her shoulders, catching the air and floating like a feather and resting by her beautiful bare feet. My heart flutters, then begins to race. It's at that point I realize my khakis are on the floor.

3

Batnaz shielded his eyes from the blinding sun peering through the cockpit glass as the helicopter slit holes through the endless cirrus streaks blanketing the Mediterranean Sea. They were en-route to Athens International Airport, where Batnaz parked Darlene, his one-of-a-kind prototype personal jet. Jacob made it pretty clear—

"Drop everything... come quickly!"

Darlene was the only way he would make it to The States as quickly as Jacob clearly wanted. Jacob had been in Palmyra, New York, overseeing renovations on the Welcome Center in preparation for the Hill Cumorah Pageant—a wonderful production put on by the church that plays out stories from the Book of Mormon in an all volunteer casted play, complete with lighting and pyrotechnic effects. Truly a sight to behold. Batnaz had not planned to make the trip to Palmyra. However, the urgency of Jacob's voice and the abruptness of his call made the change of plans a rather unavoidable one.

Buzzing on his hip caught Batnaz's attention. He grabbed his smartphone and gazed at the screen—

Get Home Now!

Immediately Batnaz started to feel something burn at his

soul. It was a burning he hadn't felt in many years. He swiped his finger across the screen and brought up President Jacob Bethsaida's number from his favorites. He pondered the message a second longer. *Could this be? No!* He pushed the thought from his mind and hit CONNECT.

"President Bethsaida," his friend answered.

"Jacob, it's Jon. Did you just receive a text?" His voice was perhaps a bit more distressed than he intended. For a man who didn't upset easily, something about this text dug at him.

"No," the president replied. "Is everything okay? Are you still on your way? Things are really getting bad here, Jon. I need your help immediately. I wish I could explain more, but—"

"Yes, I know," Batnaz interrupted, regaining his composure, "I'm on my way. However, I just received this text, telling me to go home." Batnaz paused, allowing the message to simmer.

"Who sent it?"

"I'm not sure, the sender's number is blocked."

"That's rather odd," the president agreed "However, your assistance is direly needed here, Jon."

Batnaz felt his pulse quicken as an earlier thought came rushing back to him. "You don't think this—"

"No, Jon. If it were *that*, we'd both know," the president interrupted. "You know that." The president's tone was very matter of fact. "I haven't felt *that* in a *very* long time."

The more Batnaz thought about it, the more he couldn't shake the feeling. It was a feeling he used to get often; however, lately it has become something far distant, to the point where he wasn't even sure if it was even him.

"Don't do it, Jon," Jacob said, clearly sensing his thoughts. "I need you here, right now!"

Batnaz knew the president was right.

"I can feel your desires, Jon. I always can. I also know that once it's stuck in your head, there's no stopping you."

Batnaz could hear his friend let out a distressed sigh.

"Please, Jon, at the very least, be careful."

Batnaz could hear his pleas, loud and clear. However, if there was even the slightest chance that this could be him, "I have to, Jacob. I *must* know!"

"If you're right, Jon. If *he* has made contact..."

"I know." Batnaz took in a deep breath through his nose, letting his lungs fill to capacity. "Don't worry about me."

"It's not you I'm worried about," the president sneered.

"Yes, I'm aware." Batnaz disconnected the call and took another look at the strange message.

Get Home Now!

Everything about it was screaming *no, you can't do this.* Yet, something else, something deep down in the darkest reaches of his soul was commanding that he do it anyway.

"There has been a change of plans," Batnaz told his pilot. "Please, take me home." As the chopper changed course, Batnaz considered the trials he would face in the coming hours.

President Jacob Bethsaida placed his phone into the front pocket of his slacks, and as he adjusted the sleeves of his pressed, jet-black Italian suit, he glanced at his watch.

4:00 PM.

The plan had already been set in motion, there was nothing he could do now to delay it. Batnaz needed to be in Palmyra before nightfall. He had less than six hours. He had faith that he would make it, but now that he's gone off on another one of his scavenger hunts...

Standing at the center of the freshly cut lawn in front of the Hill Cumorah Visitor's Center, Jacob studied the newly renovated facade and grinned. "Now that's impressive," he said to himself, as he admired the massive curved window, lit aglow in amber lights, the eleven-foot Christus standing graciously just beyond the spotless glass. This was a building one could easily be proud of. However, it paled in comparison to the production they were going to put on in the coming weeks. *Now that's something to tell the world about,* he thought.

Jacob walked around the right side of the building to where workers were finishing setting up the massive staging that scaled the hillside. There were only a few men remaining, picking up debris and checking the lighting and effects. This production was second to none, and the thousands of visitors who came to watch the show each night were never disappointed.

As he walked up the long, winding paved path that led up the hill to the thirty-five-foot golden monument of the Angel Moroni, Jacob considered the path that he and his fellow apostles had elected to follow to get them here. By all means, the secret they protected was worth any effort to protect.

But this?

He wondered if they were making a grave mistake.

He gazed up at the stately monument to the angel who brought forth the restoration of Christ's Church in these latter-days. The angel who visited Joseph Smith as a boy and provided the young Joseph with the Golden Plates, which Joseph translated to the *Book of Mormon*. This monument of the Angel Moroni represents this as the noble golden guardian stands upon a twenty-five-foot granite obelisk, holding the plates in his left arm while pointing to the heavens with the other.

Of all the wonderful places in this world, this very spot was one of President Jacob Bethsaida's most treasured.

"It's already done," he said, looking up at the angel as if pleading for forgiveness. "I know it was a foolish plan. But what can I do now? If Jon doesn't make it in time, I fear the worst."

4

Crystal stood in front of a massive floor to ceiling mirror, flanked in gold decorative columns, at the heart of the most spectacular spa-like bathroom she had ever laid eyes upon, much less ever stepped foot in, and she had been in some pretty fabulous spas back in America.

She kicked off her high-heels and let her bare feet relax on the smooth, heated marble floor tiles. The sensation sent chills up her spine. She had dreamt about slipping into that overflow bathtub since seeing it the night before.

So deep.

So luxurious.

She slowly walked to the tub, grabbed a packet of pink and white bath salts from a gold tray on the outer edge, and slowly poured the salts into her hand. The tub's crystal clear water cascading over its soft edges, like a silky smooth pool, beckoned to her to slip her tired-from-walking-all-day body inside. She let the salts filter through her fingers and fall into the steaming water. The delicious scent of vanilla creme swiftly filled the space as she watched them dissolve.

She took a deep breath in through her nose and felt a warmth come over her that she hadn't felt in quite some time. She smiled wide as she made her way back toward the mirror. Golden sconces, several on each wall, shone a soft amber glow, reflecting off the satin sheen of beige marble covering the walls, ceiling, and floor. In the soft shimmering light, the room looked as if wrapped in solid gold.

She stared at herself in the mirror a second, then noticed something out of the corner of her eye. It was Michael, peeking his head around the doorway. He was spying on her. She didn't react. She just stared back, as she undid the buttons on her silky white blouse, then let it slip down, exposing her slender, yet curvy shoulders and back. Her eyes never left his. She reached behind her and released the clasp of her strapless bra and allowed it to just fall. Her back was turned to the door, yet she knew that massive mirror wasn't keeping any move a secret from his spying eyes.

She had never stripped for Michael before. She had never stripped for anyone. She found it incredibly stimulating. She attempted to keep a straight face but felt her cheeks begin to lift as she struggled with the button of her tight black jeans. She quickly regained her composure, as the button popped free and she felt a bit of cool air caress her lower belly. It sent goosebumps up her middle. But she never once unlocked her gaze from his. She never felt so sexy. It could have been the setting. It may have been the city. But somehow, she knew it was something else. She was deeply in love, and her heart was swelling, almost as much as something else. It was then that she realized her eyes left his and were now drifting lower.

She slowly eased the black denim down her thighs and then, one leg at a time, exposed the delicate, yet athletic, complexion of her perfectly feminine frame. Returning her gaze to herself, she stared a moment. All that remain is a tiny pair of light pink panties—the ones that Michael loved so much—with the lacy trim and the see-through back. Even though she could no longer see him, she could feel his eyes on her. She pulled down her panties, staring at herself straight in the eyes, making sure she didn't bend her knees even a little as she lowered them down and then kicked them off her feet. Now she was really teasing. She turned and faced the bath. Its soft, flowing water beckoning her to come. She did not turn to face her husband. She slowly made her way to the tub and mindlessly eased herself into the warm flowing water and stretched out.

She gazed across the room at the lingerie she had purchased earlier at a fancy feminine shop downtown—Aubade Paris, she recalled. A friend of hers made her swear to stop and check out the store. "They sell things that are guaranteed to drive any man crazy," her friend had promised.

Crystal's mouth stretched into a face-consuming smile as she laid her head back and turned to face Michael, who was standing red-faced, hands gripping the door frame, khakis twisted about his ankles. She couldn't help herself. The corners of her lips peeled back exposing the perfectly white smile her parents had paid so much for and laughed.

Michael attempted to compose himself but instead found himself caught in his khakis, and in pure slapstick fashion, like Jack Tripper in one of Crystal's all time favorite sitcoms, bucked and twisted and fell head over heels. But her laughter quickly turned to horror as the sound of his head hitting the doorframe fired echoes throughout the stone bathroom.

She leaped from the tub, water splashing in all directions, flooding the floor and soaking the bath mat. Slipping and sliding across the heated tile, she somehow managed to make it to him in mere seconds without killing herself. She didn't even think, she just acted.

"Oh my God, Michael!" Her breath was winded and her eyes, wide with fear. He was just laying there. She grabbed his head in her wet hands, noticing a large egg forming on his right temple and cried, "Oh baby, please be okay." Her voice was shaky. This is not at all how she wanted this night to turn out. She was caressing his head, rubbing her thumbs on his face. "Wake up!" She went to stand up, needed to find the phone. "Where's the damn... I need to call—" That's when she felt something grabbing at her leg. She spun around to see Michael sit himself up, a smug look plastered across his face. He yanked her dripping wet, nude body down on top of him, right there on the hallway floor.

"You jerk!" She was laughing again.

They both were.

5

The helicopter landed in a large clearing surrounded by tall trees. It was the only way on and off the tiny tropical island. His was one of just three houses mingled amidst the luscious floral vegetation and sparkling bluish-green beaches of bamboo, palms, and sand.

Batnaz leaped from the helicopter, the blades whipping close overhead—*Woop, Woop, Woop*—and stormed up the long winding pathway to his house. As he approached the front door of the humble yet sophisticated cedar-shake cottage, he immediately saw something.

What in the world?

It was a wooden canister. It's rich mahogany color stood in sharp contrast against the soft beachy tones of his house.

It was strange indeed, about the size of a large flashlight.

Batnaz studied the canister carefully.

It was sculpted from inlaid mahogany and had six flat sides, making it a hexagon when turned just right. Strange symbols were engraved into each of its six sides, and it was capped at both ends with the same ornate wood.

He wanted to open the strange canister. However, the words of his friend and fellow apostle still rang in his ears.

"Please, at the very least, be careful..."

The canister was surprisingly light.

Could it be a bomb? he thought.

Poison?

Fear struck him as he considered all the potential dangers. Nonetheless, he had to know what was inside.

He laid the canister in the grass and attempted to twist the cap off with his feet. The further the canister was from his face, the better. It's amazing how strong the survival instinct could be, even for him. He was even holding his breath.

Don't be ridiculous, he thought.

He placed his right foot on top of the canister and using the sole of his left shoe, attempted to twist off the cap. It wasn't budging. He spun the canister and tried in the other direction, but could feel the canister buckling under his weight. *This is not working*, he thought. *Whatever it is, I'm going to destroy it, if I can't get my emotions in check.*

He picked up the canister and with all his might tried to twist off one of the ends with his hands.

Nothing, just sore hands and winded breath.

He took a good long look at the strange canister, studying the cryptic writing.

There were no latches, levers, or buttons.

As much as it pained him, he knew what he had to do. He hadn't seen or heard from her in decades. He feared how such a reunion would ultimately play out. He often thought about it, but honestly, wasn't sure if they would ever truly know one another again. However, the time had come. This is the moment they had prepared for all those years ago.

He had always kept track of her, and though she no longer knew him, he had a constant eye on her. There was little, if anything at all, that he didn't know about her. And now, it was time for her to come back home.

A quick search on his smartphone and Batnaz was able to locate the girl's current location.

"Paris!" He was excited. Paris was just a few hundred miles away. "I can be there in minutes!" All he'd have to do is trade *Elsa*, his fully custom Blackhawk helicopter, for *Darlene*, his latest, greatest top-secret fly toy, which he kept parked in a private hanger at Athens International Airport.

For an old man, Jonathan Batnaz truly adored the finest in modern technology.

Darlene was a one-of-a-kind prototype of the HyperMach SonicStar, a supersonic jet given to Batnaz as a gift for personally funding the company's development efforts. Capable of speeds greater than Mach 4 (over 2,900 miles per hour) and an altitude of over 60,000 feet, Darlene's sleek 226-foot streamlined figure and 74-foot wingspan could rocket twenty passengers from Athens Greece to Salt Lake City in under four hours—a trip that could easily take over twenty hours with a conventional airliner.

Batnaz bounded up the dozen or so steps and entered the jet, looking around the roomy, brightly lit interior, making sure no one was in earshot. Except for the pilot, Darlene was empty as she should be. He reclined in one of the bleached-white leather chairs and let his tall, slender frame—draped in a black Italian business suit—let out a series of satisfying crackles and pops as he stretched, then grabbed his smartphone. He swiped his finger across the screen, searching for a number, then pressed CONNECT. This would likely be one of the most critical calls he had ever made.

The phone rang...

And rang...

And rang some more.

Why is she not answering?

As Darlene launched down the tarmac, jerking his head hard against the headrest, the line finally picked up, but it wasn't at all what he expected. There was classical music playing in the background making it difficult to hear, but it most certainly wasn't the girl. It was a man.

"Hello?" the man said, sounding rather irritated.

A lump filled Batnaz's throat as he prepared to speak. He couldn't tell if it was the result of the jet skimming the runway at over two-hundred-feet-per-second, or if it was something else—something he hadn't experienced in years.

Fear.

6

I lay back in the plethora of oversized, plush pillows covering the massive king-sized Victorian bed and place the ice pack Crystal prepared for me on my swollen temple. I thought I could play it cool; thought I could sweep her off her feet and have my way with her, right there in the hallway, but the sad reality is, I really hurt myself.

I tap the silver panel on the bedside table and controls light up across the surface. I press the button that looks like a musical note, and suddenly *Water Music* by classical composer George Frideric Handel gently plays over speakers hidden somewhere in the room. I am quite familiar with the piece. Handel's blissful masterpiece quickly engulfs the room and my soul. But alas, *Water Music* is an all too short melody and as always it is over long before it ought to be.

I adjust the icepack and sink deeper into the pillows as another track begins. "Moonlight Sonata," I say to myself. A much longer piece and one of my all-time favorites. I mean, who doesn't love Beethoven? To me, Beethoven was the Freddy Mercury of his time—ingeniously melodic, fascinatingly peculiar, somewhat crazy, and utterly brilliant. The soft percussive tones of the piano begin to lull me adrift. The sound filling the room is all encompassing, though it isn't loud. It is so tranquil, so relaxing. As I'm about to drift asleep, the tempo changes. I knew it was coming, yet it startles me. The faster, heavier piano now pouncing out of the speakers is stimulating.

Crystal lay motionless, strapped to an altar in a dark cavernous space, as six figures cloaked in pure white robes circled around her. Black and white checkerboard tile stretched off in all directions, and dozens of lofty fluted columns strong-armed a massive structure, which was impossible to see through the blackness. Surrounding them were chest-high iron rods, upon each was a single candle—swirling whiffs of flame and smoke trailing off into the dark depths. Her eyes shot open, and the sudden jolting movement sent a wave of water over the edge of the tub and onto the bathroom floor.

The phone starts ringing and as it does the volume of the music softens. I glance at the display on the bedside table, and a number appears that I don't recognize. The phone rings several times, the music still playing in the background, getting faster and faster. *Man, I love this sonata.* As with all classical music, the melodies are progressive. In many ways, it's not unlike the heavy metal music of the 80s and 90s—another era I find myself drawn to from time-to-time.

The phone continues to ring—must have rang at least six times. Lost in the music and without thinking, I push the answer button, and as I do the volume lowers a bit more, but not completely. In the distance I hear, echoing off the hallway tile, "You better not answer that!"

But it's too late. Besides, no one has our number, and I

purposefully didn't give anyone the room number. There can really be only one explanation. The hotel is calling scheduling a wake-up call. "Hello?" I say, a bit of frustration in my voice. The line is silent. I'm about to hang up when—

"Mister DiBianco." The voice is soft, yet bold. It's obvious right away, this isn't the hotel. The man has a deep Italian accent, and his tone is severe. Something about the man's voice has me sitting straight up in bed.

"Who is this?"

"My name is Jonathan Batnaz," the man says in a soft, yet somewhat desperate tone. "I am the first councilor to the prophet of the Church of Jesus Christ of Latter-day Saints and I must speak with you and Crystal immediately."

I remain silent, unsure of what to say, the latter half of Beethoven's *Moonlight Sonata* still racing along in the distance.

"The prophet is in grave danger. Please, we must speak."

"Is this a joke?" I say snidely. "How the hell did you get this number?" I can literally feel my pulse quickening.

Everyone alive knows about my adventure in the Vatican a couple years back. It was quite the experience, to say the least. I literally found myself in a fight against the Pope and some dozen or so renegade cardinals. Much of the world credits me with stopping the largest act of terror in world history. But how does this guy know about Crystal? Her name was never made public.

"This isn't funny!"

"I assure you," the man says, "this is not a joke."

This guy is pranking me, I have no doubt, and the progressive melody speeding along in the distance is now actually making my pulse rise even more. I'm about to let the man have it, when it happens—

Crystal enters the doorway to the bedroom, a black and red teddy wrapping the contours of her frame.

She's always had this effect on me, but never to the extent that the entire world faded to black around her.

"Who's on the phone, honey?" Crystal's voice is distant as if lost in a daydream.

"Mister DiBianco?" I can barely hear the man's voice over the sound of blood raging past my ears like an out-of-control freight train.

"Honey, the phone?" she says again.

"Is that Crystal?" The man's voice is completely lost to me. I instinctively reach over and click END on the bedside display.

7

"Where are you taking me?" the old man cried, this time a bit of fear surfacing as sweat poured off his forehead, burning his eyes. He may have been The Prophet of The Church of Jesus Christ of Latter-day Saints, but by no means did that offer any amount of immunity to or relief from the terror now confronting him. Whatever it was they had placed over his head made it difficult to breathe and impossible to see.

Massive hands held him tight, two on either arm.

Another kick drilled into his ribs, forcing every bit of air from his lungs. His business suit felt taut against his body, wringing his underarms and choking him.

Dear Lord, he prayed. *Have mercy!*

He knew this day would come. To him, it was a small price to pay to protect the secret.

The hands gripped unyieldingly tight, the old man's black leather shoes slipping off his feet as they dragged him over dirt, rock, grass, and stumps—clearly in a forest.

Where are they taking me?

His body trembled, every bit of it racked with pain, but none more so than that spot in his ribs. Every time he spoke, another blow would nearly black him out.

"Where are you taking me?" he cried again. The old man knew what was coming and in a way he welcomed it. It reminded him of the sacrifice his Lord and Savior had made for him—for all of mankind. It was the least he could do in return.

He took a deep breath, his body tensing in anticipation. The hands released, and he fell to the ground.

For a brief moment, he could hear the sounds of the forest and just for that second his spirit felt rejuvenated.

But then his heart sank as the massive hands brought him to his knees and forced him to sit on his ankles. The pressure of them pushing down on him caused his knees to buckle.

Pain shot up his legs, churning and seething in his stomach, before rocketing out of his larynx in a bellow that almost brought the entire forest to its knees.

They ripped the veil from his head, a piece of wire slicing his cheek as it came off. The blood that trailed his face now was far warmer than the tears he had been attempting to ignore.

The air was hot, thick, and he immediately felt that all too familiar sensation of insects biting at his face; only in his current circumstance, he could do nothing to swat them away. Though as torturous as that was, as his eyes came into focus, he was stricken with an even deeper sense of despair.

Of all the places, he thought, as they dragged him past a familiar park bench. He lifted his head as high as he could, gazing into the heavens, through a thick canopy of massive oaks, elms, and maples and wailed, then let his head fall limp as his eyes closed and a foreboding pit formed deep in his stomach. They had taken him to the very place where a 14-year-old country boy had a heavenly vision—

After I had retired to the place where I had previously designed to go, having looked around me, and finding myself alone, I kneeled down and began to offer up the desires of my heart to God...

...I saw a pillar of light exactly over my head, above the brightness of the sun, which descended gradually until it fell upon me... When the light rested upon me I saw two Personages, whose brightness and glory defy all description, standing above me in the air. One of them spake unto me, calling me by name and said, pointing to the other—Joseph, This is My Beloved Son. Hear Him!

I asked... which of all the sects was right? ...which should I join?

I was answered that I must join none of them, for they were all wrong... that: "They draw near to me with their lips, but their hearts are far from me, they teach for doctrines the commandments of men, having a form of godliness, but they deny the power thereof."

—It was a vision that would change the world.

"Open your eyes, *Prophet.*" It was the first time anyone had spoken to him since his motorcade was attacked. The tone of the voice, the way she said, *Prophet,* sent chills down his spine.

"You!" he cried, recognizing the woman's voice—a voice that under different circumstances may have been pleasant. But as her face came into view, so did the propane torch and scalpel glowing bright orange-red in the crystal-blue flame.

"What are you doing?" he shouted, suddenly praying death would come quickly. Willing as he was, he had no desire to suffer a slow, agonizing death.

He closed his eyes and pictured Christ on the cross.

Oh, how immense was His pain, he thought.

A hand struck his face shaking him out of his vision. He opened his eyes and gazed upon the woman with despair.

"You have lied to us for far too long." She brought the scalpel close to his face, its reflection shimmered in his eyes like the sun shining off black oil slicks. "Lies, all of it!"

It was then that it struck him.

Doubt.

A deep burning fear that shook his soul.

Is it truly worth dying for?

The answer, of course, was yes.

It always was yes.

Protecting the secret was worth…

Everything.

For him, death was just temporary, and yet nothing could prepare him for the fate he was to face that sticky July morning, deep in the heart of the Sacred Grove.

"What am I doing?" the woman mocked. Her voice almost a whisper. "I'm getting what I want."

Terrified, the old man gazed at the woman as she ripped his shirt open, buttons flying through the air, and lowered the blazing hot scalpel to his thin white garment top.

"I always get what I want." Her smile grew into a full sneer. But it was her eyes. He just couldn't help staring at her eyes. Those strange, piercing eyes bore deep into his soul. *Beware of wolves in sheep's clothing.*

The woman glanced at one of her henchmen who swiftly ripped the old man's clothes off, right down to his bare flesh, then held up his sacred white garments to the flame.

The silk ignited at once.

So did the old man's spirit.

8

It's like I'm a teenager again, sitting here, mouth gaped open, looking like a fool, eyes glued to the most stunning woman I've ever set eyes upon. Ironically, Pyotr Ilyich Tchaikovsky and his whimsically majestic theme of love, *Romeo & Juliet, Fantasy-Overture in B minor*, is now filling the room.

Crystal takes those few graceful steps toward me and sits on the bed, her soft vanilla scent as captivating as her beauty. She does one of those eye-roll things. "Really," she says. "Romeo and Juliet?" She's never been much into classical music; however, even she recognized this tune. No, Crystal's a diehard classic rock fan, and not just any classic rock, the infamous power ballad.

She makes a couple selections on the satellite radio display and then places her hand on my head and smiles as the classic '80s love song starts playing. "How are you feeling?"

It's one of those melodies that are instantly recognizable; you know, the type that gets stuck in your head for days after hearing just a few bars as you pass another car on the street that's playing it? Yeah, that type. In fairness, it's probably the better of Foreigner's hits, and as the song works its way toward the first chorus I feel beads of sweat start dripping from the small of my back. After all, I have been waiting for a girl like her to come into my life.

"I feel fantastic," I lie. The truth is, my head is killing me, but who the hell cares? My heart is racing. Pounding. My body is ready for a little honeymoon action, and all she's concerned about is the lump on my head? The music, though simpleton in nature compared with Tchaikovsky, is admittedly working the mood in here. I give it that.

I embrace her, swallowing her whole with my arms, and throw her on the bed.

She smiles that perfect grin I love so much and yanks me on top of her, but I can tell there's something wrong. "What is it?" I ask. "You can try and hide it, but I can always tell when something's bothering you."

Her tiny hands frantically loosen my tie and unbuttons my shirt, then flips me around and pulls the shirt off my shoulders. She throws it mindlessly behind her and flips me on my back, then stops and grins. "It's nothing you have to worry about," she says, never breaking her smile. She places each of her knees on the bed on either side of my chest and sits on my lower stomach, just inches away from the desired location, and studies me. I can see the gears spinning, but these are the type of gears I'm more than happy to play with. She reaches for my neck, grabs my tie, and slips it off, then grabs my arms and forces them above my head, then precedes to tie my hands to one of the rails in the headboard. This is a side of her I have never seen before, but I am not stopping to argue!

She grabs my hands and gives them a solid tug, then sits up, her weight now resting uncomfortably on that previously desired location, apparently satisfied that I'm thoroughly ensnared to suffer her wicked desires. As the Foreigner song comes to an end, she glances at the radio display and her eyes light up. *My God, she is so beautiful. How did I ever get so lucky?* As the next song starts, I feel a ting in my chest. The hard rock drums, slowed down to an almost depressing rhythm, mixed with that iconic guitar sound, instantly stirs up memories of teenaged years past. I haven't heard this song in decades, and yet every word instantly floods my mind as I hear those first few notes. And of all the bands that Crystal raves about, Def Leopard is right on top.

She looks right into my soul and starts singing, "When you make love, do you look in the mirror? ..."

As she sings along with the iconic power ballad, her fingernails slowly and lightly start working their way up my chest, under my neck, and over my cheeks. The sensation sends shivers up and down my spine. The soft scent of vanilla surrounds us as she takes my right earlobe into her mouth and licks my ear. Then she sings, "I don't wanna touch you too much baby, ..."

She slowly draws her warm, moist tongue along my sharp jawline, toward my stubbled cleft chin then rubs her nose on my cheek. Her tongue presses on my closed lips and before I can part them, she takes a nibble and kisses me, slowly working her soft lips down my neck and chest.

Suddenly she jumps up and whips her long strawberry hair back and out of her face, then reaches behind her back, grinning seductively at me as she works the clasps that have been struggling to keep her priceless treasures hidden. And as the music starts to swell I see her getting ready for it—

"Love bites..."

—then it's off. The black and red teddy falls to my stomach and instantly I feel my heart rocking out, playing drums on the inside of my ribcage. Now I'm singing—

Bang! Bang! Bang!

The knocking at the door is heavy.

Rapid.

It startles the freaking hell out of me, and I pop my head up at the sound without a thought, but Crystal quickly pushed me back down. "Let it go," she demands. She then grabs my head and plants my face into her bare chest.

I have no difficulty succumbing to her whims.

None at all!

Bang! Bang! Bang!

The thrashing on the door is louder now.

Impossible to ignore.

"What the hell," she shouts, as I attempt to roll off the bed, quickly getting hung up on the headboard. "Son of a bitch!" I pause, calming myself, as Crystal loosens the bonds. "Just a second!" I shout as I grab my shirt off the floor and throw it over my shoulders—

Bang! Bang! Bang!

"I said I'm coming!" I hobble over to the chair, slip on my khakis, don't even bother zipping them, then walk to the living room—the lights coming on as I enter—and take those last remaining steps in stride. I glance over my shoulder, making sure there's no clear view into the bedroom, and then open the door as far as the security chain will allow.

"Can I help you?" I say, trying to be coy, knowing that the tone in my voice is really one of anger. But I don't care. I seriously just want whoever it is, to go away.

"Mister DiBianco," the voice is soft, yet bold and is thick with an Italian accent. "We must talk."

"I'm sorry," I say snidely. "Do I know you?"

"I am sorry for disturbing you, Michael. However, this simply cannot wait." Peering through the door, I can see just enough of the man to notice that his appearance fits his voice perfectly. Mature. Elderly, yet quite large in stature. He must be a good six-foot, four, and he's dressed a in black suit. Old, yet definitely not frail.

"Please, Michael, give me just one moment of your time." His eyes are quite sincere, which eases my anger just slightly. "Just one moment," the old man repeats. "Then, if you desire, I will leave and never return."

I close my eyes and take in a deep breath. *I can't believe I'm actually thinking of opening the door for this guy.*

"Who is it?" Crystal calls from the bedroom, but I don't answer; instead, I close the door, unhook the chain, and let the old man into the penthouse suite's grand living space.

"Please, have a seat," I say to the old man, pointing at one of the three 18th century Louis XV style chairs. I then walk toward the bedroom, enough to catch a peek in at Crystal, but as I do, she comes walking out of the bedroom wrapped in a plush white bathrobe.

The old man stands up at attention and bows, his right arm resting on his chest. Very old school. "Good evening, madam," he says. "Please forgive my intrusion."

Crystal smiles. However, it's real damn obvious that it's forced. She sits in the chair across from where the old man is standing and crosses her legs under her robe. The old man follows suit, returning to his seat and crossing his legs.

"So," I say. I'm pacing the room. The sexual frustration mixed with the anger I am feeling at the moment is making it difficult to have a cordial conversation with this unwanted guest. "Who are you?" I say, clear frustration bleeding out. I really am trying to calm myself. For all I know, there could be an excellent reason for this man being here. I shouldn't be so upset. I take a deep breath. "How do you know my name and how the hell did you find us?"

"I am President Jonathan Batnaz from the first presidency of The Church of Jesus Christ of Latter-day Saints."

Crystal and I gawk at each other. I can't believe what this man is saying, and neither can Crystal from the look on her face. "You're the prophet of the Mormon church?" I ask.

"No," he explains. "I am first counselor to the prophet." He brings his large hands together in front of him and directs his gaze skyward. "Sadly," he continues, "I am here because the prophet has been kidnapped by an adversary we cannot even begin to understand and we—I need your assistance."

"Why?" Crystal asks, standing abruptly from her chair, taking a defensive stance in front of the old man. "I'm sorry to hear about your prophet, Mister..." she pauses, apparently in a struggle to recall the old man's name.

"Batnaz," he reminds her.

"Why us, Mister Batnaz?" Clearly, she's pissed. "What do you expect *us* to do about this?"

"Honey?" I say, perhaps hoping she'll realize that she may be getting a little overly worked up.

She takes a long sideways look at me, takes a deep breath through her nose, and then returns to the bedroom.

"I'm terribly sorry about this," Batnaz says, genuine concern sweeping his face. "I did not mean any ill will—"

"Seriously?" I say to the man. "I think you should go."

"Very well." Batnaz stands from his chair and starts back toward the door. "You know, this is perhaps the most beautiful hotel I've ever seen," he declares, as he looks around the space. It sounds like he's nervous, possibly stalling. "It reminds me of our holy temples. Quite impressive."

I rush up ahead of him and open the door.

Batnaz stares at me—second time tonight someone has stared into my soul in this manner, only this time, there's a different type of urgency stirring within me. "I know you, Michael, because of what you did." Batnaz reached into his coat, and I instantly jump back. "No, no," Batnaz smiles, pausing a moment, realizing what has just happened. "What you did for the Catholic Church is no big secret."

Of course, he's right. The entire world by now has heard the stories about how this simple Harvard Divinity Professor had saved the Catholic Church and, some might argue, Christianity as a whole.

"As promised, I will leave. But before I do," Batnaz holds out an ornate mahogany canister for me, lines of strange symbols engraved into each of the canister's six sides. "I believe you may want to see this."

9

Crystal entered the bedroom in a huff, shutting the door hard behind her. This was not the way she envisioned the night going. First Michael hurt his head—and she knew he was still hurting, even if he tried to play tough guy—and now this strange visitor. His presence was severely bothering her, because Crystal had been born and, until the age of eight, raised in The Church of Jesus Christ of Latter-day Saints.

She had always known that her father had played a crucial role in the church. She remembered hearing stories about him being the bishop of their ward for nearly ten years before she was born—far longer than most people ever served in that position.

She recalled a time when her father was away a lot—months on end, for a time. She hated those years, but she now wished she could have them back. She had not yet had the chance to develop her own spiritual testimony when tragedy struck.

Her father died in a horrific accident flying home from overseas for her eighth birthday. He had been visiting Greece, on duty for the church, and was returning home to baptize her when it happened. They never found his plane.

What made matters worse for the very young Crystal, was that her mother was unusually old—fifty-one when she gave birth to Crystal—and she struggled, tremendously, trying to cope with her husband's passing. Crystal and her mother tried to survive together after her father died. But her mother just wasn't the same anymore. Something had completely changed in her.

She was never part of the conversation. Always off in another world in her mind. At just eight, Crystal was clueless to what it was, but today, she was sure it was broken heart syndrome. Crystal's mother reluctantly placed her in the custody of a couple whom she knew would take care of her, the way she would have wanted to herself.

Her mother died a few weeks later.

Like that, Crystal's world was turned inside out.

That couple adopted Crystal on August 8th, 1991. They were so good to her. Gave her everything she ever needed or wanted. Crystal graduated two different colleges before eventually enlisting in the United States Army at age 21 to work as a Cryptologic-Linguist. To say that Crystal was an overachiever was somewhat of an understatement.

She never returned to church. "We're spiritual, not religious," her adopted parents would often say. They just weren't the church-going types. Weren't much into scripture-reading, or praying either. But she knew, in her heart, they believed, and they did their best to raise her with good morals and standards.

Crystal's belief in God wavered a lot after the death of her parents. However, those little tidbits of knowledge that she gained from all those Sundays spent in Sunday school began to grow stronger after spending nearly eight years in the middle-east, breaking codes for the military. After all, how could a nation the size of New Hampshire possibly survive in an area of the world where billions of people surrounding your every border want you wiped off the face of the planet?

It only proved to her that God was not only real but truly Merciful and *all* Magnificent and Powerful.

10

The sight of the artifact takes my breath away and immediately I wish I hadn't seen the godforsaken thing.

The last thing I want is for this escapade to continue on any longer, and yet, that's exactly what this strange canister—plastered over in cryptic writings—is going to do.

I glance back toward the bedroom. Crystal is clearly pissed off and in no better mood than I; however, this could be just the thing to remedy that. Though still, I hesitate.

I recently published my fourth book which focuses on the many secret codes and agendas surrounding Freemasonry. Some could say I've become somewhat seduced by Masonic lore, and wouldn't you know, before me now is one of the most amazing things I've ever seen.

"Fascinating," I say as I take the canister in my hands and examine it carefully, studying the code, trying to decipher it in my head. "I have only heard about these." It's clear that the strange symbols are an early Masonic cipher known as a PigPen. However, I haven't quite caught the cryptology bug, as strong as Crystal has. No, she lives and breathes this stuff. "Excuse me," I say, as I run over to the coffee table and grab a notebook and pen. I scribble out a series of tic-tac-toe grids and two large Xs, then I write the alphabet within the grids, placing dots in the alternating tic-tac-toe and X grids.

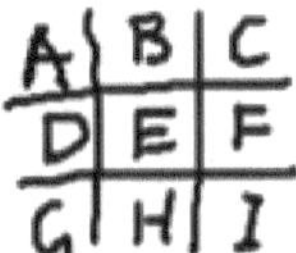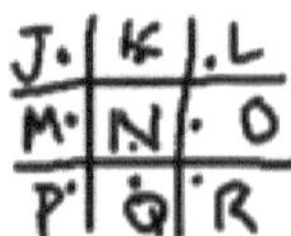

"Crystal can do this in her sleep," I mumble under my breath. *I'd bet she does.* I know, this is her gig, her lifework. I really should go and get her. But the intrigue has me ensnared, held captive to its mystery. "This is not just any ordinary canister, as you may well see. However, what you may not know, is that these have only ever been used to conceal the most vital of secrets." I write out the strange symbols that appear to be written in the form of a sentence underneath the tic-tac-toe and X grids—

—and my wheels immediately start spinning. Almost on impulse, a nervous glitch perhaps, I start rambling. "The Freemasons created the Pigpen cipher hundreds of years ago." I can hear the excitement in my voice, but it has little to do with what I am saying. "But stopped using it for serious applications in the 1900s since it quickly became too easy to crack." I am writing out the translated text when it occurs to me, it's too easy. I stop writing and stare up at Batnaz, who's standing over me, waiting for me to write out the answer. *Something is wrong.* "This either predates 1900," I say, "or we're about to discover something unwelcome." I take the canister and study it closer.

It's immaculate as if made yesterday. Whatever's inside, it's not locked very well. "This is either a joke," I say, unable to hide my concern, "or a trap."

Batnaz looks impressed. "I wasn't aware that you were a cryptologist." His calm suddenly strikes me. How could this not bother him? For all we know this could be a bomb.

"She's rubbed off on me, I suppose," I say, gazing at the Masonic symbols. It only took a second to crack the code. Even though I stopped writing halfway and had made a mental effort to stop looking at it, it made no difference at all. There it is, plain as day before me.

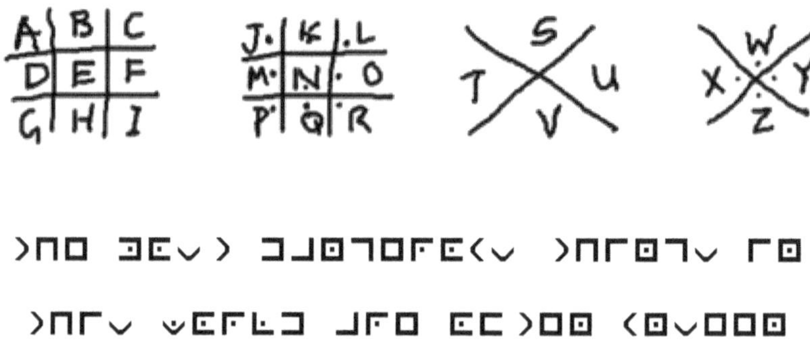

I return my gaze to Batnaz, a strange blend of intrigue and worry finally filling his face. *About time*, I think. I was beginning to wonder if the man was even human.

"What is it?" he asks. "What's the answer?"

But I know better. The answer was far too easy. I finish writing it out so Batnaz can see and then I place the pen on the coffee table. Something feels very wrong. Something is missing. I was expecting instructions on how to open the canister. But this... *this* sounds more like a warning.

THE MOST DANGEROUS THINGS IN
THIS WORLD ARE OFTEN UNSEEN

"The only thing unseen is inside that thing," Batnaz says. "Perhaps it's a warning to us, not to open it."

"To me, it sounds like an invitation," I say, my desire to know outweighing any potential dangers. That's the story of my life. No matter how crazy, no matter how dangerous, I'm impulsively and compulsively drawn toward the answer. "The canister itself is what makes this mystery so fascinating," I say. "This is no mere PigPen cipher, but one tiny layer of a much deeper mystery." I see now, without question, how beyond my capabilities this task truly is. I look over my shoulder toward the bedroom. I have to show her this.

"You have incredible chemistry," Batnaz says, clearly identifying what I am thinking, "and apparently you *both* are skilled beyond measure in the art of deciphering code." Batnaz smiles warmly. "Please, our church desperately needs you."

"We'll do it." Her words surprise both of us, firing out from beyond the bedroom doorway. Batnaz and I simultaneously turn toward her voice, shock in our eyes. She emerges from the bedroom, fully dressed, holding her phone up so I can see a photo of President Batnaz. It's the church's official website. The man is for real. "But I am only doing it because your church meant so much to my parents."

"Splendid," Batnaz says with relief, standing abruptly from his chair. "We shall meet in the lobby in ten minutes."

"Ten minutes?" I say, glaring at Crystal who stares back in dismay.

President Batnaz clamps his hands together and grins. "Plane leaves Charles de Gaulle in thirty. Driver's waiting!"

As Batnaz entered the elevator, he grabbed his phone and dialed a number he knew from memory. "It has begun," he said. "Yes, I found her." He paused. "Indeed, he is with her." Another pause. "It appears they are both on board." Batnaz gazed at his reflection in the polished stainless steel panel as he pressed the button. There was nothing anyone could do now to change their path. "You know what you must do." As the elevator doors closed, there was a beeping in his ear. "Hello?" He looked at his phone.

No Service.

Batnaz had made a solemn promise to do everything in his power to protect her throughout this mission. Ever since the day she left, she had been different. However, that didn't change anything—he knew to expect that. She was still the woman he knew, even if *she* was no longer aware of that fact. And now that the mission had taken this new direction, he would have to find a way to bring her back home.

Sure, he would still work diligently to keep her safe, but reality is—and sadly always has been—there are things in this world more important than promises.

11

Sitting in the back seat of the Lincoln Town Car, racing down the steaming tarmac in a private section of the Charles de Gaulle Airport, I can feel my palms getting moist.

Not again, I think, wiping my hands on my pants.

There's a whole lot of aircraft parked up ahead, and just the sight of the massive rocket-shaped plane takes me back to the time when I was kidnapped and flown to London on a private jet. I woke up a week later in a drug-induced stupor.

But this—this is something altogether different.

Easily two hundred feet long, the fuselage is thin, coming to a long needlepoint at the front. Two stubby wings and tail make this thing look more like a missile than a jet. Twelve round windows sprawling the length are all that separate it from something that looks like it should be launched off the coast of Cape Canaveral.

Moments later I'm cruising along at 60,000 feet above the earth's surface at nearly Mach 4.

With the hum of the jet engines and the craziness of the evening coming to a head, I find myself nearly collapsing from fatigue. I recline the chair back into sleep position, with my feet propped up in the air, and rest my eyes. The sun has fully set, but in my state, the light shining off the moon is enough to bring on a headache. I open my eyes and study the window. *You've got to be kidding me*, I think, then turn to Batnaz who is just now sitting in the seat one row over. The lights are low, except for a few track lights aiming at a small, knee-high table affixed to the floor between where Crystal is sitting and where Batnaz just sat. "There's no shades on these windows?"

"Oh, silly me," he says, then grabs a small remote control that was stuck to the arm of his chair with velcro and pushes one of the buttons. Instantly, my window goes black, I mean, completely black, like the window wasn't even there. "There's a controller next to your seat if you wish to adjust it," Batnaz says. "Catch them if you can. This won't be a very long flight."

I seriously have no desire to sleep at the moment, but if I could just rest my eyes, even if just for a few minutes. I stare at the window, push the button on my remote, and watch as, slowly, the moonlit sky beyond materializes. It's not a shade or a blind. The actual glass changes from clear to opaque. *Interesting*, I think, as I close my eyes. The moment I do, the vision of the cylinder come into view, along with the Masonic symbols. In my memory, I examine the cylinder.

All my life I've been told I have a photographic memory. I would never be so arrogant or bold as to state such a claim; however, even I must admit, I remember things with some degree of ease. The thing that stands out most is how flawless the cylinder is. For something made hundreds of years ago, it looks brand new, and yet, the color, size, shape, and weight, even the woodgrain, appear to be perfect for the period.

The cylinder looks to be a solid piece of wood, except for a hairline circling the circumference at one of the ends. It's obviously a cap. Clearly, there is a way to open it.

But how?

There are no levers, no latches, no combination lock. *I suppose it could simply twist off*, I think, but something tells me Batnaz would have tried that. There's clearly a reason why he brought this to us. He tried, and he can't open it. So, if there are no visible signs and no... Wait. *No visible signs!*

The most dangerous things in this world are often unseen

In my work, unearthing the mysteries surrounding the world's many theologies, sacred orders, higher-powers, and the like, it's impossible not to also discover some very real, very alarming scientific mysteries—harsh realities, which are only truly a mystery to the victims. Mysteries, such as those found in the hidden realm of the Spectrum.

A world almost completely unseen and most certainly unknown—or at the very least, misunderstood—by us mere mortals. Everything from the lights and colors we see, to the gadgets we cook with, to the recorded music we listen to, it's all found within a space many scientists call the Spectrum.

While we all live with it and utilize it and build our worlds around it, nearly none of us understand it or the very real dangers it presents to our way of life and in many cases, our very lives. It is this invisible world of electromagnetism that some believe is humanity's weakest point of entry for all breeds of crime and terrorism.

Anyone who educates themselves on how to manipulate the Spectrum can truly wreak havoc. These havoc-seekers often get away with it, too, because the rest of us are so oblivious—even the best of us. Thieves line bags with foil, blocking antitheft alarms from sounding; hackers steal information straight off your credit cards as they pass you on the street. Some believe that a single strategically placed electromagnetic pulse could wipe out the entire power grid of a country, causing mass chaos and violence in the streets.

Nowadays, technology rarely seen, much less used by the general public, has resurfaced and is used by millions to protect against what's been labeled cybercrime.

The Faraday Cage

But it's not actually cybercrime at all, but rather, it is the criminal manipulation of the Spectrum.

Yet today's Faraday Cages come in the form of credit card sleeves or metal-lined wallets and purses. People are beginning to understand the dangers of the Spectrum without even realizing it. I say this because people are starting to see the dangers, but haven't the slightest clue why or how they exist. What's arguably worse, is that people don't even realize that the mandated changes to the lighting industry, banning incandescent light bulbs for those curly fluorescents things, has made the average person's health fail in ways they may never understand, and may likely never recover from.

My eyes open wide, "I've got it!" The excitement in my voice startles even me as I sit up and jump to my feet.

Batnaz and Crystal jump at the sudden outburst—Batnaz nearly spilling his glass of cola—and gaze at me with concern.

"The cylinder," I say, as certain as anything that I'm right. "I know how to open it!"

The looks on their faces are priceless. Apparently, I was out longer than I thought. Crystal is shaving slivers of material off the outside of the cylinder with the blade of a small pocket knife, tiny mahogany-colored shavings litter the table. She even has a few in her bar glass—still full of cola.

"What's going on?" I ask.

"It's not wood," she says.

"What do you mean, it's not wood?"

"I mean, it's not wood, Michael." She hands me a small pile of the shavings.

They feel familiar in my fingers. "Plastic?" *That makes perfect sense,* I think to myself. "I'm even more certain now," I say, grabbing the cylinder off the table. Crystal gets a defensive look in her eyes and instinctively reaches for it. She's invested in this now, I get it. Perhaps too invested. "You, of all people, should understand the dangers of tampering with something like this." I examine the areas where she was scraping. She was careful not to scrape in the area around the cap. Perhaps I was too quick to judge.

"I'm well aware," she replies, not looking much pleased. "I'm also aware that it's plastic." Her eyes are not the typical wide, sparkly blue. Instead, they are darkened with concern, worry, maybe even fear. "It's the type of plastic, Michael."

I put the shavings to my nose. The odor emitting from the fresh shavings is distinctive and terrifying. "But how?" I ask, returning my gaze to the cylinder itself. I don't know how, but someone managed to create an intricate, perfect replica of a hand-carved mahogany Scytale cipher, out of Semtex.

"My guess," she starts, "is that they printed a rugged outer shell over top of the C-4 with a high-tech 3D printer."

"Oh, that's peachy," I say, my original thought momentarily lost to the terror of the new reality staring me dead in the face. I freeze. I know how to open it. I am more certain now than I was before. Not only that, I am equally confident that the way to open it, is the way to disarm it.

"What are you thinking?" Batnaz questions, still looking far too calm for a man who was just told there's a bomb on his plane. "You said you knew how to open it. Are you sure?"

"Positive," I say as I grab the pad sitting in front of Crystal and flip back to my notes from earlier. I hold up the page for them to see, and I read it aloud.

The most dangerous things in
this world are often unseen

"The Spectrum," I exclaim.

Crystal's eyes light immediately with recognition. "Of course," she says. "The lock is electromagnetic."

"Not just the lock," I explain. "The bomb." I feel the smile blossom on my face. I know I'm right, and I know that Crystal knows I'm right. "If we shut down the Spectrum—stop it from making contact with the cylinder in any way, it will simultaneously disarm and unlock."

"But how do we do that?" Crystal asks. "We would need some sort of electromagnetic shield."

"It's not a difficult as you might think," I explain. "All it takes, at its fundamental level, is to completely surround it within a steel cage."

"Faraday Cage," Batnaz says. "The elevator."

"What?" Crystal asks.

"As I was leaving your hotel room, I started a phone call, and as the elevator doors closed, the call dropped. Clearly the elevator acted as a Faraday Cage. Perhaps we could open it in an elevator?"

"Indeed," I say. He isn't wrong. "That very well could work. However, most buildings with elevators also have massive electromagnetic fields. Even if we cut all the power in the building, traces could still get through."

"Darlene," Batnaz says. "Yes, I know how we can do it." His voice rises in excitement as he stands and glances about the interior of his plane. "Absolutely, yes! It will work!"

"What," I say. "What will work?"

"The hull of an aircraft is a perfect Faraday Cage, and Darlene is no exception. However, she has a few other tricks up her sleeve that make this perfect." Batnaz's voice gets more excited the more he speaks. It's the most humanity I've seen come out of him. "Her windows are equipped with state-of-the-art conductive resins. When the power is on high, the glass is transparent—clear as any window you've even seen. But adjust the current slightly and the transparency changes. Cut all power and the windows become like metal plates."

"It won't work," I explain. "There's still power in the plane. Electromagnetic fields are emitted from practically every single energy source, not to mention light itself. Even the slightest bit of light—even invisible light—will prevent the lock from releasing."

"Yes," Batnaz says in a bit of a nervous tone. "Well, that's where the last part of this plan comes in. There is something else Darlene can do something most aircrafts cannot."

"I'm afraid to ask," Crystal says, giving me an uncertain glare. I can only imagine what she's thinking, and yet, I have the distinct feeling that what he's about to say could be worse.

"My Dearest Darlene," he says with a proud grin. "She can fly in the dark."

Crystal and I gaze at each other in disbelief.

"That's right," he says, tapping his right index finger on the tabletop, as if finally convincing himself that it's a good idea. "We're going to cut the engines and go lights out."

12

"Put all your electronic devices in here," Batnaz said, holding out something that closely resembled a large bank deposit bag.

"That's perfect," Michael agreed, recognizing it as a shielded security bag used to protect sensitive electronic equipment from hacking or any form of outside influences. Michael dropped his iPhone in the bag and then started removing his watch. "Make sure everything is in that bag, even your watches. If it has a battery or any wound up or moving parts whatsoever—if it has even the slightest chance of generating an electrical charge—it needs to be removed."

Crystal placed her phone and watch in the bag, then bent down and removed something from under her pant leg.

A pistol.

Michael looked at her incredulously.

"It has a battery-powered laser pointer," she explained, not looking very pleased that she had to reveal her personal defense weapon. She dropped the tiny Smith & Wesson in the bag, then stood there with a strange look on her face. Clearly something was on her mind.

"Is that everything?" Batnaz sealed the bag with an audible zip and then turned and walked into the cockpit. "Charlie," he said to the pilot. "Prepare for stealth mode."

The pilot's face went white. "It's never been employed in real-world conditions," he argued. His posture was that of someone about to stand his ground. "I've never even seen it tested. There is no way I can do this safely, Sir."

Batnaz immediately closed the cockpit door, leaving Crystal and Michael out in the cabin. "I've seen it done, Charlie," he declared, trying to keep his voice down. "While there's still a few flaws in the prototype, I've seen it work in the facility."

"I know you've seen it, Jon," the pilot said, apparently not caring much about keeping his voice down. "But I haven't, and I'm the one who has to fly this damn thing!"

"Look, I understand the risk," Batnaz said, getting real close to the pilots ear, nearly whispering. "But if there is anyone in this world whom I trust to keep this bird flying, it's you."

But the pilot, a Vietnam veteran with nearly fifty years of flight experience, over a decade of those in combat, was clearly no where near as convinced, nor as confident.

As Batnaz slid open the cockpit door, Charlie crossed his right hand over his chest and closed his eyes.

The voices inside the cockpit fall silent. I glance at Crystal who looks terrified.

"It's never been employed in real-world conditions," the pilot argued. "There is no way I can do this safely, Sir."

"I'm not so sure I like this plan," I say as I approach Crystal with the intention of embracing her. But before I reach her, the cockpit door slides back open and Batnaz steps out smiling.

"I have full faith in you, Charlie," he says. "I also have full faith in Darlene. She'll be fine." Batnaz slides the cockpit door closed, and I hear the pilot latch it from the inside.

"If anyone can handle this," Batnaz says, "it's Charlie."

"Sixty seconds till Stealth Mode." The pilot's voice does not sound nearly as confident as Batnaz seems.

He almost sounds scared.

I grab the cylinder off the table where Crystal and Batnaz had been sitting and almost immediately the lights flicker out.

This surprises Crystal, who reacts with an audible gasp.

"It's just Darlene getting ready for a full shutdown," Batnaz says. "Don't be alarmed."

"Thirty seconds," the pilot announces. "Once we go stealth there'll be no further announcements until we're back online."

I run over to the emergency light and twist out the bulb. Surprisingly, it burns my fingertips. *Youch!* I cry internally. *It's only been on a few damn seconds.* But now it's dark. Real freaking dark. However, as my eyes adjust I begin to see something—another light, coming from the back of the plane.

"Ten seconds," the pilot announces.

"Crap!"

"Eight, seven, six—"

There's going to be an ultra slim window of opportunity for us to pull this off. "There's a light in the back," I shout. "There can't be anything... not a single thing with power going to it!"

"—three, two, one."

There's a noticeable *thunk* as the cabin quakes and dips suddenly, the sound of breaking glass fills the space—

Smash! Crash! Ting, ting, ting-ting-ting...

—obviously the glassware Batnaz and Crystal have been drinking from. Then... nothing.

Total silence.

Not even the air, racing by us at 3,000 miles per hour can be heard from inside this ultra soundproofed jet.

It's eerie, surreal even.

Out of the corner of my eye, I see a tall silhouette creeping its way toward the back of the plane. I turn my head, and it vanishes. "All set," Batnaz says.

Now, there's absolutely zero light on this plane. If not for the sickening feeling in my stomach—like trying to keep food down on the whale-watch cruise we took last summer in Boston—I'd swear we were back on land.

"Did you open it?" Crystal's voice attacks from my left. "Well," she says, sounding excited. "Did it work?"

That's when it hits me, "Um, guys, I think we may have a problem." *It was in my hands a second ago.* It had to have slipped out when the engines cut out. "I don't have the cylinder!" I drop to my knees and start feeling about the floor. I hear a winching sound fire off from Crystal's direction, then—

"Son-of-a-bitch," she shouts.

I'm just about to ask what happened when my left-hand brushes against something. The pain hits me slowly, much slower than the feeling of blood as it quickly gets between my fingers and starts to coagulate, making them stick together.

Crap! I think. *Broken glass! It's everywhere!*

In the darkness of the cabin, Crystal heard something—

Is that chanting?

Suddenly, three cloaked figures circled around her, chanting something unrecognizable to her ears. They spread their arms wide, blocking out the flickering candlelight which came from somewhere off in the distance with their pure white robes. They closed in, tightening their circle around her, all the while sidestepping, counterclockwise, around the altar. It was as if they were performing some tribal dance. But this was no tribe. These figures were cloaked entirely in white, with smooth silver masks covering their faces—even their eyes.

"Ouch!" Michael shouted, bringing her back.

After a couple seconds, the pain hits—it's strange how, in the dark, sensations feel so much different. If I didn't know better, I would think I had just been bitten by a snake. There's no way for me to know just how bad it is, but the sensation of blood is tremendous. It must be bad, but I must keep looking.

I do my best to ignore the pain and the smell of blood and keep searching. Only now, I move my hands with a bit more caution. No more mindless sweeping about. No, now it's more a gentle patting along the floor. But still, each time I move my hands I wince in anticipation of what I might touch next.

A sudden feeling attacks the pit of my stomach and quickly works its way up my throat. It's an intense sensation, one that makes me feel like I'm about to puke. "What the hell was that?"

"We're losing altitude," Batnaz says. In the pitch blackness, his voice sounds kind of different. Younger, maybe. It's really strange, but I also hear something else.

Nervousness?

"We have little time," he shouts. "Michael, our window of opportunity is quickly closing!"

The plane takes another sharp dive and starts to shake and roll violently. My body feels as though it might leave the floor. The plane then rolls sharply to the right, and I lose balance, falling over against one of the tables. I feel like I've just been stabbed in the leg. I grab at my upper left thigh with both hands, a wedge of glass is sticking out through my khakis.

God!

I'm just about to yank it out when—

Tap, Tap, Tap...

It's the sound of something not quite round, rolling or tapping across the floor. It has to be the cylinder, I think, its six hexagonal edges knocking on the floor as it tries to flee my grasp. I instinctively give chase and bump into something. I feel hair—long wavy hair. "Crystal?" I say. But there's no response. *Oh dear God,* I think. Another nose dive and the knocking sound grabs my attention again. *God, why?* I chase after the sound, this time on my hands and toes, running across the floor like some kind of crazed baboon. I feel around with my hands. I swear, there's not a single pinprick of light in here. I have never in my life experienced darkness like this.

Then I feel something. "I've got it!" I shout. I sit on the floor, stabilizing myself between what I think is a chair and the hull of the plane and feel around for the hairline in the plastic, indicating where the cap should be.

"Where are you?" Batnaz's voice is distant. I don't respond. I grab the cylinder at both ends and give it a solid pull, my fingers covered in blood slipping on the now wet plastic—

Nothing!

It's amazing how much it actually feels like plastic now. Again the plane hits turbulence, and the cylinder jumps out of my hands and slams into my forehead, smacking me straight in the goose-egg still throbbing at my temple from earlier in the evening. *My God,* I think. *How much abuse are you going to put me through tonight? What have I done to deserve this?*

"This cannot continue, Michael!" It's definitely nerves I recognize in his voice. "Only seconds remain!"

"Michael?" It is Crystal. Her voice is soft, weak. "I can barely breathe." It sounds like she's crying. I hear her soft whimpers coming from somewhere to my right. I hadn't noticed the air until now, but suddenly I'm struggling to breathe myself.

Cabin pressure, I realize. *Just freaking great!* The urge to drop the cylinder and run toward my wife is overwhelming, but so is the knowledge that we must get this cylinder open.

Only seconds remain! Batnaz's voice repeats in my head.

"Michael!" Batnaz snaps. He's getting closer to me and quickly. I hear him scurry up the center isle, then pause. "For the love of God, get that thing open!" I hear Crystal make a soft groan as she is lifted to her feet. I can actually see it all happen in my mind. Amazing how much one actually can see in the dark, when your senses are all on hyperdrive.

I grab the cylinder in my hands, and twist it hard—

Again... Nothing!

My hands are so slippery with blood. I wipe my hands on my shirt and grab on again. I pull, then I push and pull, and then I push and twist, and I pull and—A deafening, high-pitch whine roars through the plane as the lights flood on, blinding me, forcing my eyes closed. The collar of my shirt lifts off the back of my neck as fresh air blows against my back, coming from a vent somewhere behind me.

My eyes aren't even open yet when I hear her voice creep up to me. "Oh God," she says, her voice stronger. I feel her slide beside me and take the cylinder from my hands. "Michael..."

I wipe my eyes with my right hand—the one that I can tell is not covered in blood—and then open my eyes to see Batnaz kneeling on the floor inches in front of me, and Crystal, sitting cross-legged to my right, the open cylinder resting in her hands.

"...You did it!"

13

The prophet was naked and forced to kneel at the feet the most beautiful woman he had ever laid eyes upon.

His broken knees throbbed in pain. He could feel the bones slipping and grinding under his weight.

As the woman took the glowing scalpel out of the torch flame and brought it toward his flesh, the man braced for the pain. At first, he didn't feel anything. It actually felt a bit cold. Then, as the blade dug in deeper, slicing through his tender breast muscle, it finally hit him—a deep, searing pain that could not be measured in this world.

The beautiful woman studied the old man closely, careful to bring him right to the very edge of consciousness, and just as he knew for sure that he was about to black out. She stopped, brought the blade to his lips and smiled.

"How about a taste, Prophet?" She put the blade to his lips. "Go ahead, have a taste of your own medicine?"

That is when the smell struck him. It was a grotesque blend of sulfur, burning flesh, and singed hair.

"What's the matter?" she said in a tone that mocked sympathy. "Not painful enough?" She returned the blade to the torch, waited long enough for it to start glowing again, then returned it to his chest, this time, the pain was far more intense than before. She made thoughtful, yet agonizing slices, as if sculpting—up, down, and to the right. "We are far from done, my beautiful subject," she said, pleasure filling her voice. "But you already knew that, didn't you? ... Prophet."

Her henchmen clenched on to his arms tighter.

Even in his senior years his fight was merciless.

The pain of the blade searing through his flesh was like nothing he ever imagined, and yet it paled in comparison with the anguish Christ felt, taking upon Himself the sins of the world. The sins of every soul who ever lived and who ever will.

For decades, people had looked at him with awe and wonder. He wasn't at all what they thought he was. In fact, he was far more. And today he would make the ultimate sacrifice to protect The Secret. He only prayed it might make up for his many shortcomings.

One of the woman's henchmen twisted the old man's arm too much, and he felt a pop. His vision blurred. Darkness crept in. He longed to be with God.

"Father," he cried.

He wanted to die.

Take this pain from me... Please!

That's when he noticed the railroad spikes, the sledgehammer, and the crown of thorns—

"Good God ... NO!"

14

With the cabin lights back on and my eyes finally adjusted I'm astonished to see that there's no blood on my hands. True, there's a minor abrasion at the base of my left index finger, but it's hardly a cut, and there's no bleeding to speak of. Most of the fluid soaking my shirt and pants is diet cola, spilled in the turbulence. Even the massive shard of glass sticking out of my leg is little more than a fragment no larger than my pinky nail. Oh, how the mind plays such ridiculous tricks when the lights are out and your fear level is on maximum overdrive.

Crystal stands, and Batnaz helps me to my feet. There is broken glass all over the floor, most of it managed to scatter away from where I had been scurrying about the floor. Crystal and Batnaz head back to where they had been sitting, and they place the open cylinder back on the table.

I follow, adjusting my clothing so it's not all bunched up and sticking to me. *What just happened?* I think. It really is pretty hard to absorb what just took place. It was like something out of an action movie—not a day in the life of Michael DiBianco. Sure, I've been in some hair-raising situations before: like the time I scaled down a dilapidated wrought iron ladder on the side of an old hospital building wearing nothing more than a medical gown; and the time I jumped off a cliff in the Old London Underground, into a snake infested subterranean river... but this?

I remove my medication bottle from my inner jacket pocket

and twist off the top. My anxiety has improved exponentially since starting this prescription. I hardly ever take them anymore, perhaps once or twice a month. I pour the contents of the bottle into my hand and grimace.

Only two left!

I toss them both in my mouth a let them dissolve.

God! It tastes like... I can't even finish my own thought. The doctor told me chewing them was by no means recommended, that these would absolutely wreck my stomach, but he also indicated that doing so may help in extreme cases.

Well, it doesn't get much more extreme in my book.

I approach Crystal, who scoots over in her seat, making room for me. I sit on the edge of the chair and she places her right hand on my knee. "Look inside, Michael," she says, a wide smile on her face. I can tell that she knows what we're looking at. I can also tell that she has fallen into another one of her test modes. She wants me to show Batnaz that she's not the only one with brains on this ship.

I pick up the cylinder and carefully unfurl the thin strip of cloth stored inside. It's delicate but holds together as I run it through my fingers. There are symbols written all along the strip. I have seen this before. I'm not talking about the Masonic symbols—that much is obvious—but there is something else. This is more than just another PigPen cipher.

Fascinating.

As I study the strip of cloth and the wooden canister it was kept in, I start talking, but it's more a nervous, unintentional rambling than anything. "The earliest use of cryptography was discovered in hieroglyphs carved into monuments from the Old Kingdom of Egypt circa 1900 BC. But it wasn't really any type of secret language."

Batnaz is staring at me. It is a look of surprise. Perhaps, even disbelief. "I knew that Crystal was a master at cryptology," he says, grinning ear-to-ear. "However, it would appear that we have truly hit the jackpot with you two."

I shake my head in disagreement. "Crystal is the master. I am simply her student, her husband, and a fan." I take the cloth strip and start wrapping it around the outside of the wooden canister. "The first known account of *secret* writing—real coding—was developed by the Roman leader Julius Caesar. His cipher took two rows of letters, the top row depicting the letters of the Roman alphabet in their proper order..." I rest the canister down and jot out the letters of the alphabet on a clean sheet of paper—Batnaz never once turning his eyes away—and continue, "and the lower row listing the same alphabet with the last three letters (X, Y, Z) placed at the front, followed by A, B, C, like this."

A B C D E F G H I J K L M N O P Q R S T U V W X Y Z
X Y Z A B C D E F G H I J K L M N O P Q R S T U V W

"Caesar would write out his secret messages using the lower letters in place of the upper ones. For instance, the letter X would take the place of A, G would take the place of J, O for R, and so forth. The result would look something like this."

E B I I L   Z O R B I   Z L O I A

It didn't take long for Batnaz to see the pattern. I can tell by the look on his face that he has figured it out.

"Hello cruel world," he confirmed, inquisitively.

"However, this clever way to keep information secret quickly became obsolete, because Caesar never changed the cipher. So once it was cracked it was cracked for good.

"But it paved the way for later, more advanced ciphers, such as the cipher wheel, invented in 1466 by an Italian man named Leon Battista Alberti, and the infamous Enigma and Hagelin ciphers of the WWII era, which took the art of cryptology into the realm of Popular Mechanics."

I grab the thin cloth strip and continue wrapping it around the ornate wooden canister, and Batnaz glows with pleasure. I know that he's up to something.

But what?

I push the thought aside and continue. "Even the ciphers we're all used to today—often times never realizing we're using them, the encryptions used to keep our emails and websites safe from hackers—all stem from these earliest forms of cryptology. The only difference is that these days ciphers are generated and hacked by supercomputers and are constructed out of endlessly complex arrays of numbers."

I finish wrapping the last bit of cloth around the outside of the canister and hand it to Batnaz. "This is fascinating," I say. "It combines the Masonic or PigPen cipher with a transposition method known as a Scytale cipher."

Batnaz looks at the cylinder, now with the cloth covering its entire surface, the six equal sides of the canister, perfectly separating clearly defined lines of characters. The only problem is, it's still written in Masonic code.

"The Scytale cipher was one of the first truly successful ciphers because the Scytale—or 'baton' as translated from the Greek word σκυτάλη—is actually the key. It must be precisely the right girth, length, and have the correct number of flat sides—this one has six—otherwise the code would be quite tough to crack. Add in the further complication of Masonic cipher and this code is nearly uncrackable without the Scytale."

I set the cylinder down and immediately start writing out the symbols:

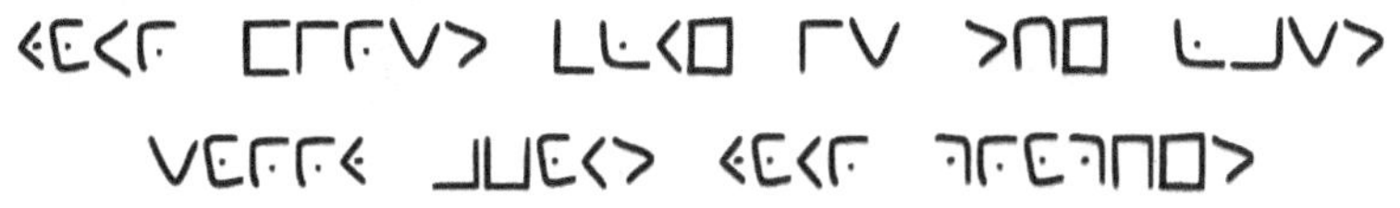

I then write out the basic Masonic PigPen cipher key:

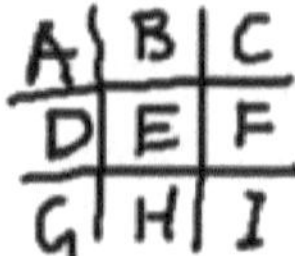 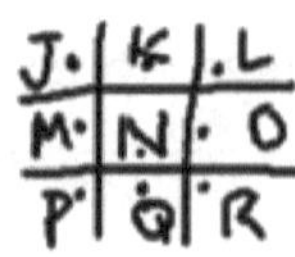  

It doesn't take long for the message to become clear and as it does, it strikes terror in all who can see it:

YOUR FIRST CLUE IS THE LAST
SORRY ABOUT YOUR PROPHET

Batnaz could only stare at the deciphered message that Michael had written out on that notepad.

The silence onboard Darlene was mind-numbing. Batnaz's mind wondered as Crystal and Michael tried to figure out what the message meant. Batnaz had known for many years that this day was coming. He could feel it in his heart. Everything that was happening and about to happen had been long foretold. But the sudden realization of what his dear friends would have to go through—the very image of it—in the manner by which his visions had foreseen terrified him.

Dear God... Forgive us!

The humming from Darlene's engines was beginning to enter his consciousness when a sudden vibrating at his hip startled him back to the present.

It was a text message:

We've found the prophet... It's not good.
Drop everything... Come to Palmyra!

He looked at Crystal and shook his head.

She looked up at him and smiled, before realizing that something was wrong. "What is it?"

Oh, my dear, he thought. *I pray that one day you'll forgive me.* "The prophet," he said, solemnly. "He's dead."

15

The stretched SUV speeds down a series of winding country roads racing toward Palmyra. Toward the Sacred Grove.

Crystal stares at me with heartbreak in her eyes. "My parents brought me to the Sacred Grove once. It was so long ago, and I was so young," she says. "I might have been six. I couldn't stop crying the whole time. My mother had told me it was the Holy Spirit making me cry, and I remember thinking, Why the heck would the Holy Spirit want me to cry?"

I wipe her tears away and gaze into her eyes, the whites surrounding those crystal blues are bloodshot red. I can feel the Holy Spirit here. Right now… burning inside. Its extraordinary power bleeding out of her soul and into mine. The feeling in my chest is one I haven't felt often in my life. It is the sense of peace and of comfort. Strange coming at a time such as this.

"How could anyone murder such a great man—a prophet of God," she cries. "And in a place so sacred to so many people?"

Batnaz says nothing, but I can tell that somewhere inside, he has got to be feeling the effects of the situation as well. How can he not? He's the senior apostle of the Mormon church. Besides, I can see that look in his eye—the look of someone who has just lost the love of his life.

For the first time, I really feel sorry for the man.

The car swerves off the country road into the Smith Family Farm Welcome Center parking lot and screeches to a halt. Without a word Batnaz exits the car where a man dressed in black slacks, a white shirt and tie, and a small name badge had been standing patiently waiting.

The man grabs Batnaz by the arm like a young man might assist an elder and immediately starts off down a long, well-groomed gravel pathway. The path is flanked by stones and small fruit trees, winding through a field of freshly trimmed bright-green grass, away from the welcome center building, through a wide open field, towards a small log home in the distance.

What the hell? I think to myself, looking at Crystal with confused eyes.

But almost as quickly as the men start down the path, Batnaz turns and waves for Crystal and me to catch up.

Crystal and I run by the Smith Family Home—it's tiny.

It's hard to imagine a family living in such a tiny space. "That was Joseph Smith's house?" I ask, stopping briefly, distracted by the meticulously built, hand-hewn log structure.

I turn around, and Crystal is off in the distance, nearly caught up with Batnaz and the mystery man, who are now sprinting. I run towards them, just as they all disappear into the gaping mouth of the larger than expected forest—

The Sacred Grove.

It was hot. Even with the dense shade provided by the grove, sweat puddled in the small of Batnaz's back.

The guide quickly led them down a series of heavily wooded trails, ending in a small clearing several hundred yards into the heart of the grove—an area closed off by streamers of yellow caution tape. The guide paused for a moment, making sure the entire party was present, then lifted the tape, gesturing for the group to enter.

Several men dressed in sleek black suits stood around the area. *Church leaders*, Batnaz recognized.

A couple of them were taking pictures, one was picking up something, but Batnaz couldn't quite tell what it was.

"Where are the police?" the guard asked the suits as he approached. "I called the authorities an hour ago." The guide was visibly distraught. "Leave that alone!" He shouted to one of the suits who was picking up pieces of something that looked like burned silk. "Nothing can be disturbed until the authorities tag and bag it. This is a crime scene, damn it!"

"It's okay," Batnaz said to the guide as he grabbed him on the shoulder and gave a gentle, yet authoritative squeeze. "I am all the authority needed here." Just then a foul stench blew across Batnaz's nose, causing him to waver. His vision blurred momentarily as the stench grew more distinct. Even in all his many years, and all his countless experiences in death and destruction, this smell hit him particularly hard.

"Where's the body?" Michael asked, looking confused.

Just then, Crystal ran back toward the yellow tape and toward a bush, dry heaving.

Michael grabbed his nose and gawked at Batnaz and the guide with inquiring eyes. "My God... what's that smell?"

The guide lifted his hand and pointed into a small grouping of tall oak trees.

Everyone looked up in unison.

Batnaz let out a loud gasp and quickly looked away. There wasn't a shadow of doubt in his mind, the sight before them would haunt him, and anyone else with a soul within them, for the rest of their lives.

The body of the Prophet had been sliced up and burned and strung cruciform from a tall oak. Blood was still dripping from the old man's toes, oozing out from the cuts and burns on his chest and running down his legs and feet. His face was barely recognizable under rivers of blood which streamed down from the crown of thorns that had been driven into his head.

From where they stood, approximately twenty feet away, on the ground, looking up into the tall oak tree, the first thing that struck Crystal was the large triangular formation of symbols etched into the man's bare, bloody chest.

Even after years of serving in Iraq, witnessing some of the worse acts of terror she had thought imaginable, this... Well, she had a difficult time just looking at the body, let alone focusing any attention on what was carved into it. She spotted a bit of silvery gray hair peeking out of the caked blood, and she turned away. "I think there are symbols carved in his chest," she said. "I just can't look anymore."

Michael grabbed his phone and zoomed his camera nice and close on the man's chest and snapped a few pictures. He then ran one of the photos through a special filter that removed the red tones and increased the exposure of the cuts in the flesh. As the filters rendered, a much clearer picture began to appear. "You're right," he confirmed. "Not just symbols, but symbols inside of symbols. Take a look!"

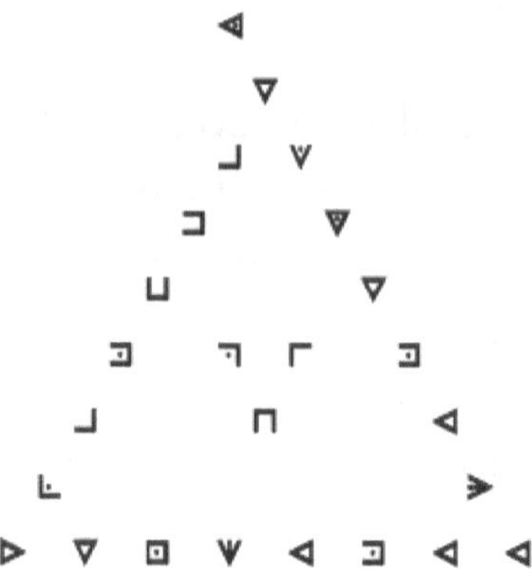

There were Masonic symbols meticulously carved and arranged in the shape of a large triangle taking up most of the area of his chest, with a smaller triangle at its center. Even in a photo, the sight was nothing less than demonic to Crystal, and for the first time in her life, she felt truly out of sorts.

The prophet of The Church of Jesus Christ, she thought. She looked back up at the body and quickly turned away.

How can this even be real?

Her chest tightened and her throat burned. She closed her eyes and put her hands over her nose and mouth. She thought she just might throw up again. She felt her legs start to tremble and quickly bent over and placed her hands on her knees. "I think I need to sit," she murmured.

Then something touched her hand.

It was Michael.

He took her hand into his and held tight.

It was then that she realized just how apparent her inner feelings were on the outside.

She forced out a smile for her husband, squeezed his hand, and then took his phone and focused on the photo, at the markings carved into the Prophet's chest.

"It looks like another PigPen," she managed, then handed the phone back to Michael and grabbed a pad and pen from her back pocket and started writing something out:

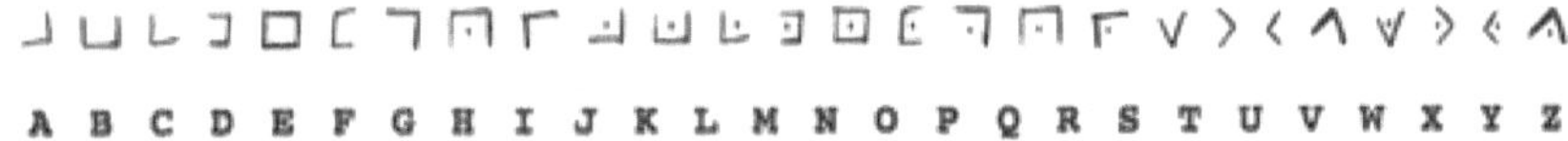

It was the same PigPen key that Michael had written earlier, but then she added something else. Something Michael hadn't used when breaking the code back on Darlene.

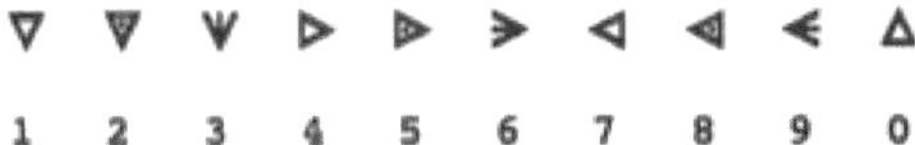

Michael looked at the key Crystal had written out and shook his head, thinking, *I have a hard time decoding PigPen ciphers without writing out the grid lines and X-patterns. I can't even begin to write it out from memory like you just did. And, for crying out loud, I always forget the damn numbers!*

"Why all the Masonic codes?" Batnaz questioned, pulling the Scytale cipher from his jacket, exploring the Masonic code plastered thereon, and then returning his attention towards the prophet's chest, also covered in Masonic code. "I understand about as much as anyone about Freemasonry, yet I fail to see any logical connection."

"That surprises me," Michael said. "The history between the early Mormon Church and Freemasonry is rich, and many argue, ripe with the blood of prophets." Michael continued, "The links between the two are fascinating and go back to before the Mormon Church was even founded."

"Joseph Smith was a Mason," Crystal said. "I remember my father telling me that once."

"It's true," Michael said. "So was his brother Hyrum and his father, Joseph Smith Sr, as well as many of his closest friends. And when the church was in its infancy, thousands of members were Freemasons, even Brigham Young, who some believe remained a practicing Freemason long after he denounced the practice, after moving the church westward, finally settling his people in the vast no man's land that would later become the great state of Utah."

"Isn't it true that Mormon temples are actually Masonic temples in disguise?" Crystal questioned.

Batnaz let out a groan, "Absolutely not!"

"He's right," Michael confirmed. "Mormon temples are not the same. However, early Mormon temple ceremonies did rather closely resemble Masonic ceremonies. Even today, Mormon temples are decorated with images often associated with Freemasonry. So there is an undeniable connection."

"Sure there is," Batnaz started. "However, you must understand that Freemasonry is not, in itself, a religion. It is merely a brotherhood. A fraternity whose primary prerequisite for membership is the profound belief in a higher power." Batnaz paused, looking at Michael with inquisitive eyes. "How do you know so much about Mormons?"

"I actually know very little about Mormons," Michael explained. "My focus of research has been on Freemasonry. I've done a fair amount of digging around over the years, researching for my latest book, *The Secret Freemasons*."

"That's right," Batnaz recalled. "You're a bit of a scholar, aren't you? A college professor and an author."

"Yes, Sir," Michael admitted. "My last book focused on Freemasonry and their dealings with several rites and orders through the centuries. Mormonism is just one of many."

"Yes, well, most of the symbols people associate with Freemasonry," Batnaz continued, "have been around for centuries, long before Freemasonry existed. They are merely images that have been used through the history of mankind by people to symbolize God, the heavens, and creation."

Crystal wrote out the decoded message, happy that the boys were chatting it up. It was helping to keep her mind off of what it was they were actually doing out there.

"Joseph Smith climbed the ranks of Freemasonry with fervor," Michael continued, "receiving the 32nd Degree after just two years, quite an achievement—"

"And the highest one can achieve, without the graces of the Grand Master," Batnaz injected.

"Yes," Michael agreed. "However, even though Smith founded the first Lodge in Nauvoo, and later founded several others, with membership in the thousands, the Mormons would ultimately be thrown out of Freemasonry entirely. The Grand Master declared that all Mormon Lodges had gone clandestine and that all Mormon memberships were suspended.

"There are those who believe," Michael continued, "that this abrupt severance of Masons and Mormons is what ultimately led to Joseph Smith's martyrdom just a few months later. Many claim that Joseph cried out in his last moments, "O Lord, my God, is there no help for the Widow's Son?"—a distress call every Freemason is exhorted to honor—only to be murdered by those very Freemason brothers."

"Something isn't right," Crystal said, as she finished writing out the code. She began to think that perhaps she had it all wrong. *Is this something more than just a PigPen?*

The deciphered message did not make sense:

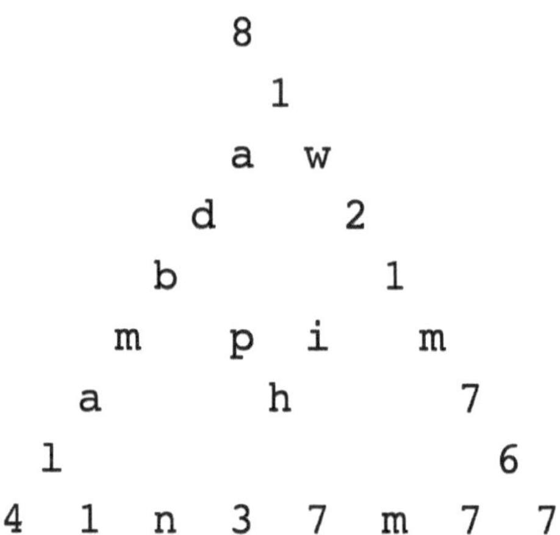

There must be a key? she thought.

"What is it?" Michael asked, concerned.

"Even though the transposition appears to be complete, the message makes no sense."

Something was definitely wrong.

Almost immediately, something stands out. "I see it," I say, unable to control my excitement. *It's so obvious,* I think. *How can she not see?*

"What the hell am I missing?" Crystal asks. Her face testifies that she actually doesn't see it. I'm feeling proud. Then I remember where we are, and that sick feeling returns.

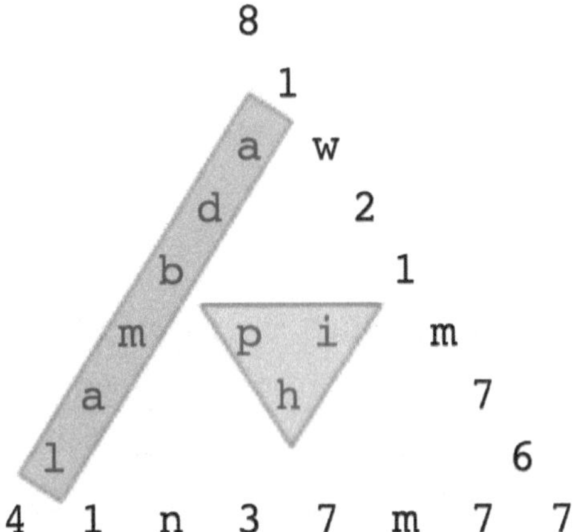

"PHI and LAMBDA," I explain, clarity of the situation—the code painted in blood on canvas once the vessel of a Prophet—hitting hard. "There's no way it's a coincidence."

Right away I can see that Crystal understands. She casts me that proud grin that I feed off of and she allows me to continue explaining what I have found.

I write out the Greek character for PHI and explain, "PHI is the twenty-first letter of the Greek alphabet."

I then write out another Greek character. "And Lambda is the eleventh letter of the Greek alphabet."

Looking at the Greek characters, I almost immediately realize a similarity to the triangles.

The smaller triangle, which the letters PHI created, and the Greek character φ , both are pointing down, to the bottom row of numbers, and the larger triangle, with that oddball character hanging off the top-left, corresponds with the Greek character λ , indicating a connection with the right set of numbers.

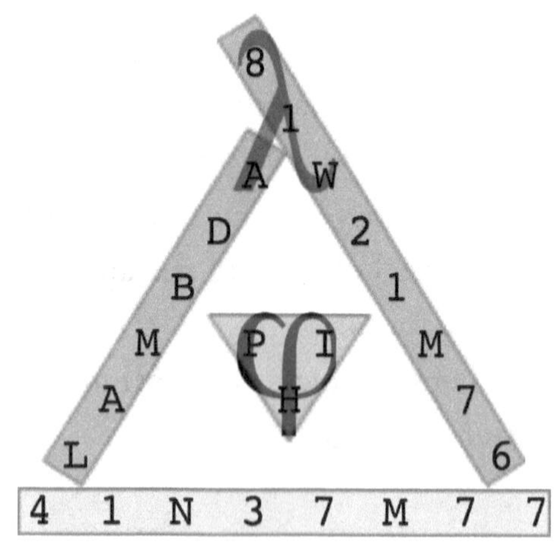

"Well, these Greek symbols are used for another purpose as well," I say, as I write out the remaining numbers and letters. "I'm sure this must look familiar to you?" I look over at Batnaz, whose eyes light up just as I remember my students' eyes lighting up back when I was teaching at Harvard Divinity School. It was somewhat child-like, yet still serious.

φ 4 1 N 3 7 M 7 7   λ 8 1 W 2 1 M 7 6

"Coordinates," Batnaz says, sounding excited.

I write out the string of code into something a bit more recognizable and smile. "You would be right, my friend."

$$\varphi\ 41°\ 37.77N$$
$$\lambda\ 81°\ 21.76W$$

Crystal enters the digits into her smartphone's GPS app, and the coordinates bring a tiny red dot on the Google map. She pinches her fingers together on the screen and then spreads them out, zooming in on the map until a satellite image of a small white church building begins to appear.

Batnaz lights up again at the sight. I've never seen him so excited. Kind of strange, considering the situation. "The code," he declares. "It's pointing to the Kirtland Temple."

16

Batnaz held the door to the back seat of the stretched SUV, still parked in the Smith Family Welcome Center parking lot, and allowed Crystal and Michael to slip inside. He didn't say a word. At the moment he had just one thing on his mind.

He closed the door with a soft smile and discreetly grabbed his smartphone from his breast pocket. He selected a number from his favorites and started walking around the front of the SUV, out of sight of the others. *Come on,* he said to himself. *Answer the phone!* "Is it done?" the man who finally answered asked, his voice gentle, yet authoritative. "They cracked the code, as I predicted they would," Batnaz quietly answered. This was not a conversation he wanted the others to hear. "I'm more confident than ever. This is going to work."

"You're positive she doesn't know any—"

"Yes," Batnaz interrupted, eager to end the call before the others grew suspicious. "I assure you, this will be well worth every last bit of your... of *our* sacrifice."

Batnaz ended the call as he opened the door and slid into the passenger's seat beside Crystal. "Make haste," he said to his driver, patting the palm of his hand on the driver's headrest. "We need to get back to the airport, now."

As we settle ourselves back into Darlene's reclining cushy seats, skimming along the Earth's stratosphere, Batnaz takes it upon himself to start explaining a little Mormon history. I suppose it could prove useful as we try to figure out this baffling case, but, truthfully, I'm exhausted. The last thing I want to hear is a load of mind-numbing church history.

As Batnaz starts talking, about how within a year of forming the Church—founded in the Smith family room in Fayette, New York—Joseph received revelation to move his family and the church to Kirtland, I adjust my seat into a semi-reclined position. I'm playing with the controls to the window, making it as clear as it will go. The view at 60,000 feet is like nothing the average man ever gets to experience. I certainly never have. There isn't a cloud to be seen at this height. Just an ocean of intense dark blue. At times it almost looks black. The curvature of the Earth is clearly visible, making it all too easy to imagine that we're in space.

"One reason many believe Joseph Smith moved his family and church to Kirtland," Batnaz continues, "was because he had sent missionaries westward who converted a Reformed Baptist pastor from Kirtland named Sidney Rigdon."

I'm barely listening. However, Crystal is all ears, sitting upright in her chair absorbing every word as I gaze out the window at the surreal otherworldliness taking place outside.

Batnaz continues, never skipping a beat. "Sidney Rigdon would later convert his entire congregation, plus countless souls from his community. There were more members in the Kirtland area than there were in the entire state of New York at the time."

"Well, that explains why he moved then," Crystal says.

"Indeed," Batnaz confirms. "Realizing this, Joseph felt that the church would grow faster, and his followers would be happier if they set up their church headquarters in Kirtland. Joseph and his followers experienced a burst of growth and peace for several years after they settled in Kirtland. Some members would also settle in areas around Missouri, which would later prove a blessing."

The sound of Batnaz's rich melodic voice lulls me to sleep. I close my eyes and rub my head. The lump appears to be subsiding a bit, but it still hurts like hell. I start to drift off and Batnaz's words begin to flow out like a fine chardonnay.

"Membership in the Church grew from a few hundred people in 1830 to well over 15,000 by the time they were forced to leave everything behind for yet another promise of peace, growth, and blessing in another land."

"What do you mean?" Crystal asks. "Why were they forced to leave?"

"I'll get there," he explains. "But first, you need to understand where we're going right now. Kirtland is a special place. Sometime during the winter of 1832 Joseph received revelation to build a house of God. But this was not just another church. No. God instructed him to build a temple."

"Like Solomon's Temple?"

"Not quite," he explains. "Solomon's Temple was basically a monument. Some believe it was built to house the Ark of the Covenant, keeper of the tablets bearing the commandments of God. In reality, Solomon's Temple was a place where ritualist sacrifices were made as a means of communicating with God. Mormon temples are quite different. Joseph Smith was instructed to build a holy temple where he, and other worthy members, would receive higher authority in the priesthood and become enlightened to greater knowledge in the doctrine of Christ."

I feel as if I'm floating in space. Am I outside the plane? I can see Batnaz sitting in his chair speaking. His voice sounds a lot like Berry White now, but I can hear every word. But I'm floating, looking in the window from outside. How can I hear him? Clearly, I'm trapped within that tripping realm, caught somewhere between consciousness and dreaming.

"It took three years to complete the first temple," Barry White says, in that deep baritone that almost sounds like singing, "and on March 27, 1836, the Kirtland Temple was dedicated. From that day on, the veil had been ripped away from the barrier between heaven and earth. Joseph Smith knew that building a temple was important, but until it was finished, and the pursuing revelations and blessings flooded him and his people, he had no real clue as to the magnitude of what he was doing. By the time the Saints (as his followers were known) left Kirtland, Joseph was a new man. He was a restored priest, a restored Prophet. He had a renewed faith and an intensified focus on his life and purpose of this mission. Nothing was going to stop the building up of the Kingdom of God on Earth."

Darlene's tires hit the runway and startle me awake. Even at one-quarter of its top airspeed, thirty minutes is all it took for us to arrive at Classic Jet Center at Lost Nation Airport in Willoughby, Ohio, minutes north of the Kirtland Temple.

17

The Kirtland Temple is surprisingly plain, as are the well-maintained grounds, accented with modest, yet beautifully arranged flowerbeds and shrubs.

As for the building itself, it looks old. Cracks in the stucco spiderweb off in all directions. And rather than displaying the typical markings or symbols that most would associate with Mormon temples, *this* temple looks, well, ordinary. Granted, it's pretty damn big. Easily over a hundred feet tall, and yet still, it just looks like a typical church you might see in any small town. There are many large arched windows plastered across the sides and front of the building, and though their frames are clearly in need of a fresh coat of paint, they are beautifully designed and masterly hand-crafted.

Standing on the curb of the main road—Chillicothe, I believe—merely a few dozen steps away from the main entrance, it's easy for me to tell just how proud the Saints must have felt after completing such a grand structure. I mean, it's pretty massive even by today's standards. But a hundred-and-eighty years ago, this must have looked like a mountain unto itself.

The main entrance of the temple consists of two oversized forest-green doors, which are propped open. These entranceways nest atop two large pyramids, which make up the three concrete steps leading into the building. Several feet above the doors at the center of the wall is an arched window, bigger than the rest, and just above that is an equally large millwork placard that reads—

HOUSE OF THE LORD
Built by the Church of the
Latter Day Saints. A.D. 1834

Even higher still, above the placard, towering at least a hundred feet over my head is a proud, stately tower, capped off with a tarnished, green copper dome and simple wrought-iron weathervane. All and all, it is definitely an impressive bit of hand craftsmanship from A.D. 1834.

There's a decorative sign on a green post sticking out of the ground just a few feet away from me. The researcher inside my soul compels me to check it out.

Dedicated in 1836, the "House of the Lord," commonly known as the Kirtland Temple, served as the center of community life for the thousands of church members in and around Kirtland. Distinctive design features include two large assembly rooms with tiers of elaborately carved pulpits at both ends, and windows on every interior and exterior wall. Members and friends gathered on the first floor to worship. The second floor was devoted to church leadership education and training. The third floor housed additional schoolrooms and administrative offices.

According to a local minister, life for many members was difficult. They lived in what he described as an "assemblage of hovels and shanties and small houses." They overcame their hardships through great sacrifice, with some giving up "even the necessaries of life" in order to build what was then one of the largest buildings in northern Ohio. Kirtland Temple symbolizes the empowerment that comes from spiritual preparation and dedicated stewardship, while inspiring continuing efforts to build up the communities in which we live.

"Hey, are you coming?" Crystal's voice startles me and I look up to see that she is with Batnaz, starting down one of the concrete pathways that wind through a wide open park. I quickly catch up to them. The grounds really are lovely in their simplicity. I've visited a couple of Mormon temple grounds before, while researching Freemasonry. The markings on Mormon temples are fascinating, and the grounds, absolutely breathtaking. But here, everything is subtle. Elegant. Simple. The pathway is lined with black cast-iron benches, and the scent of mixed flowers, shrubs, and evergreens fills the air.

"There's no one around," Crystal says. "Is this normal?"

"I'm afraid not," Batnaz expresses, then quickly makes his way back toward the front of the temple. Crystal is right on his heels as they disappear around the front of the building. I'm not far behind, but as I leave the path and step onto the red inlaid herringbone brick circling around the front of the building, I get this strange feeling in the pit of my stomach.

I look over at Crystal and Batnaz who are both standing at the top of the pyramid of steps waiting for me to catch up. Batnaz looks impatient, but Crystal looks at me with eyes that say something isn't right. Suddenly the atmosphere around me changes. I feel a heaviness fall on my shoulders.

I take those few steps up the pyramid to the massive green

door and do my best to brush off the feeling, but it is weighing me down. I mean, I'm actually beginning to feel ill by this.

Batnaz enters the temple and Crystal just stares at me. She knows. I can tell.

"Are you okay?" She places her arm around my shoulders and pulls me close. "Is it your head?" She gently kisses my temple. "Are you dizzy?"

I honestly haven't considered that. "Perhaps," I agree. "It must be that." But I'm not so sure.

Something is wrong. I can feel it in my soul.

I give Crystal one last look, to see if perhaps she also feels something. But she doesn't. She truly is just concerned about me. "You don't feel anything?"

"What do you mean?" she asks, sounding somewhat confused. "You're starting to scare me."

Maybe it's my head. "Nothing," I say. "I'm okay." Then I enter the temple.

We catch up to Batnaz who's standing in the foyer looking skyward. As my eyes adjust from the momentary sun-blindness, I'm immediately taken aback. The interior of the temple is far more impressive than you would imagine looking at it from the outside. We're standing at the center of a massive, pure white, wide open vestibule. On either side of us are two beautiful oak staircases twisting up the walls to a second-floor loft, wrapped in golden oak banisters and rails high overhead.

In front of us are two large closed doors.

Batnaz turns his attention to these doors and opens the one right in front of us, which happens to be the left door, leading Crystal and me inside the heart of the temple. *Where church members would meet to worship,* I recall from reading the sign posted out front.

Crystal's face is one of pure awe as she gazes upward at the massive scale of the space. I'm taken by the pure whiteness of everything, though I still can't shake the feeling that something is very wrong here.

Immediately upon entering, I notice on my right a massive, hand-crafted, tri-tiered set of white podiums. Just opposite those podiums to my left is a set of quad-tiered platforms. Eight fluted Greek columns, motiffed at the top with richly crafted moldings and floral designs, flank either side of an arched ceiling giving an almost magical depth to the center of the hall. Straight ahead there's an isle leading all the way to the back wall of the temple. To the right of the aisle are row after row of pure white pews, lined in that gold millwork. And to my left, all along the length of the aisle, are those stunning arched windows, made even more impressive by the light now beaming through, casting a magical glow over the space.

"Something is not right," Batnaz finally says. "The doors are open. This place should never be empty like this." He turns and heads back into the vestibule and stops dead in his tracks. Crystal and I move quickly behind him.

A woman's cries echo throughout the large space, traveling down from somewhere upstairs. Batnaz starts up the stairs with haste but stops as the woman appears. She's walking slowly down, gripping the railing with her left hand and holding a tissue to her face with the other. She's draped in a long rose-red dress and is wearing a sunhat of the same color. Her face is flush and wet with tears. Her hair is long and as white as the interior walls of the temple. "There's..." she starts to say, then coughs to clear her throat. "Something horrible has happened."

Just then a police car races by the front of the temple, the sound of the sirens screaming through the open doors as it skids to a stop.

"What's happening?" Crystal asks, and as she runs to the door a second police car streaks by. Directly behind that car follows a fire rescue vehicle and an ambulance. Almost immediately the sirens go silent, and doors slam in rapid fire.

Without another word, we run toward the commotion.

"It's a cemetery," Crystal says as we run around the street corner and everything comes into view.

But to me, the strobing lights from the plethora of emergency vehicles, along with the frantic movements of the rescue personnel, give what should be a quiet and peaceful graveyard, the appearance of some kind of morbid carnival.

18

It was that smell again. The same smell they experienced back in the Sacred Grove. Only this time it hit them all simultaneously and paid no mercy whatsoever.

As they approached the scene, marked off by yellow crime-scene tape, a man looked their way and immediately came running over. Noticing this, Batnaz walked up ahead and met with the man, who lifted the tape and waved to them to enter. "President," the man said with a subtle bow as Batnaz crossed under the tape. "I'm so very sorry, sir." Something about the man appeared strange to Crystal. The man looked sincere, perhaps a little too sincere. It was almost as if it were rehearsed.

"What has happened?" Batnaz questioned, waiting briefly for Crystal and Michael to cross the perimeter, then making no further attempt to prolong the inevitable, he sprinted toward the huddled mass of rescue workers and officers. "Damn it, Fitzgerald!" he shouted. For the first time, Crystal sensed anger bleeding from Batnaz, and it startled her. "What's going on here?"

Black vultures circled high overhead, swooping down as opportunity broke. They were pecking at the ground—or rather, something on the ground. The man called Fitzgerald ran up to Batnaz, still moving quite fast toward the scene and said, "He was just giving a joint tour of the temple not thirty minutes ago." The man sounded nervous. "I don't understand how this could have happened."

When Crystal finally realized what it was the vultures were

picking at she ran behind the nearest monolith and emptied her stomach. In all of her years breaking codes as a cryptologic linguist in the military, witnessing people get murdered, women and children shot in the crossfires of an endless middle-eastern conflict, never did she once experience a sight as horrific as what lay before her now.

"I'm sorry." The voice was Michael's. Crystal didn't turn to look at him, she just kept her head low, behind the monument, unsure if it was over. "None of this would have happened if I hadn't picked up that phone or answered the hotel room door."

"It's not your fault, Michael," she said, finally turning to look at him. "I'm the one who said we would do this." She composed herself and then stepped back out into the open, stepping a bit closer toward the scene, where a couple of police officers quickly stepped in and blocked their way.

"Excuse me, folks," one of the officers said, looking at Crystal and then at Michael. "I realize you're with the president, however, I must insist that you stay back—"

"It's okay," Batnaz interrupted. "I need them here."

The officers obliged, which struck Crystal as odd. Why would Batnaz hold authority over this scene more than the police would? She and Michael cautiously stepped closer.

There was a gaping hole in the man's abdomen, long strips of fleshy, bloody webs were scattered about. It was as if something had exploded inside and the guy's innards had blown out in every direction. One of the vultures swooped down at that moment and grabbed a piece of the intestine in its beak and flew off, the intestine, still attached to the body, stretched at least ten feet before snapping off, sending a large section springing back toward the corpse like a rubber-band. One police officer flinched as a line of blood splattered across his face. It took several seconds for it to sink in what had just happened to him, and when it did, he turned pale and stumbled a bit, before sitting himself on a grave marker.

Though the body lay chest up, the head was twisted face down. The neck was clearly broken. His arms and legs were mangled, twisted in disturbing positions, and blood...

Blood soaked absolutely *everything*.

Batnaz slowly made his way toward the body, suddenly not looking so sure that he really wanted to know. He very carefully turned the man's head and let out a loud gasp.

"Oh, God!" he said, tears welling in his eyes.

"Who is it?" Crystal asked.

"It's Jacob," he said, choking back tears. "My dear, Jacob, apostle and second counselor to the prophet." He closed his eyes and bowed his head, then turned and looked straight at Crystal and Michael, who were standing just a few feet away, subconsciously holding hands. "I'm all that's left."

19

Her name was Lilith and she was quite possibly the most beautiful woman to ever walk the Earth.

But her attraction went far deeper than mere beauty. Men who looked upon her fell at her feet, granted her every wish. She was the personification of female sexuality. Her eyes, a heart-piercing olive green so stunning, even women couldn't help but stare.

She had a power over people that was almost godlike, and she used it to get whatever she wanted, and right now she had her sights on President Batnaz, Michael DiBianco, and young, pretty, blue-eyed Crystal.

She donned a press badge, an expensive Nikon camera, and was dressed in a light-peach blouse and a light-grey skirt which draped her sleek curves with perfect elegance. A navy-blue cap with the words The Kirtland Gazette sprawled across the top—which helped keep her silky blond hair out of her olive green eyes—was a clear statement that she was ready to make her move.

She watched the scene unfold before her from a distant secret location, zooming in close on her three targets with her camera as they examined the body and the surrounding area.

Why haven't they found it? she thought.

They examined the body and the area surrounding the body. Now they were just chit-chatting like school children.

What fools!

"They're not doing anything," she grumbled. "They're just scrambling about like idiots. They're wasting my time!"

How could they miss it?

She snapped a few pictures, feeling the temperature of her body rise. *It's right under your noses!*

She could see it plain as day from all the way across the field. Sure, that could have been because she planted it. But she had all but convinced herself that it would be too easy.

"Boy, was I wrong!" she sneered, no longer able to watch.

20

There was no denying that this heinous slaughter was connected in some way with the equally gruesome murder of the Prophet. However, it was Crystal who made the Biblical connection. "The Prophet's death clearly mimicked—"

Mocked, really, she thought.

"—the crucifixion of Christ," Michael finished.

"Yes," she confirmed, glad that he was paying attention. "And though this may look just flippin' out of this world crazy," she said, trying hard to ignore the morbid stench and fighting off the continual urge to get as far away from there as she could, as fast as she could, "this well-orchestrated display is very clearly, in my opinion, mimicking the death of Judas."

"How so?" Fitzgerald chuckled. "Everyone with a brain knows Judas Iscariot hung himself after he betrayed Christ."

Michael sneered at Fitzgerald's disrespectful tone and looked as if he might say something, when—

"There are actually two accounts of what happened to Judas," a beautiful young journalist said, startling them as she snuck out from behind a tall monument.

She was calm, pleasant, and very sensual. Her seductiveness wasn't totally in their face, but it was clear, at least to Crystal, that this woman was trouble.

Crystal gazed upon the beautiful woman with disdain, while Batnaz and Michael welcomed her into their little group as if they had known her for years. And the police... it was as if they didn't even notice that she was there.

"The second and likely more accurate account," the beautiful woman continued, "is found in Acts 1:18, which explains that Judas purchased a large plot of land with the silver he got for turning in Jesus and that it was somewhere on that land where he fell headlong off a cliff, his body spilling out over the land."

Batnaz gazed sharply at the beautiful woman.

"The name is Lilith," she said, reaching for his hand. But Batnaz didn't bite.

Michael was the first to take the bait and shook her hand firmly, his full attention swallowed up by her piercing olive green eyes.

"Pleased to meet you," he said with an awkward, almost child-like grin, holding on perhaps longer than he should have.

"Yes," Crystal said, a bit of sarcasm bleeding through as she stole the woman's hand from Michael. "A pleasure."

"You sure know a lot about Judas," Michael said, prying his gaze away from hers to look back at the body.

"If Judas fell from a cliff," Crystal considered, "then that means this man must have also fallen from somewhere."

As if on cue, everyone looked up, except for Batnaz, who just glared at the beautiful woman.

High within the branches of a red maple hung a frayed rope, a broken noose dangling at its end. Tucked inside the knot was a tightly rolled piece of paper.

"What is this?" Crystal said to the beautiful woman.

But she was gone.

Crystal works the small piece of parchment from the knot and carefully unrolls it. I recognize the cipher right away.

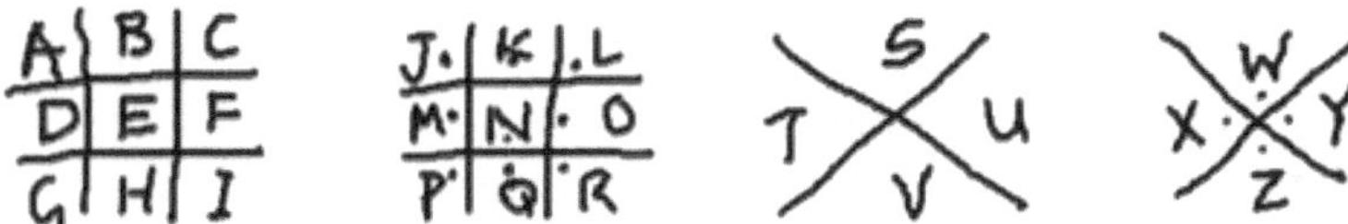

"This should be easy to crack," I say, with perhaps a bit too much confidence.

"Who was that woman?" Crystal asks, but I barely hear.

I grab a pen and pad from my jacket pocket and draw out the PigPen cipher codex, as I had earlier.

"Don't worry about that woman," I hear Batnaz say under his breath as Crystal steps closer to hear him.

I speak up, perhaps a little too loud. "Seems obvious that it's just another Tic-Tac-Toe cipher."

Crystal gazes at me. I can't quite tell if it's pride—knowing that she had taught me well—or aggravation.

"So, what does it say?" She says, with a smile. Actually, it's more like a smirk.

I take a closer look at the Masonic symbols and suddenly realize the error in my hasty declaration.

My lack of code breaking experience has made me look a little like a fool. Not only can I not crack the code, but I failed to notice the upside-down T's before trying to show off.

This isn't part of any Masonic cipher I've ever seen.

"I have to admit, this is not at all what I thought." I wipe a bit of sweat from my brow and stare at the codex.

She must realize how foolish I'm feeling because she quickly breaks the awkwardness. "You're not entirely wrong, Michael." Her voice is soft. "It is Masonic, you are absolutely correct about that. However, this is a variant that few people have ever seen. It is no wonder, really, that you missed it."

"How do you mean?" Batnaz says.

"Yeah, I've done extensive research on Freemasonry," I say, perhaps looking a bit bewildered. "You of all people can attest to that. How many times have I picked your brain on the subject? How could I have missed this?"

"It's okay, Michael," Crystal says. "I nearly missed it myself." She points to the piece of paper, specifically, at the upside-down T's. "But this is not a typical Masonic cipher. It fact, it's a rare Brigham Young variant of the Royal Arch cipher—"

"Royal Arch?" I say all of a sudden positive that the alarm in my voice had been noticed.

"And what exactly is the Royal Arch?" Batnaz asks.

"It's one of the highest levels of Freemasonry," I explain. "Bearing strong ties with such notable groups as the Templar Knights and even the Illuminati."

"Illuminati?" Batnaz's tone is abhorrent. "You are not trying to say that Brigham Young was a member of the Illuminati?"

"While Michael is technically correct," Crystal says, "not every Mason in the Holy Royal Arch was involved in, nor even was aware of, many of the darker activities held within those fringe groups."

Batnaz gazes intently at both of us. "Brigham was a great man." His tone was both stern and powerful. "I assure you, he was *not* Illuminati. As for the Templar Knights, noble as they may have been, Brigham was not involved there, either."

Crystal looks relieved, as am I.

She grabs the pen and pad from my hands and starts writing something down. "The Brigham Young Royal Arch cipher looks like this."

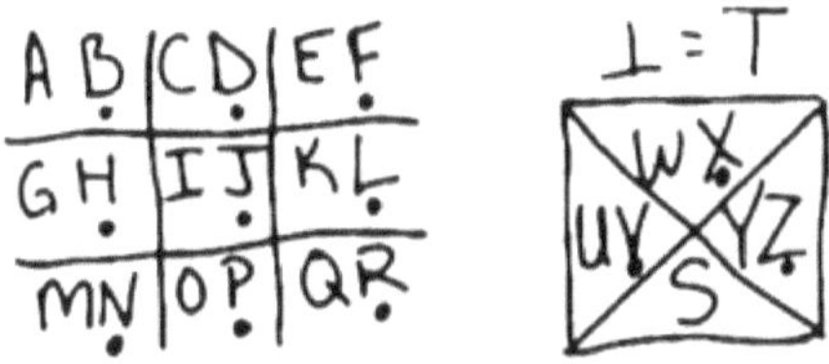

Batnaz and I gaze at what Crystal has just written out, and well, it's times like these when I realize that my wife really is the superhero I often see when I look at her. She is easily the most incredible woman I have ever met.

Crystal hands me the pad and pen and gives me the honor of writing out the answer for us all to see.

THE LIAHONA EFFECT

"Where have I heard of that before," she says. "Liahona. It

sounds so familiar."

I shrug my shoulders. "Certainly nothing I've heard of."

"The Liahona was a mystical compass used by the *Book of Mormon* Prophet, Lehi—father of Nephi," Batnaz explains. "It helped Lehi lead his people, known as the Nephites, out of the wilderness, across the ocean, and to the Promised Land. The Liahona was special, a truly unique device, because its godly power could only be used in the hands of a worthy soul."

Crystal could only remember bits and pieces from her childhood. Her parents were devoted to the Church and yet, for some reason, she just never connected on that level.

It didn't help much that her parents were stolen away when she was just eight years old.

She never returned to the Church after that. "Okay," she said, trying hard to remember the story.

"But, it is more than just that," Batnaz continued. "The Liahona Effect is something altogether different."

"How so?" said Michael.

"I've heard about this only once before. It's not something many people know about. Indeed, I am but one of three still alive who are aware of its existence—until now, that is."

"What are you talking about?" Crystal said.

"Remember, the Liahona is a compass that only works if you are truly worthy and is a useless hunk of metal in the wrong hands. Lehi was a chosen prophet, called by God, and he was given the Liahona as a means to guide his family out of the wilderness and to the Promised Land." Batnaz hesitated, unsure of how exactly he should proceed.

"What does any of this have to do with what we're talking about?" Michael said.

"Joseph Smith created an inspired roadmap, designed to guide one special person—someone who is worthy—to something truly amazing. I am speaking of something that can only be compared with the Holy Grail. It is both an artifact and a great secret. This roadmap was designed specifically to work only in the hands of the one person who has been chosen by God. Just like the Liahona led Lehi in the *Book of Mormon* stories. Brigham Young called this—"

"The Liahona Effect," Crystal finished.

"Yes, my dear." Batnaz nodded.

"So, if this is merely the name of a map," Michael said, "what are we supposed to do with it?"

"Where's the map?" Crystal said as she started pacing about, drifting further and further away from the grisly murder scene. "Excuse me," she said, lifting the yellow tape and ducking under. "I need some fresh air."

Michael started off in her direction but was quickly stopped by Batnaz who took him by the shoulder and turned him around. "Your wife is very special."

"Excuse me?"

"Please, forgive me," Batnaz said, taking a step back. "Your wife has a gift. She's been described by everyone that I have spoken with, as simply the best cryptologist in the world. She also has a strong connection with the Mormon church. I doubt that even she realizes the extent of it."

"Hey, guys!" Crystal called out from afar. "Come up here!" She was several yards off, on a slight hill, gazing down at a small tombstone. "I think you might wanna look at this!"

It was the tomb of a small child, and it sent chills down Crystal's spine.

Carved into the pink marble was a small toddler bed. Upon the bed lay a child, lost in eternal slumber.

It was clean—the tomb.

Relatively new.

A name was chiseled below the masterfully carved child:

Savanna Mary Ellen Smith
2014 - 2016

My God, she thought. *She's just a baby.*

She wondered if the child could have been a descendant of the Prophet Joseph. But then, as she looked below the name, something else arrested her attention.

It sometimes takes a weary
female to lead the world!

Weary Female?

At that moment she was transported back to Iraq.

Less than a year before meeting her husband, Michael, she had helped the US Military break a series of encrypted messages that were flooding back and forth between several middle-eastern countries. The cipher had been written using an archaic form of Latin.

During those days, sweating off more liquid then you could possibly take in, trying to break codes in the back of a fast moving Humvee or in one of the dozens of dust-filled, claustrophobic tents they had her working in, she had learned far more about Latin than she had ever learned in college.

She had convinced herself that she'd never again use that knowledge. Now, she was grateful to have it.

Lia, she thought for a moment, recalling that it's a Latin variant for the word *Leah,* derived from the Hebrew name *Lā'āh,* which is a girl's name that literally means—

Weary.

And *Hona,* she remembered—digging deeper into memories that she had sworn to keep buried away, back to her less than admirable college days—is a very little used archaic word, meaning *female.* Oddly enough, it is a Swedish word. It is so obscure that many scholars who have tried to understand the Mormon Liahona, simply choose to ignore the word *hono* altogether, instead focusing on just the first, more common word—*Lia.*

How could Joseph Smith have understood this? she thought. *World-renowned scholars, men and women with PhDs, have struggled to understand, and many simply choose to ignore the conjunction of the seemingly at odds words.*

But Joseph?

Somehow, he knew.

It sometimes takes a **Liahona** *to lead the world!*

As Batnaz and I arrive at Crystal's side, she's just standing there, pointing down at a rather haunting infant tombstone and the inscription carved thereon.

"Liahona," she says, still pointing. She looks as if lost in a deepening thought.

"What is it?" I say as I notice something odd and run my fingers down the cool stone. "There's blood here." I raise my hand to my nose, rubbing the warm, sticky fluid between my fingers. "And it's still fresh!"

Crystal must have been so taken by the inscription that she hadn't noticed. But now, as she turns her attention lower— "There must be a deeper purpose for me."

I knew from the start that Crystal had reservations about this whole thing. And the look on her face right now speaks volumes. "What is it?" I ask.

"You might say, I've been a bit of a weary female since the start of this venture. It just now struck me that there may be more to all this than I first considered."

"What do you mean?"

"Liahona," she says. "It literally means, weary female."

Batnaz looks at me with impressed eyes, however, frankly, I'm not sure what to think of it, so I get back to the blood, even though I know that it would be pointless to try to find the perpetrator. "Whoever did this can't possibly have gone very far," I say. "This had to have just happened." But there are far too many people hanging around the cemetery. Anyone could be the murderer.

That goes for us, I suddenly realize, panic threatening to set in its dastardly claws. I glance over at law enforcement—

My God, I think, just noticing for the first time. *There must be dozens of them.* They are still down by the body, taking photos and collecting evidence. One of the officers glances over at me, and I feel my pulse rise.

Damn it!

Relax!

We don't have a damn clue who or what we are looking for and suddenly—perhaps because I'm out of anxiety medication and I'm starting to lose it—I'm getting the unyielding feeling that we're not welcome here.

"Guys?" Crystal says. "There's a code!" Crystal pulls away some tall grass and gazes at the blood which is forming a string of Masonic characters along the base of the marble:

Crystal could tell immediately, due to the upside-down 'T's, that it was also written in Brigham Young cipher, like the code from the broken noose.

As Michael snapped photos of the tombstone and the code eerily written in blood, Crystal grabbed the pad and pen from her jacket and went to work decoding the text.

U	G	N	H	E	T	Q	E	E	T	H	R	R	B	B	H	T	U
U	T	S	T	E	O	O	S	N	A	N	C	Y	E	I	E	E	R

Crystal explained that it was a transposition cipher, and to break it they would need to count the number of characters in the code and divide that number into equal parts.

"Here we have thirty-six characters, which divides perfectly by six," she explained. "And six happens to be a special number to Masons. Freemasons are obsessed with certain numbers: zero, three, six, nine, thirteen, et cetera, and multiples thereof."

She reorganized the code into a 6 x 6 square:

U	G	N	H	E	T
Q	E	E	T	H	R
R	B	B	H	T	U
U	T	S	T	E	O
O	S	N	A	N	C
Y	E	I	E	E	R

"Once you figure out the size of the square," Crystal said, "you simply examine it much like a word search puzzle."

Immediately, she saw a light go off in Michael's head.

"I see it!" he said and took the pen from Crystal's hand and circled the word YOUR which he found in the lower left corner of the square, flowing from bottom to top.

"And here, also!" he said, circling the word COURT found at the top right of the square, again flowing bottom to top.

But then, almost as quickly as the excitement flooded him, the light of inspiration went dark.

"That can't be it."

"You're so close," she said, retrieving her pen. "It's not exactly a word search. With these ciphers, once you figure out the direction of flow, you just follow that same direction through the entire square."

She drew arrows from bottom to top beside each of the columns within the square and then allowed Michael to study the puzzle a bit longer.

She had no doubt that he would figure it out now.

U	G	N	H	E	T
Q	E	E	T	H	R
R	B	B	H	T	U
U	T	S	T	E	O
O	S	N	A	N	C
Y	E	I	E	E	R

Michael studied the square a moment. He followed Crystal's arrow up the left side, again finding the first word.

YOUR

He then examined the next couple letters—

QU

—and combined them with the letters in the second column, again following the letters up, from bottom to top. He found that combining the last two letters from the first column and the bottom three letters from the second column, gave him the second word in the decoded message.

QUEST

He continued this process throughout the entire square until the message finally revealed itself.

Your Quest Begins
Beneath the Nether Court

Right away, Batnaz's eyes lit up. "The Melchizedek Priesthood Pulpit," he started to explain, "located on the western side of the temple. It's known as the Lower Court." He looked dead certain. "It has to be the place."

21

Lilith stood motionless in the cool dark cavernous space as two figures cloaked in pure white robes stood before her. Black and white checkerboard stretched off in all directions beneath her feet and dozens of lofty fluted columns strong-armed a massive structure—impossible to see. Surrounding them all were chest-high iron rods, and upon each was a single candle—swirling whiffs of flame and smoke trailing off into the dark depths.

"I have done what you asked," she said in an arrogant tone. "Why have you summoned me here?"

The cloaked figures spread their arms wide, their white robes draping at their sides. The action blocked out much of the light from reaching the center of the room where Lilith stood. One of the figures spoke in a bold voice, "You can have no further contact with the subjects."

"I was just trying to—"

"Do you understand, Lilith?" the voice retorted.

She said nothing.

She simply nodded.

22

Batnaz, Crystal, and Michael ran to the temple.

The two adjacent doors were still open, and there was no sign of anyone on the temple grounds or standing about the entrance. They all must be caught up in the commotion at the cemetery. *Oh, Jacob,* Batnaz thought as he led Crystal and Michael up the pyramid steps, through the open door, and back into the heart of the Kirtland Temple, *I'm sorry.*

"That's it," Batnaz said, pointing up ahead.

On the far wall was a set of tri-tiered podiums, flanked by stairs with bright golden oak railings, which were themselves flanked by even more quad-tiered choir platforms filling all four corners of the room.

"When the choir sings from those platforms," Batnaz said, gesturing to the four corners, "it transcends anything you've ever experienced in your life. Nothing less than heavenly."

Crystal believed it.

"But that," he said, pointing to the podiums. "That's the Melchizedek Pulpit, also known as the Lower Pulpit, simply because it is on the lower floor."

your quest begins beneath the nether court

They frantically climbed the dozen or so steps on either

side of the massive triple-tiered lower pulpits, searching on their hands and knees, combing the walls and floors for anything out of the ordinary. "There must be something here," Batnaz said, sounding sure.

About halfway up the right staircase, just before the first tier of pulpits, barely noticeable in the hardwood floor behind the sacramental altar, Crystal found something that looked like a panel. It was large, easily big enough to be a doorway.

They got on their knees and tried to work the panel out of the floor. There was no handle, no visible hinges, but still, with little effort and a lot of help from Crystal's longer fingernails, it finally lifted out. It took a few attempts before she finally got her nails under it enough, but the moment she did, Michael grabbed the panel and lifted it out of the way. It was a lot lighter than he expected, just a few pieces of hardwood glued together into a solid square tile of flooring. He rested it against the backside of the sacramental altar and quickly shined the flashlight on his phone into the hole.

Nothing.

Only a dark empty space.

A bone-numbing chill rushed up at them as they just knelt there at the edge of the hole, staring into the blackness. Along with the chill followed a strange odor. Old, decrepit. Maybe there was something down there, but Crystal sure as hell couldn't see it.

She shivered.

"We have to do this quickly," Batnaz said, looking over his shoulder.

"Do what?" Michael asked. "There's nothing there?"

"Why quickly?" Crystal questioned, looking as though she didn't want to get in the hole at all, let alone quickly. Not to mention, she could clearly see Michael starting to sweat at the thought of climbing inside this tiny space. "You're the senior apostle. Don't you pretty much own this place?"

"I'm afraid not," Batnaz explained. "Most of the historic sites of the Church in this area belong to The Community of Christ. They're the reorganized sect of Mormonism, founded by Joseph's wife, Emma." He quickly directed them to climb down inside the hole. "We really should not be here."

"You've got to be kidding me," Michael whined as he turned and gawked at Crystal, who simply returned her typical, reassuring smile. "Fine," he said, finally. "But I'm completely on board with that *quickly* part."

Crystal grabbed Michael's phone and lowered herself into the hole. It wasn't all that deep, perhaps four feet where she first entered, but it was quite extensive, crossing the entire length of the pulpit—at least twelve feet—and it was completely overcome with dust and spiderwebs.

Oh just freaking great, I think as I brush a mass of cobwebs away from my face and hair. I close my eyes and try to count to ten, but it doesn't work. I can't even make it to four before getting attacked by another spiderweb, and I didn't even move. They're attacking me from everywhere and nowhere.

What I wouldn't give right now for just one anxiety pill.

"Hey guy," Crystal says. In the tiny space, her voice sounds so different. Almost like she's talking in a box. But amplified a hundred times.

But again, perhaps it's just my nerves right now.

God, I've got to get out of here!

"Over here," she shouts, making my head feel like it might explode. "I think I found something!"

We're all crouching down as low as we can, exploring the tiny space. Even Crystal, who's almost a foot shorter than me. I'm trying to find her, but I can just barely see the light from my phone that she stole from me, through the thick webs.

"Over here, Michael." She shines the light right into my eyes, and suddenly I know where she is. I can't see a thing anymore, but I know where she is. "Look at this," she says as she grabs my hand and guides me toward what she's found.

I clear more cobwebs from my face and study the wall, waiting for my eyes to readjust after being blinded. After a few seconds, I start to see something shiny. It looks like a metal door covering something inside the foundation wall.

It's clearly old. It appears to be secured to the wall with just a couple of rusted out bolts.

Doesn't look too complicated, I think, focusing all my attention on the task at head, instead of the godforsaken pit I have been thrown into.

I grab ahold of the metal cover and try prying it off.

That's clearly not going to work.

I build up my strength and really grab hold. The bolts are wiggling around, and the door feels like it might come loose. Putting all of my weight into it this time, I yank on that thing hard. Pushing. Pulling. Rocking it back and forth.

Sweat is building up on my forehead, dripping into my eyes. Eyes I already could just barely see out of. It suddenly doesn't feel all that chilly down here. I rock that metal plate back and forth several more times and then—

It breaks loose.

It's going to come!

Even more determined now, I give that little sucker a piece of me, and when it finally gives and crashes to the concrete floor with a clang, sending concrete and rust particles into the already heavy air, I give way myself, crashing into Crystal, who just barely keeps us from tumbling to the floor.

Batnaz looks at me as if I had just shouted—

HEY, LOOK AT US… WE'RE OVER HERE!

At least Crystal is smiling.

I peer into the foundation wall and hidden inside is a thick iron pipe, about a foot long, capped at either end with ivory pegs carved into impressive replicas of the Liahona.

Without question, this has been buried here for quite some time, likely since the temple was built.

The ivory pegs are stuck in place.

The iron pipe, caked in a thick layer of rust.

I place the pipe up on the ridge of the opening in the floor and quickly crawl back up through—Crystal and Batnaz following close behind—then we carefully shut the panel, grab the pipe, and run toward the temple entrance. We run the entire length of the worship hall in under four seconds. Batnaz disappears out into the vestibule and is already out the large green door when—

"Hey!" The voice fires down at us from above. It's the old woman in the long rose-colored dress and sunhat again. She's walking down the stairs only, this time, she's not crying, and she's accompanied by two uniformed officers. "That's them!" she spits, pointing at us. "They're the ones who were snooping around when President Bethsaida was murdered!"

23

There are moments in our lives that change everything. We call them pivot points. For me, one of those moments is now. Crystal grabs my hand and runs out the door. My life has finally found its end. *I'm a damn fugitive!*

"Another apostle is going to die," Crystal shouts, as we run as fast as we can, trying to keep up with Batnaz who is quickly closing in on the idling SUV. "In all likelihood, that next victim is about to open the door for us."

I realize at that moment that she is right. But it does little to cull the anxiety of now being wanted by the police.

"We cannot let that happen!"

"Things have all of a sudden become personal," I shout, as I glance over my shoulder and see the police running behind us, quickly catching up. "For Christ's sake, Crystal, we're running from the police!"

We finally reach the SUV and practically jump inside. Batnaz gets in and slams the door, and without a word, the driver peels away from the curb. I watch through the back window as the police officers give up the chase and collapse, palms to their knees, huffing and puffing. One of them grabs his radio. He's clearly reporting us.

I can't believe this is happening!

I glare at Crystal who just stares back without a word. I shake my head and turn to Batnaz. "What the hell are we supposed to do now?"

"Don't fret, Michael." There's not an ounce of worry in his voice. "Everything will work out as planned."

What the hell is that supposed to mean? Suddenly I'm not sure any of this was a good idea. Frankly, I'm feeling played, and Batnaz is the player. I just look at him, as he turns and faces the road ahead. "Don't worry, Michael."

I feel Crystal grab my left hand, and I turn to face her. She apparently doesn't feel right about this either. However, I sense something else in her. She is calm. She smiles warmly at me and her spirit instantly drains the anxiety from my body. "Don't worry," she says. "I can't explain why. But I just know that everything will turn out right."

Throughout the brief time that we've spent in the SUV, I have felt the driver making several odd turns down several streets. He drives us down a tight alleyway, which then opens up into a large parking lot. There's a large white building up ahead. "Where are we?" I ask.

"Kirtland Historic Center," Batnaz explains, as a gate automatically swings open letting us drive through, then closes behind us. "The Church owns this place. We'll be safe." The car drives into a small underground parking facility and comes to a stop right next to a set of double doors. "At least until we figure out our next move."

We sit down around a large conference table inside a private office space and lay the pipe out in front of us. Clearly, none of us want to break the ivory pegs—I know I don't—but seriously, what other choice do we have?

We *must* see what's inside, and we have very little time.

While Batnaz makes a few calls on his phone, trying to plan our next move, I tap one of the ivory pegs on the edge of the table, and to my shock, it breaks instantly, without the slightest bit of hesitation.

I remove the remnants of the peg. There is still a bit of rotten cork stuck in the end of the pipe that won't come out.

Someone had hoped the ivory and cork would keep the contents safe, and from the look of things, they were right.

"Is there anything I can use to dig this cork out?" I ask.

Batnaz motions with his hands to a sink in the corner. Crystal runs over and finds a fork and rushes it back to me.

It makes quick work of the remaining cork. I then carefully work the parchment out and unfurl it on the table. It's small. Tiny compared to the pipe. It's old, brittle. Clearly hand inked, and of course, just to make sure we haven't forgotten, it's written in Masonic cipher.

Batnaz hangs up the phone, walks up to the table and sits and Crystal studies the page. "We need to get this done quickly," he says. "Our time here is about to expire."

"There's a keyword needed," Crystal says, visibly upset. "I can't solve it."

There's nothing else written anywhere on the page or

anywhere inside or on the pipe. I literally have nothing.

"I'm not joking around here," Batnaz says, sounding a bit agitated as he rises up from the table and walks toward the door. "It's time to go. We have another flight to catch."

As Crystal starts rolling up the parchment and I grab the broken pieces of the end cap and cork, it occurs to me.

That's it!

Suddenly I am overcome by a feeling of confidence that Crystal notices even before I can get the words out.

The pipe! I know. I can hardly contain myself.

"I know what the key is," I say. "The end caps—"

"The Liahona," Crystal realizes, knowing that I'm right. "Well done!" she says proudly.

"We can figure this out later," Batnaz demands as he opens the door and walks out. "We have to leave!"

24

As we walk out those double doors into the parking garage, I feel a sudden ping of fear in my heart as two police vehicles come speeding into the facility and stop directly in front of us.

Batnaz opens the back door of one of the cruisers.

"Get in," he says. "Don't worry. Everything is fine."

I swallow the lump that's blocking my throat and reluctantly get in. *We were just running from the police, and now we're getting into the back of a squad car?*

Crystal slides in next to me, and Batnaz closes the door. "What the hell is going on?" I say to Crystal who just burns me right back with her eyes. Clearly, she's worried too.

Batnaz walks up to the second police car, says something to the officer inside and then returns to the car we're in and gets in the front passenger's seat.

"I don't know what you've gone and done this time, Sir," the officer says. "But it's a real whopper. The entire police department is after you guys. Hell, Governor Patrick even has the Ohio Stateys' on the prowl."

"Yeah, well," Batnaz says, sounding almost tongue in cheek. "You know how it is."

I sure as hell wish I knew how it was, I think to myself.

"We'll have no trouble making it to Darlene with these fine souls as our escorts," Batnaz declares.

"I do hope this makes us even, Sir," the officer says.

Batnaz nods his head in agreement as the officers take off out of the garage and through the open gate leaving the Kirtland Historic Center.

Crystal lays the parchment out on her lap and starts decoding the message. "The key is Liahona," she says under her breath, apparently talking to herself. I watch as she struggles to write out the letters—using 'LIAHON', omitting the duplicate 'A', as is customary with cipher keys. It's shocking just how uncomfortable the back of a police car is. The seats are hard plastic, absolutely zero cushioning. And every single bump feels like a damn earthquake.

I continue to watch Crystal as she translates each Masonic symbol into its decoded alphabetic sequence, and quickly the message starts to materialize before my eyes.

the lords hand is fair
unveiled with alluring psalm
twice holiness to the lord exalted
deep beneath the comely home

I repeat the lines in my head several times and quickly realize that cracking the code was likely the easy part. "What the heck does it mean?" I say.

Crystal looks at me like she's about to say something, but then just scratches her head.

Realizing that Crystal has broken the code and has written out the answer, Batnaz says, "Read it to me."

She does.

"Hmm," he sighs. "It would appear that this little bit of poetry is actually a clue that needs to be further deciphered."

"I am sure you're right," Crystal says. "But without context, I see no way for us to figure this out."

"Perhaps there's some secret message in a song that we need to find," I say, pointing at the second line of the poem.

unveiled with alluring psalm

"I think you may be on to something," Crystal says, grinning that *oh yeah* smile at me. "Too bad there's like a quadrillion songs in the world."

"The third line," Batnaz says, looking over his shoulder at the work Crystal is doing. "Please read that again."

twice holiness to the lord exalted

"Holiness to the Lord is an important phrase found on nearly every Mormon temple." He taps his index finger on his chin and appears to get lost in thought for a second. But then a light turns on, and excitement fills his voice. "I think I not only understand this line but the first line as well."

"What is it?" I say, feeling a bit of relief that we're getting somewhere.

"Twice exalted could literally mean twice raised." Batnaz's sudden excitement was almost shocking. "There is only one place in the world where the Mormon church has built a holy temple on the same ground twice."

Batnaz is truly on to something. I can feel it. This is finally beginning to make sense.

"And the first line only goes to solidify my theory."

the lords hand is fair

"When Joseph Smith found the place where he knew his people could flourish, many members believed the place was a bug infested hell-pit," Batnaz explains just as a bump in the road tosses him about, and he grabs the roof overhead with one hand and the dash with the other. "Seriously?" he says to the officer.

"Sorry, Sir, these back roads are not the greatest."

Batnaz quickly recovers his senses. "But Joseph knew better. He knew the spot would be perfect for them at that time and so he called the place, Nauvoo, meaning to be beautiful—or in Old English, which Joseph spoke—fair."

"Wonderful," Crystal says. "So the first and second lines tell us where to go—"

"And once we get there," I interject, feeling the need to push my theory on the second line of the poem, "we need to find a message hidden in a song."

"So that's it," Crystal says as she rolls the parchment and places it back into the pipe. "How far is Nauvoo?"

"With Darlene—" Batnaz grins, as we pull off of a rocky dirt road into a massive clearing. *The airport,* I realize, spotting Darlene a few yards ahead. "—Hardly time for a nap."

25

The Nauvoo Temple, the second built in the days of Joseph Smith, had been burnt to the ground by anti-Mormon mobs shortly after the Saints were driven out of Illinois. "Even though the temple has long since been rebuilt," Batnaz explained as they exited Darlene and made haste toward the tarmac. "We won't find any secrets there." He thought about the situation a moment, then looked for his driver. "We are going to have to turn this town on its head."

A black SUV pulled up and Batnaz opened the rear door and ushered Crystal and Michael inside. He then took another look around the small private airstrip, thinking about the magnitude of the task at hand, and finally got inside the SUV with a loud sigh. It was impeccably clear that the decoded message was leading to Nauvoo. *But, where exactly?* That is what baffled him.

"Nauvoo was a massive hub of Mormon activity in the days of Joseph Smith," Batnaz said as he continued to ponder what they should do next. "Thousands of people flocked to the area from around the world to be close to the prophet and to help build up the Kingdom of God on Earth."

"Wasn't Joseph Smith the Mayor?" Crystal asked.

"Indeed," Batnaz confirmed. "And he led the largest militia in the entire state of Illinois," he elaborated. "The result? A slew of Mormon history now stands proudly in Nauvoo, Illinois." Batnaz knew that the area would be thronged by visitors this time of year. There was only one place he could think to go. A place where, at the very least, he might capture some inspiration. He patted the back of the driver's seat. "Nauvoo Visitors' Center."

"Where the hell are we?" I ask as our SUV speeds past endless fields of cornstalks and the occasional utility pole. With the speed limit being a dismal 45 miles-per-hour and the road conditions making it difficult to handle even that, the fact the driver has us riding along at over 60 is either a true testament to the man's driving abilities or proof that he's both suicidal and homicidal. After all, he has a car full of people. Or did he forget that fact?

"Shouldn't we be worried about getting pulled over?" Crystal asks. "We did just run from the police."

Batnaz shakes his head. "No need to worry about them," he says with certainty in his voice. "I've taken care of it."

What the heck does that mean? I ask myself. Something is really strange about this. I glance over at Crystal who gives me one of those looks. You know, the one that says, *what the hell?*

"How?" I mouth to her, not really sure what to make of it.

She responds, *I don't know,* with an involuntary shrug.

"You must be wondering how I have influence over the authorities," Batnaz volunteers, apparently sensing our concern.

We don't say anything, but I can imagine that our faces are not nearly as silent as we're trying to be.

Batnaz smiles and gives a little chuckle. "You can't be as old as I am, having had the mantle of the first presidency of the Church for nearly a decade, and not make a few friends along the way."

Friends? I think. *This almost feels criminal.*

"We did nothing wrong," he declares. "And the fate of the Church and the lives of our leaders hang in the balance. It was a choice that I had to make, and I do not regret it." He is right, of course. We did nothing wrong, and lives *are* at stake.

"So the police are not after us?" Crystal begs for clarity.

"Trust me," Batnaz promises. "All we need to worry about is solving that riddle you decoded." But as the fields of corn suddenly morph into oceans of grass, and the first signs of habitation emerge in the form of small-town shops and converted farmhouses, Batnaz begins to look nervous.

This, of course, kicks up my own anxiety. I mean, I'm *really* starting to not trust this guy.

As we enter the heart of Nauvoo, the driver eases our speed to a reasonable 30 miles-an-hour, just five over the limit. The town looks ordinary, like any other American small town. Tiny homes, run-down shops, the occasional well-maintained business, gas stations, general stores... We just passed the Nauvoo Inn. There really doesn't appear to be anything all that special about Nauvoo. But then, out of nowhere on the right side of the road, just past a dinky Insurance Company, The Fudge Factory, and The Bank of Nauvoo, a vision of pure white materializes.

The Nauvoo Temple.

Now, *this* is the type of temple people think of when they hear Mormon temple. A monumental structure, lined with dozens of windows of varying shapes and sizes. Judging by the orientation of the windows it is pretty clear that this temple has at least five floors, not counting the tower. Eight arched windows peak up at the ground-line—clearly basement windows. Above those are eight more arched windows making up the main floor. Then there's a row of eight round windows, and above that, another row of arched windows. In all, there have to be over thirty windows on the side of the temple. Flanking each set of eight windows are these monolithic columns. At the base of each is a carving of a large crescent moon, facing the ground, and at the pinnacle of each a rising sun. But what really catches my eyes, and what has always fascinated me about Mormon temples, are all the Masonic symbols scattered about its facade. All along the roofline, above each set of windows, are small, circular stained glass windows depicting an inverted five-pointed star. And capping it all off, at least an additional five stories above the main roofline, atop a stately multi-tiered clock tower, is a golden statue of an angel, glowing in the sun.

The driver passes the temple and then takes a right turn just in front of it, and as we pass by the front of the temple I feel my breath escape from my body and refuse to return, yet only for a moment. Something about this building—its pure majesty perhaps, or maybe, it's something else, something far more powerful—just has me in a state of awe. As we turn down Young Street, I find myself looking over my shoulder, to study the beautiful building a moment longer.

"It truly is a work of wonder," Batnaz says. "Is it not?"

All I can do is nod. Admittedly, until today, I've never seen a Mormon temple in person. I've never desired to learn a great deal about the Mormon church, was only really interested in the Church's use of Masonic symbology on early temples. I've seen pictures, but never have I been stricken by anything the way that this temple is hitting me now. It's a feeling I've never felt. Something deep. Something unexplainable. It's not the Spirit. This is something else. Something much stronger.

The SUV pulls off to the side of the road into a small paved area marked by signs as "Bus Unloading Zone."

"Keep it running," Batnaz says to the driver. "We shouldn't

be long." He gets out of the car and directs us down a red brick pathway, through some thick trees, and into a luscious flower garden almost unnoticeable from the road. "Welcome to the Monument to Women," he says, with arms wide open. "One of my favorite places in the world to meditate and contemplate life's grandest mysteries."

I watch Crystal as her eyes brighten up and she walks into the heart of the magnificent flower garden, full of life-size sculptures, toward one of the many bronzes of women in all mannerisms of a female life. She stops at a statue of a woman in a long flowing dress, holding hands in a circle with three small children, dancing in the manner of the old nursery rhyme, Ring around the rosy.

"It's the largest commissioned display of sculpture in the world dedicated to women." The look on Batnaz's face is one of pride, but also admiration. Something tells me that he paid for this magical oasis in the middle of nowhere. But it's not just the incredible sculptures that make this place so special, it's the mass quantities of meticulously kept plants and flowers of nearly every color of the rainbow. It's no wonder it's one of Batnaz's favorite places in the entire world.

The statues truly are impressive too, of course. There's one of an adorable old lady in a rocking chair, a quilt draped over her lap. She's either knitting it or hemming it. I can't really tell. There's one of a woman and her husband, teaching their baby to walk. That's where Crystal is right now. Other monuments depict women in all manners of teaching, working, and fellowship. With such immense beauty surrounding us, it's all too easy to forget why we're here.

"Excuse me," I say to Batnaz, who is sitting on a concrete bench looking off into some other place. "Shouldn't we be discussing the decoded message? Two men are dead, leaders in the First Presidency. Frankly, as I see it, you're most likely the next target. Doesn't that worry you?"

He doesn't respond. It's like he's in another world. I pull the decoded message, written on a torn-out page of Crystal's notebook, out of my pant pocket and study it some more.

> *the lords hand is fair*
> *unveiled with alluring psalm*
> *twice holiness to the lord exalted*
> *deep beneath the comely home*

I look up at Crystal, who's a ways off now, looking at what appears from here to be a statue of Joseph Smith talking with a woman. Just beyond that statue is a large brick building with many columns of large, ground-to-ceiling arched windows. Just beyond the glass, I spot a massive white statue. *The Christus*, I recognize. By no means is the Christus a uniquely Mormon monument. Christians around the world treasure the open-armed depiction of the Christ, the most famous of which being Christ the Redeemer, at the peak of Corcovado mountain in Rio de Janeiro, Brazil.

"I'm going inside," I say to Batnaz. But still no response. I guess he was serious when he mentioned meditation. I quickly walk up to Crystal, now examining a statue of a man and a woman in the act of courtship, and wrap my arm around her. "Seems like just a few hours ago, doesn't it?"

She chuckles. "It's actually not funny, Michael."

"I'm going inside," I say. "Batnaz is in some tripped-out

trance. He refuses to snap out of it, and we need answers. I'm going to see if I can find anything in the Visitors' Center." I grab her hand, and she doesn't hesitate to follow me.

"I thought they'd never leave," Batnaz said under his breath, and as they entered the Visitors' Center, he grabbed his phone and selected a number from his favorites. It rang only once.

"We're close," Batnaz expressed. "I can feel it." His eyes brightened up as he listened. "Yes, we found the roadmap. We have never been so close, Simeon. It will not be much longer now. The Revealer will surely be pleased with us this time."

26

The inside of the Nauvoo Visitors' Center is like a museum of all things Joseph Smith and early Mormon culture. The walls, made up of the same red brick as the exterior, are lined in pristinely maintained relics of the past.

Straight ahead at the far end of the hall is the Christus I saw through the windows. The light flooding in, reflecting off the white marble sculpture is magical.

At the center of the room is a large twelve-foot octagonal display case housing a scaled three-dimensional map of Nauvoo. Just beyond the showcase is a three-dimensional model of the Nauvoo Temple, arranged in a manner that, like the Christus, it looks over the model of the town.

Every wall in this magnificent building is packed with artifacts to explore; yet, it's the temple that lures me in. I walk toward it as if it's the only thing in the room. There's something truly fascinating about this marvelous work of art. One doesn't need to be a Mormon to appreciate its splendorous architecture and design. Then, of course, there're those Masonic symbols, which only add to my intrigue.

As I admire the many symbols and details of the model rendering of the Nauvoo Temple, Crystal explores the town, searching for anything that could possibly be a clue. "This is crazy," she says, clearly getting frustrated. "We're not getting anywhere. There is no question that we missed something."

"Can I help you?" a woman asks. She's smiling genuinely

and wearing a formal woman's dress suit, with a little black name tag that reads, Sister Williams. "The temple truly is a beautiful place, isn't it?"

No question about it, the temple is beautiful. However, I can't shake the feeling that's been sinking to the pit of my soul. I can't tell if it's bad or good. All I can say is that it's cooking up a brand new batch of anxiety. "What answer does the Church have for all the Masonic symbolism on their temples?" I finally ask, doubtful that she'll have a satisfactory answer.

"What a great question," she says, radiating that typical Mormon glow. A classic response from someone who hasn't a clue how to answer. "And one we often get around here, since the Nauvoo Temple was and is one of only three Mormon temples to display such symbology, the others being the Logan and Salt Lake Temples."

"What do you mean, was and is?" I ask, taken aback by the oddity of the statement.

"Well," she says, pointing across the room toward a showcase of a fragment of gray stone. Immediately I remember what Batnaz told us, but I listen to her remind me. "The original temple was burned to the ground by arson after the early Mormons were forced out of the area."

It's truly a horrific story, when you think about it, which makes it even stranger that this woman can tell it with such a bright smile on her face. I imagine that's what happens when you tell the same story, over and over again, to countless numbers of inquisitive schmucks such as myself.

"So, can you please explain the use of Masonic symbols?" I repeat politely, returning my gaze toward the model of the Nauvoo Temple, specifically to the series of tiny, stained glass windows in the shape of inverted pentagrams.

"The pentagram," she starts, apparently noticing what I was focusing on, "is one of, if not *the* oldest symbol known to mankind. It was discovered in ancient Babylon and for millennia was tied to light, creation, and healing. It is because of these divine connections that for centuries the symbol was used to represent Jesus Christ."

"It's true," Crystal agrees, still examining the model town and the key historic building marked off by placards. "It wasn't until 1855 when the pentagram was hijacked by a spirit of wickedness." Crystal grabs a piece of paper from her pocket and starts toward the woman. "Alphonse Louis Constant," she continues. "A Mason who had been excommunicated by the Catholic Church and disbarred from Freemasonry for delving into witchcraft—Eliphas Levi, as he would later become known—took the pentagram and perverted it into something evil, something satanic. Ever since, the pentagram has been used by occultists for satanic rituals and has made its way into the mainstream consciousness as a symbol of the occult."

"And it is because of that history, that I am made to answer this question at least once every day." The woman smiled, but timidly.

"Ma'am," Crystal says, handing the woman the piece of paper, "can you make any sense out of this?"

The woman grabs a pair of reading glasses from her breast pocket and stares at the piece of paper for a long moment, then suddenly a spark of recognition appears. "This is odd," she says. "Where did you get this?"

It's not a question either of us are prepared to answer.

"Why?' Crystal asks. "Have you seen it before?"

"No, I don't believe so. However, I might understand what it means." The woman removes her glasses and scratches her head, just above her right ear, with its unfolded temple tip.

I can see rays of hope beaming from Crystal as the woman contemplates what she's looking at.

> *the lords hand is fair*
> *unveiled with alluring psalm*
> *twice holiness to the lord exalted*
> *deep beneath the comely home*

"We are in Nauvoo because we believe that the first and third lines of this message has led us here," Crystals says. "In fact, we're certain of that. But we're struggling with the rest."

The woman smiles and walks around the octagonal display of the town of Nauvoo, stops next to one of the large placards, and places her right index finger on the glass. "There," she says.

Crystal and I both walk curiously to her side and look at where she's pointing. It's a large, half brick, half stone building at the end of a cul-de-sac, on the banks of the river.

"That's the place," she says, with certainty in her voice. I read the name on the placard—*The Nauvoo House*—and suddenly hear Batnaz's voice ringing in my head—

Joseph called the place, Nauvoo, which means Beautiful.

Comely, I think to myself, and instantly, I know that she's right. *Comely means beautiful.*

deep beneath the Nauvoo House

"But good luck getting inside," the woman says. "It's been closed all summer for restoration."

"I think we might have that covered," I say as I look Crystal straight in the eyes and as if connected by some neurological link, we start running for the exit.

"So glad I could help," the woman yells in a library voice.

27

"Joseph Smith never lived in The Nauvoo House," Batnaz said, as he led them around the back of the large stately building where they had a choice of several large windows and doors to enter, each leading somewhere into the lower level of the grand structure. The building clearly had its share of improvements and upgrades over the last hundred or so years.

Michael admired the look of the gray stonework, which covered the lower level of the structure, as well as the red brickwork lining the two top levels.

"He never even saw it completed," Batnaz continued. "Joseph received revelation a few years before his death. He'd been instructed to build a boarding house, 'a delightful habitation for man, and a resting-place for the weary traveler' he had said, and later wrote in the *Doctrine and Covenants*."

Batnaz led Crystal and Michael around to the far back of the building, where there stood a small doorway, hiding between two tall bushes and slightly protected by an overhead brick archway.

Wrought-iron fire escapes lined this side of the building. Obviously a more recent addition. Most every city and town these days mandates fire escapes, even on historic buildings. These massive eyesores are typically thrown on the least visible side of a building, and this is the side of the building Batnaz had brought them to.

"This door," he explained, "goes straight to where we need to be." He paused, recalling the last line again—

deep beneath the comely home

The door is locked. However, Batnaz has it covered. Sure, the Nauvoo House, like just about every historic church site in Nauvoo, was owned by The Community of Christ, but he just happened to be close with the curator of these particular buildings and knew exactly where she kept her backup keys.

"Michael," he said, wrapping his arm around his shoulder and bringing him close. "See this emergency staircase?"

Michael nodded. It was a very steep set of wrought-iron steps with a nearly microscopic iron railing that scaled up at least twenty feet to one of the second story windows. More an elaborate ladder, than a staircase, but yeah, he saw it.

"At the top of this staircase, just to the right of the window, almost in line with the center sash of the double-hung glass, you will find a loose brick. Carefully pull out that brick and grab the key from behind it."

Michael didn't move at first. He just stared at Crystal.

"Go on," he said, nudging him onto the first step.

I take that first step, feeling Batnaz's hand finally release my shoulder, and a lump surfaces in my throat.

Heights have never been a strong point in my life. And even though you may be thinking *twenty feet, that's not so bad,* trust me, it is. As I make my way up the narrow treads, the entire thing starts to sway and bounce. I grasp the railing so tightly that my knuckles hurt. The steps are so thin, so flimsy under my feet. They creak and bend with each step, raising my anxiety level that much higher. I try to keep my focus on the platform above, but I just can't seem to stop looking at my feet and at the fact that I can see right through the steps to the ground below. Let's just say, for Crystal's and Batnaz's sake, that there is nothing in my stomach to throw up right now. It's been a while since we've eaten.

Great, now I'm hungry.

"Am I getting close?" I beg to Crystal, unable to look up.

"Just keep going, honey; you're almost there." Crystal's voice has always had a bit of a soothing effect on me. I really wish it would soothe me now.

Suddenly I feel the railing level out, and my eyes instinctively look in front of me. I'm on the platform, right outside a large double-hung window.

I glance inside the window into a dark room.

Thank goodness, I say to myself. Then I look down the steps and reel back. *Oh, crap!*

I turn my focus on the brick wall and run my hands along the side of the window, feeling for the loose brick.

"I don't feel anything!"

"Look closer," Batnaz says. "You may not feel it, but you should see gaps in the mortar."

I study the bricks that are in line with the center sash like Batnaz had said, yet I just can't see any—

"Wait a second," I say. "I got it!"

I work the brick out of the wall and as promised, there's a key, a few actually.

I grab all three and push the brick back in place, then slowly back step my way down the ladder.

With each step, I feel my heart sink.

Then suddenly I feel a hand on my back.

"Great job, Michael." Batnaz looks proud. "You should have told me you are afraid of heights. I could have done it myself."

28

As updated as the outside of The Nauvoo House looked, the inside—at least the basement—was like stepping back in time at least a hundred years.

Batnaz slipped the keys Michael had given him into his pocket and found the dangling light switch and pulled it. An old-fashioned Edison light bulb glowed a light orange-amber and a long set of dusty old wooden stairs—a single handrail hung loosely on the wall to the right—came into view.

Batnaz led Crystal and Michael slowly down the stairs, holding tightly to the handrail that felt as though it might suddenly rip right off the wall.

"This is obviously not part of the tours they give visitors of this building," Crystal surmised.

"I would certainly hope not," Michael said.

The basement was old, somewhat dusty, and the air felt dank, but remarkably, it didn't smell all that bad, which was clear enough evidence that the owners at least cared to keep this historic landmark free of mold and mildew.

At the bottom of the stairs, Batnaz searched for another light and pulled the string. As the old Edison filament began to glow that orange-amber hue, the basement, for the first time came into view.

To everyone's surprise, it was completely empty. It was not as large as Batnaz remembered, either. It had been many years since he last visited the place, even longer since he'd been in the basement. It didn't have the same footprint as the building itself, which took up far more space.

"I have a bad feeling about this," Michael said, turning on his phone for a bit more light. "Perhaps we were wrong."

"We can't be," Crystal declared, recalling the last line of the poem again and repeating it out loud.

deep beneath the comely home

"This has to be the place," Michael said. "Explore every nook and cranny." Michael shined his phone's flashlight along the foundation wall, looking closely for anything out of place. "Something has to be here. I know it."

"Michael," Crystal said. "Come over here." She was standing next to a newer-looking furnace, tucked into the corner of the basement.

Michael started walking her way, shining his light into the corner, when he noticed what she was looking at. Behind the furnace was an extremely old wood burning stove—the original heat source for the building he was sure—and directly behind the wood stove was a large hole in the upper part of the foundation, just large enough for someone to crawl through, leading into a crawlspace.

"I'm not going in there," Michael said. "No way."

Crystal didn't say a word, she just rolled up her sleeves and pulled herself up and disappeared through the hole.

"Give me your light, Michael," she said, reaching down through the hole and stealing his iPhone.

The crawlspace was tiny, perhaps ten feet deep by ten feet

wide, and there was maybe, barely, three feet of clearance between the ground and the floor joists above her head. And the entire space was littered with everything from old mason jars full of something certainly less than appetizing to piles of old rags, newspapers, and furniture stuffing, apparently the byproducts of past, or present, rodent habitation.

"Oh Michael, you would love it in here," she said smugly, as she dug around through the debris, waist-deep in some parts, searching for *what...* she hadn't the vaguest clue. She grabbed a massive pile of wet paper and cotton batting and tossed it aside then spotted something on the floor. It looked like a piece of stone set into a frame on the floor. She put Michael's phone in her teeth and grabbed at the stone, pulling as hard as she could. Whatever it was, it was in there good and did not want to come out. She gazed at the stone, breathing hard from the tugging. There was a hand print somehow pressed into the center of it. She placed her left hand into the hand print; it almost fit perfectly. Sent chills down her spine, but nothing happened. She felt kind of silly for even doing it. She looked around for something to pry it open with. She dug her hands through the mash of debris, shining that light in every corner of the tiny space until she found what she was looking for—a three-foot piece of iron bar, leaning against the far wall, half buried in whatever the heck that crap was. She grabbed the bar and stuck it into the small crack that she had worked her fingers into and pried that stone out in the first shot. It tipped over and fell to the ground with a—*THUD!*

There it was. Exactly what, she had no clue, but she was sure this is what the message had brought them to.

"And the bugs," she said, as she poked her head out of the hole. "Michael, you would just flip for all these bugs." She was really letting him have it now. "You have no idea what you missed in there." She leaped out of the hole and brushed herself off. In her left hand was a small metal box. "Good thing bugs hate metal."

Crystal sits on the dusty basement floor and places the small metal box down in front of her. It looks like an old jewelry box with all its stylized trimmings and inset gemstones. It's about the size and shape of a standard shoe box, and aside from the classic, early 1800's decor, it bears no markings making it stand out as something special.

Batnaz and I kneel on the floor in front of her as she examines the box. The hinges are rusted almost entirely away, so the cover comes off effortlessly in her hands. Inside is a charred fragment of stone about the size of a softball, a couple half-burnt white candlesticks, some candle bases, an old yellowed magazine titled Juvenile Instructor with a single sheet of folded paper laying on top, and a few other small personal looking trinkets—photos, lockets, and jewels.

I carefully take the magazine in my hands. The cover almost has a green tint to it in the bright light. There are two Greek-style columns; between the columns, along the top of the cover, it reads Holiness to the Lord. Below that in bold print it says Juvenile Instructor an Illustrated Magazine. In each corner, in the bases and headers of each column, are portraits of, I assume, the Prophets who had served up until the time of printing, since in the top left is Joseph Smith, and across from there is Brigham Young. The two on the bottom I don't recognize, but it only makes sense that they'd be prophets, too. Along the bottom, between the columns it says VOL. XXVI. AUGUST 15, 1891. NO. 16.

I carefully flip the cover over and start examining the pages. They are extremely brittle and nearly fall apart in my fingers. It kind of reminds me of a magazine I used to get as a child, *Boy's Life*. It's a resource packed with youth activities, personal stories, testimonies, and pictures—though they aren't the most inspiring pictures. By that, I mean, there's no color. No kids biking the grand canyon. No teens shooting each other up with paintball guns. Nothing a child stuck in today's world would find the least bit entertaining or interesting. As I flip to the last couple pages, about to place the magazine back in the box, I see a piece of sheet music. It's the only one in the magazine, and it has a very peculiar title.

"Hey, check this out," I say, carefully laying the magazine open on the floor so not to damage the frail page. I shine my iPhone's flashlight on the text and Crystal reads it out loud—

The Unknown Grave

There's an unknown grave in a lonely spot
But the form that it covers will never be forgot
There the Heaven tree spreads and the tall locusts wave
There snow-white flowers over the unknown grave
Over the unknown grave

And near by its side does the wild rabbit tread
And over its bosom the white thistles spread
As if placed there in kindness to guard and save
From intruding footsteps the unknown grave
Guarding the unknown grave

And there reposes the Prophet, just
The Lord was his guide and in Him was his trust
He restored the Gospel our souls to save
But he now lies low in an unknown grave
Low in an unknown grave

God grant that we may watch and pray
And keep our feet in the narrow way
Our spirits and bodies in purity save
To see him arise from the unknown grave
God bless that unknown grave

"I've seen this before," Batnaz says. "This is not just any old hymn. Almost no one in the church has seen it, or even knows it exists." He goes on to explain that the hymn was never added to any church hymnbook. He points to the name of the person who wrote the hymn and with eyes weeping, says, "It's a story so fascinating, and yet so incredibly sad."

After Joseph Smith's death his wife, Emma, had a major falling out with Brigham Young, the man her husband had appointed to take over leadership of the Church. She did not take Joseph's death well at all, and she and Brigham argued ad nauseam over what should be done with her husband's remains, about which parts of Joseph's estate were personal and which belonged to the Church, and of course... there was polygamy. Brigham actually called her out as a liar during a session of General Conference, saying, "Emma Smith is one of the damnedest liars I know of on this earth; yet there is no good thing I would refuse to do for her, if she would only be a righteous woman; but she will continue in her wickedness."

She had become dysfunctional and perhaps with good reason. After all, she had just barely turned 40 years old, and already she lost her mother, her father, her father-in-law, three brothers-in-law, five children, and now... her husband. And, she was five months pregnant when Joseph died.

She had had enough and when Brigham Young ultimately led the body of the Church, who would later become known as The Pioneers, westward out of Nauvoo two years later, Emma stayed behind with her five living children and what scraps of spirit she had left in her soul.

David Hyrum Smith was born four months after his father died. He never joined the church; instead, his mother taught him that Brigham Young led the church astray. By far, her biggest grievance had to do with polygamy. She even went so far as to testify that Joseph never preached or lived the law in any way shape or form, even though Joseph, in fact, did have several women sealed to him, and Emma not only knew it, she supported it. These marriages had nothing to do with sexual desire, rather, they were a way to open the heavens to women who had no one. Mormon doctrine teaches that in order to achieve the highest degree of glory in Heaven, one must enter into an eternal marriage, which is a temple marriage, or sealing. But after Joseph's death, Emma swore to the ends of the earth that she knew nothing of this. She ultimately went on to start her own church—the Reorganized Church of Latter-day Saints, or RLDS—of which her eldest son, Joseph Smith III, would later become president.

David grew up a devoted member of the RLDS, a well-loved and respected preacher, and an accomplished artist, poet, and musician, known as the Sweet Singer of Israel.

Never having known his father, David penned this sad ballad, The Unknown Grave, which tells of the death of his father. How after his martyrdom he was secretly buried in the night by close friends, while his enemies anxiously sought to steal his body. "What might surprise you," Batnaz said, looking solemn. "Is that it was not just the murderers Emma was hiding the bodies from, it was Brigham Young."

At age twenty-three, David was called to serve a mission with his older brother Alexander. They would travel west to Utah, to convert people they called, the Brighamites back to the ways of

God. But, shortly before leaving, he was stricken with a deepening sadness, and while on a trip to General Conference with his brothers, he wrote this disturbing letter.

Batnaz picked up the piece of paper that had been laying on top of the magazine and read it aloud.

Dear Mother

I must tell you I feel happy sometimes, most always; but today and last night I feel very sad and the tears run out of my eyes all the time and I don't know why. I have to work away as tight as I can clip to keep the rest from seeing it. I wonder if something sad is going to happen, strive as I will my heart sinks like lead. So I must go to work or I will make you feel sad too. I must tell someone my troubles or I should, well I don't know what,

God bless you Mother,
from your Child

"I believe this letter forecasted things to come for David," Batnaz said. "While on his mission he experienced several run-ins with the leaders of the Utah church, including Brigham, and had exchanged some rather harsh words. David's biggest grievance, like his mother's, was polygamy. Emma had taught David that polygamy never appeared in the Church until after Brigham took over. So, it's to be expected that David had it out for Brigham. However, after spending time with the Utah

Mormons, hearing the heartfelt testimonies of people who had been close to his father, his heart became softened. Their testimonies weighed on his soul.

"While on his mission David later grew ill. It was at the same time that his brother was called home to serve his wife, who had also fallen ill. They both returned to Nauvoo. David was nurtured to health by his mother, then shortly after, got married to a woman who had captured his heart. On March 8, 1871 David's son was born.

"In July of the following year he was called to return to Utah. It was during this trip when things began to fall apart for David. During his efforts to learn more about his father, through interviews with folks who knew him and research into census reporting, he discovered many truths about his parents.

"Joseph Smith did, indeed, preach polygamy and in fact did have a multitude of wives—as many as forty of them.

"Knowledge of this and other facts began to deeply erode his faith. He started exploring spiritualism and more liberal religions, such as the Godbeites—a sect of Latter-day Saints who not only believed in polygamy, but other sexually liberal acts, and practiced witchcraft and mysticism.

"He drifted between speaking with and befriending the Utah Mormons and exploring other religions. It was likely during this period when David met in private with Brigham Young, who told him about the prophecy his father had made, about how one day, his youngest son would rise up to lead the church.

"Brigham Young introduced David to three elder gentlemen who explained to David that he would one day lead the Josephites back into the fold. They gave him a special task to perform. A task, he was told would save his people.

"Shortly after, he returned home to Nauvoo to confront his

mother about the things he had learned. Sadly, his concerns fell on deaf ears. To his family, David was confused. In time he would succumb to his mother's nurturing.

"During this brief period of wellness, he was called to serve as councilor to the president of the reorganized church. But David couldn't let go of the knowledge he obtained on his mission. He couldn't get past the fact that his mother had lied, and the RLDS church had been founded on a lie.

"In his deepening confusion, and with all the constant questions and confrontations with his family, it was determined that David had fallen mentally ill, and when his relentless frustration had finally sank him down to the point of mindless violence, his eldest brother and president of the RLDS church had him admitted into an asylum.

"For the rest of his life, David hovered between moments of lucidity, extreme sadness, and bouts of anger. Emma often referred to David's condition as her living trouble. He died just shy of his sixtieth birthday."

As Batnaz places the letter back into the box, I rise to my feet. There's no question, unlocking the next piece of the roadmap involves finding the location of the unknown grave.

"Fortunately," Batnaz says, also returning to his feet, "finding the unknown grave shouldn't be difficult. The initial grave was located by the RLDS Church in 1928, and the bodies of Joseph, Hyrum, and Emma were relocated to their current resting place, just down the street from here."

I do a quick Google Search for the initial burying place of

Joseph and Hyrum Smith and click on the first listing.

Death of Joseph Smith - Wikipedia

I scroll down. The page is plastered with information, but it's what I see half way down that grabs my attention. I read it aloud.

Interment

Joseph and Hyrum Smith's bodies were returned to Nauvoo the next day. The bodies were cleaned and examined, and death masks were made, preserving their facial features and structures.

A public viewing was held on June 29, 1844, after which empty coffins weighted with sandbags were used at the public burial. (This was done to prevent theft or mutilation of the bodies.) The coffins bearing the bodies of the Smith brothers were initially buried under the unfinished Nauvoo House, then disinterred and deeply reburied under an outbuilding on the Smith homestead.

In 1928 Frederick M. Smith, president of the Reorganized Church of Jesus Christ of Latter Day Saints and grandson of Joseph Smith, fearing that rising water from the Mississippi River would destroy the grave site, authorized civil engineer William O. Hands to conduct an excavation to find Joseph and Hyrum's bodies. Hands conducted extensive digging on the Smith homestead, and located the bodies, as well as finding the remains of Joseph's wife, Emma, who was buried in the same place. The remains—which were badly decomposed—were examined and photographed, and the bodies were reinterred.

"The initial burial ground was here?" Crystal says, a look of concern flooding her face as she glances about the basement.

Batnaz shakes his head, "No, no. There were several locations where the bodies were hidden before actually being buried. That Wikipedia listing doesn't mention that the caskets were stored in the basement of the Nauvoo Temple, before being stolen by Emma and put in her basement."

Wikipedia is about as accurate as a warped arrow, I know; however, I typically find it to be a good starting point, since there are a plethora of links to other resources.

"Stolen?" Crystal says.

"That's right,"Batnaz explains. "Not only was Emma—like everyone else—afraid that Joseph's enemies would steal and defile the bodies, but she was *not* going to let Brigham Young control what happened to her husband. It was just one of several things that came between Emma and Brigham, ultimately ending in her staying behind with her children when Brigham Young led the Saints westward to Utah."

Batnaz reiterates his thought. "The initial burial was not the brief time they were stored in the temple, nor the time they were stored here. The initial Burial was under the out-building of the old Smith homestead."

Crystal thinks about that a moment and then asks, "How could they bury their Prophet under an outhouse?"

"No," Batnaz says, snickering. "Not an outhouse. An out-building was more like a shed. It was an extension of the home, really, used as storage or a workshop."

Crystal nods, but still has a strange look on her face.

"Unfortunately, there is nothing remaining. The president of the Reorganized Church was right for doing what he did. The river has since washed the entire area away."

"So what do we do?" I say. "Can we even find the key to unlocking the next verse?"

Batnaz returns to the decoded verse.

"The key MUST be hidden in the hymn itself," Crystal says.

But I'm not so sure about that. I look at the line again and something entirely different occurs to me.

unveiled WITH *alluring psalm*

"Perhaps the key is not hidden in the hymn," I say. "But rather, WITH the hymn."

At once I can see it in their eyes, they know I'm right.

Crystal grabs the letter out of the box and holds it up to the light bleeding in through the tiny basement window and something strange appears on the back of the page. It's barely visible, but it's there. "Is that a—"

"It's a watermark!" Batnaz interrupts, stealing her discovery.

"There's just one problem," I say, realizing the same thing they must have been thinking. "Watermarks didn't exist when this letter was written."

Raising the sheet of crumply old paper closer to the light, Crystal says, "What the hell?"

"Is that—" Batnaz starts.

"It looks like another code," she finishes.

But then I notice something else in the box. It hadn't occurred to me, until now, what this small trinket might be. I pick up the tiny piece of colored stone, which looks almost like a piece of hardened amber, and I hand it to Crystal, who smiles, knowing what I'm thinking and clearly agreeing.

She places the letter facedown on the lid of the box, and lays the small amber stone directly on top of it, and like magic the code appears clear and vibrant through the stone.

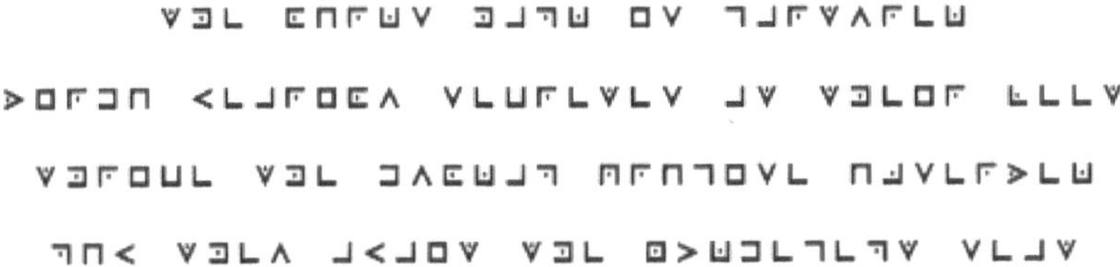

Crystal quickly writes down the coded message and attempts to crack it. She tries to use SAD as the key, but it doesn't work.

"What about SICKNESS," I ask. "Or MENTAL?"

Batnaz thinks a moment. "Try DAVID or EMMA."

"Nothing's working," Crystal says in frustration. She returns her attention to the box. She grabs the fragment of stone, the candles, the trinkets. She pulls everything out of the box and lays them out on the basement floor before us.

When it finally hits her, the spark in her eyes almost lights up the entire space. "We have a piece of the original Nauvoo Temple," she says. "An old magazine featuring a hymn by Joseph Smith's youngest son, which was never again published, and also this heartbreaking letter."

Batnaz looks bewildered. But I think I understand.

"These are all items that were sacred to someone," she continues. "Sacred to Emma!" Crystal's smile's growing and her excitement level is at a height I haven't seen in over a year. She's really getting into this. "This isn't just a box of stuff, guys," she says, looking like she is unsure why we aren't getting it. "It's a shrine!" She grabs her pen and writes out the cipher using

SHRINE as the key to unlock the code. But as she writes out the message, Crystal and I can only stare in disbelief. It makes no more sense decoded than it did before.

> *the lords hand is martyred*
> *virgo wearily secretes at their feet*
> *thrice the gyldan promise observed*
> *now they await the judgement seat*

Batnaz could hardly contain his excitement. The moment he saw the deciphered text its meaning flooded his mind.

"I know where we have to go."

The only problem was that the message was taking them nearly eight hundred miles away—to Richmond, Missouri.

"How can you make any sense of that?" Michael asked.

"We're going to have to pay Darlene another visit," Batnaz said. "Come on, let's go! I'll explain on the way."

29

the lords hand is martyred

"I assume that we all think the same thing when we hear the word martyr," Batnaz says, as the SUV races along at highway speeds down Nauvoo's winding country roads. "What comes to your mind?" He is talking to Crystal.

"Someone who is killed in the name of their religion."

"And you, Michael?"

"That's basically it. But I'd say more like a prophet or a religious leader who is slain in defense of their beliefs."

"And you would both be right," Batnaz explains. "However, there is a deeper meaning—a much simpler meaning, really. One that has been lost or at the very least, diluted, over these many, countless generations."

I'm all ears, and I can tell that Crystal is right there with me.

I live for this stuff.

I'm constantly chest deep in research for my books and student projects, all of which are right in line with this type of stuff.

"You see," Batnaz continues, "even though martyr is a word used by millions of people around the world almost every day, it is actually a Greek word that literally means *witness*."

I can't believe it, I think.

The moment I hear him say it, I know it's true.

I already knew the meaning, and yet, for whatever reason,

the standard definition is the one that stuck in my mind.

Funny how that works.

I failed a simple test and cannot believe it.

"Knowing that," Batnaz continues, "we can move on to the next line, which seems very clear to me." Batnaz, for the first time, seems to almost be enjoying himself.

thrice the gyldan promise observed

"I think we all know that the first word means, three times," I say. Then I consider the last word for a moment. "I suppose there is no coincidence that *observed* means the same thing as martyred." It's not really a question.

But Batnaz answers it anyway. "No, I suspect there is no coincidence at all. In fact, I believe, just as with the last poem, the first and third lines work together to give us the location of where we must go next."

"And where's that?" Crystal asks. "You said you know where we're going next. So tell us."

"Please, let me explain why I've come to my conclusion, so you know if I am right or I am wrong." Batnaz's excitement does not wane. "Gyldan is an Old English word, meaning golden," he continues, "and even though they were not actually made of gold—but rather, brass—I reason with you that the term gyldan promise is referring to the Golden Plates—the book of promise."

Crystal nods her head in agreement. However, I'm not sure. "Seems to be somewhat of a stretch, don't you think?"

"Actually, I don't," Batnaz says. "I believe the first and third lines of this poem are telling us that The Golden Plates were Witnessed by Three individuals."

And then, just like that, it makes perfect sense.

Again, so weird how that happens.

"So where does that bring us?" Crystal says.

"Well, I have a good idea," Batnaz starts, "but let's take a closer look at the second line for a moment."

virgo wearily secretes at their feet

Batnaz explains that virgo is a latin word that means virgin, principally used to describe a young girl.

"What comes to mind when you hear the word, secrete?"

Crystal sneers.

"Spit, more specifically, saliva," I say.

"Sweat," Crystal offers. "And other nasty body stuff."

"Again, all good answers," Batnaz confirms. "However, the word secrete, is actually a derivative of the latin word secretionem, better known today by the word, secret, which of course means to set apart, or keep hidden."

That one I did not know.

"There's a monument in Richmond, Virginia," he explains, confidence abound. "It's called the Three Witnesses Monument. I am certain that is where we must go next."

Batnaz explained that the Three Witnesses Monument was dedicated by Heber J. Grant—the last leader of the Mormon Church who was also the head of The Order and the last member who was actually a Mormon—seven years before Grant would become president of the Church.

Even though Batnaz knew there was a metal box packed with artifacts sealed in the base of the monument—leaders of the Church have done this since the days of Joseph Smith and still do to this day—he never considered this to be a place of any serious significance. After all, Grant was not even aware of The Secret during the time this monument was dedicated.

Batnaz was stunned at the simplicity and brilliance of Grant's plan. *He must have gone back and altered the contents of the vault. No one would ever suspect that one of the biggest secrets in the world would be hidden in the base of a humble monument in a private cemetery on a quaint neighborhood street.*

Even if he had considered this location to be a possible place to hide The Secret, how could he justify ripping apart the monument, in search of something that no one in the world is supposed to know exists?

How could he explain such an effort?

Frankly, the location never entered his mind until now. But seeing this text excited him. They were about to rediscover something... something of vital importance!

Could this actually be it? he thought.

virgo wearily secretes at their feet

30

We board Darlene and immediately take flight. It's downright terrifying to me, how quick this personal jet is. The moment we reach altitude—just a few minutes later—Batnaz leaves his seat and walks to the bar.

Batnaz grabs a few pieces of stemware and places them on the counter. "Drink?" he asks, grabbing a bottle of Diet Coke from the small refrigerator and holding it up to show us.

"Nothing stronger?" Crystal asks.

"Afraid not," he says, with a look on his face that clearly says that he wishes he had something stronger. "It goes against the Word of Wisdom."

"What is that?" Crystal asks in a somewhat sarcastic tone.

"The Word of Wisdom are guidelines for good health and mental well-being," he explains. "But even more important, it is a commandment passed down through revelation. Believe me, as much as I may desire a good stiff Scotch right now." He smiles, then pours the diet cola into Crystal's glass. "Please, allow me to come clean on a few things."

I don't like the sound of that, and by the look on her face, neither does Crystal.

"I haven't been entirely honest about something." Batnaz hands Crystal and me the glasses and then makes his way back to his chair. "This is really pretty difficult for me. I only ask that you hear me out."

This cannot be good.

"Your father did not die in a plane accident, Crystal."

This takes Crystal off guard, and she goes quiet.

"A rather unique set of circumstances forced your father to leave," he continues. "And leave in a hurry, I might add."

Crystal's face is growing harder by the second. It's easy to tell that she's fuming hot. I am *not* about to intervene.

"It was a tremendously difficult time for him. He was confronted with a decision that no man should have to make, and during a point in his life when he was already preparing for other changes—changes that are not so easily explained."

Crystal starts swaying in her seat. My goodness, she's going to blow and yet Batnaz is completely oblivious of the impending terror. "Your father was a man like no other—"

"Enough!" she shouts, as she jumps out of her chair. I have never seen her this angry. "You come to Paris, rip us away from our honeymoon—I've never once trusted you—then you're always acting so damn shady... now you're saying you've been keeping secrets?" She was pacing about the cabin now. "My father would have never left us!"

I attempt to comfort Crystal, but she snaps at Batnaz again, causing me to back off. "Why are you doing this? Why did you bring me here? My father died coming home to baptize me when I was eight years old! My mother died just a few months later. She was a broken woman!"

"Your mother did not die!" The thunderous tone in Batnaz's voice as he jumps to his feet sucks all other emotion from the cabin. Crystal goes silent in shock. He takes a deep breath then slowly settles back into his chair. "After finding you a suitable home, your mother returned to be with your father," he says, his voice slowly easing, settling back into a gentle calm.

Crystal is clearly bewildered.

So thick is her confusion, that she apparently hadn't heard what I had just heard.

Crystal's mother didn't die?

"Your adoptive parents were sent a letter explaining that your mother had passed away. Please. You must understand. We could not have you attempting to find her."

Crystal stops pacing and freezes, gazing at Batnaz.

"Because finding her, would have led you to me."

Her mouth falls open and as if on cue, Batnaz's phone rings, and Darlene's tires hit the pavement with a chirp and squeal to a sudden halt on the shorter than desirable runway.

Batnaz waits for the cabin door to open then brings the phone to his ear and runs ahead of us, quickly making his way down the stairs and across the tarmac.

Crystal just stares at me.

"What the hell just happened?" I ask. I mean, seriously, did Batnaz just confess to being her father? Sure as hell sounded that way to me. However, I didn't want to be the first one to say that. She was still just gawking at me. Shock, I guess. I put my arm around her and look out the door as Batnaz disappears into the airport terminal building.

"Did he just say that my mother was still alive?"

"I do believe he did."

She shakes her head and takes a deep breath, then pulls away from me, walking out the door and down the steps. "Come on, Michael," she says as she pauses a moment on the stairs. "We seriously need to finish that conversation!" She takes off running, and it takes me a second to mentally catch up. I chase her down the stairs and across the tarmac, finally meeting up with her as she's about to open the double doors into the terminal.

The terminal is surprisingly small and almost entirely void of activity. Just a few people are hanging about. The place actually looks closed.

"Where is Batnaz?" Crystal asks, glancing about the tiny space, no larger than a typical mall food court. From the entrance, we could easily see all areas of the terminal, even the only boarding counter and baggage area. "How the hell—"

"Men's room," I say, making my way toward the large *Restroom* sign off in the rear right side of the building.

Crystal starts following me but then spots a security guard and stops to ask him something. "Did you see an older gentleman come in here within the last five minutes?"

"I saw someone enter the restrooms just a few moments ago," the officer says. "Haven't seen him come out."

I enter the men's restroom. It's small and dark. Barely lit by a scant trace of sunlight bleeding in through a single, small nautical-style window. I turn the light on. "President?"

There is no answer.

I push open each of the three stall doors.

Nothing.

Not a sign that Batnaz, or anyone else, has even been here. It's sparkling clean and still smells of lemon cleaner and bleach. I look out the window, far too small for an adult to climb out. *Besides, why would he climb out the damn window? I ask myself. Why would he try to evade us at all? Something is definitely very wrong here.*

I exit the men's room and have Crystal check the women's room. He's getting up there in age; he could have made that simple error. But he's not in there either.

We quickly leave the restroom area and head back toward the main entrance. "Batnaz!" Crystal yells. Security takes notice and immediately comes our way, but Crystal keeps moving toward the entrance. "President?"

I follow her out the front entranceway to the main street and begin searching the grounds. "President?" Seriously, where the hell could he have gone?

Crystal runs out into the nearly empty parking lot, looking for anything that might grab her eye. "Where is he?"

Just then a black SUV drives up beside us, nearly hitting Crystal, and squeals to a stop. The passenger window slides down, and a male voice spits from the driver's seat. "Get in!"

The back door swings open, and a woman dressed in a dark suit beckons us inside.

Crystal snickers. "I think not!"

But I know this woman—those striking olive green eyes.

"If you want to see that old bat again," Lilith says in a smug tone, "you'll do as he says."

31

The car takes off out of Curtis Airfield and heads north on Curtis Road at a speed that has me grabbing at imaginary handles on the back of the seat and above my window.

My heart's racing.

Lilith is talking, but I can't hear a single word.

The mounting anxiety is playing pizzicato on my nerves.

My panic attacks, I think to myself. *Damn it!*

I had thought for sure they were a thing of the past, but having just taken the last of my meds during the attack earlier on Darlene, and now this.

I take several deep breaths as the car turns left onto State Highway F and eats up an entire mile of road in seconds, before turning south on MO-13.

My hands grow anesthetized on the headrest in front of me and I can feel sweat dripping down the small of my back.

God, make it stop!

"Do you understand what I have told you?" Lilith says.

I glance over at Lilith and nod, praying to God that Crystal is taking in whatever it is she's saying.

The car takes a sharp turn into a peaceful, small-town neighborhood, and mere blocks later pulls off the road, barely stopping before the door swings open and Crystal and I are thrown out into the street and the car squeals away.

Crystal jumps to her feet and pulls me off the scorching pavement. She looks perplexed, as if she's just been told something absolutely incredible—something that might change everything—if she could just somehow put the pieces together.

Without a word she runs across the street.

I just stand there, my breathing finally beginning to calm, and look around. We're smack dab in the middle of a typical small-town neighborhood, complete with modest homes, minivans, and beautifully manicured grounds.

She's running toward what looks like a garden nestled on the street corner. It consists of a couple robustly flowering trees, pristine bushes, and a tall, yet stocky monument. But it's not like any obelisk I've ever seen—looks more like a gravestone.

Strange place for a grave, I think.

"Are you coming?" Crystal says, stopping just shy of the monument, next to a sign that reads Richmond Pioneer Cemetery. She turns and waves, trying to hurry me along. "What's wrong with you?" she says, clearly annoyed. "Didn't you hear what she said?" No, in all seriousness, I didn't. *Oh man,* I think as I run toward my beautiful wife and the large granite monument towering over her head just beyond.

The monument to the three witnesses is a massive chunk of granite with messages chiseled into each of the four sides. Not your typical obelisk. This monument is girthy, about half as wide as it is tall, which makes it look quite a bit shorter than it actually is. Even with me standing at nearly six feet tall, the monument towers over my head by several feet.

"What are we doing here?" I say. "What the hell did that woman say?"

Crystal's scoping the area.

She scans the cemetery parking lot.

There's a small motor bike parked in one of the spaces, but there are no visitors around anywhere.

It's a very humble, very quaint neighborhood. "On the plane Batnaz said there's a box hidden in the base of the monument," she says, without once looking at me.

She keeps looking around. Watching.

What the heck's she doing?

"What about the woman?" I ask.

Crystal finally looks at me, her eyes full of fear.

"She said that if we're ever to see Batnaz again, we need to retrieve whatever's under this monument and bring it to her."

"What?" There's no way I heard her right. "Not only do we know nothing about this woman, but we're going to turn over whatever secrets we find here... to her?" All I can manage to do at this moment is stare right into Crystal's eyes.

I'm waiting for an answer.

But I don't get one.

"This is crazy," I say. "Even if we do this," and there's just no way I can bring myself to even consider it, "how do we find her?"

Crystal is terrified. I can see it all over her face. "Michael. We can't allow anything to happen to Batnaz."

"I know," I say, then think, *but we can't just give whatever we find under this monument over to that woman.*

"However," she continues, her eyes fiercely determined, "we cannot hand whatever it is we find here over to that woman."

I knew there was a reason I married you.

With Crystal standing watch, I get down on my hands and knees and try to lift one of the massive concrete pavers along the front of the monument. But it won't budge. I look around for something, anything, that can help me pry the damn thing up. But I can see nothing.

Crystal runs over to the motor bike and is taken aback by something she sees. "Hey, there's a note here," she shouts back to me. "And there's a key attached!" I can see her put the key in her pant pocket, then she takes a closer look at the note. "You're not gonna believe what it says!"

I stare at her from across the small lot, waiting for her to tell me. She takes a moment to absorb the message, then turns and gazes at me. "It says, It takes a weary female!"

How's that possible? I wonder. "How the heck could anyone know that we just discovered that phrase?"

It's clear to me by the look on her face that she's just as clueless on this as me. However, it's equally clear that she has solved our paver-prying problem as she grabs a long breaker-bar from the side of the bike and holds it in the air like Excalibur. "Will this work?" Her sarcasm is bleeding.

She brings me the breaker bar and I take it and immediately start wedging it between a couple of the pavers. I lean all my weight into it, and suddenly the paver stone pops up just enough for me to get a few fingers under it. "Give me a hand with this, would ya," I snap.

We heave the massive paver with a loud grunt and lean it carefully against the side of the monument, and as I stand up to relieve my lower back I spot an old couple standing on their front porch watching us. "I think we'd better hurry."

Crystal agrees with a quick nod as she places her hand on the hard rocky soil that was hidden beneath the paver. "It's solid as a rock," she cries.

I'm not really sure what I was hoping for. A hidden chamber? A pre-dug tunnel? But whatever it was, the reality is most certainly the opposite.

I flip the breaker-bar around and start smashing and digging out the earth beneath the base with the steel claw.

It's moist and very heavy, with large rocks throughout. As I break it apart and pull it out with the breaker-bar, Crystal kicks away the debris with her shoes.

"Michael?"

I don't look at her. Instead, I keep digging as quickly as I can. "Yeah?"

"Please hurry. We're acquiring a rather large audience."

My hand's cramping and sore. I glance up and notice that there are people gathering. Many are on their phones. We clearly haven't much time. I take the long end of the breaker bar and drill it into the hole. "I hit something!"

It's metal.

The box!

"Hey, Crystal. I think I found it."

Together we dig out those last few handfuls of dirt and frantically pull the metal box free from its tomb. It's about the size of a shoebox—large enough for a pair of work-boots.

Crystal attempts to open the box, but it's rusted shut.

"We don't really have time for that." I grab the breaker-bar and start toward the motor bike. But Crystal doesn't follow. "What are you doing?" No doubt, my anxiety is showing strong. "We've got to get out of here, now!"

Crystal grabs the metal box off the ground and starts running toward me, when the sound of sirens starts blistering the air. I slap the breaker bar back on the bike and jump on. As I sit there waiting what feels like an eternity for Crystal to catch up, I can hear the sirens growing louder. They are very close now. "Let's go!" I shout, feeling my heart racing and my palms sweating. I hold out my left hand. "The key!"

As she puts her hand in her pocket she trips. The metal box flies through the air. In my mind's eye time slows, nearly dead still. The sound of the sirens fade into obscurity as I witness Crystal fall to her knees, one hand still stuck in her pocket. My mind wants to jump and help, but my body is frozen in place. The metal box flies several feet away from her, finally smashing open on the pavement, mere feet from me.

The box had to have been severely degraded from age and many decades of relentless water damage. It literally falls to pieces as it hits the ground. As the dust settles and my mind's timeline finally catches back up with reality, I spot what has rolled out from inside the box. A small, perhaps softball-sized, golden spherical object. It has made its way out of the box and rolled several feet away, resting gently against the curb.

Crystal runs over to the object, brushing herself off from the fall, and quickly removes it from the gutter. I can see now that it's a little bigger than a softball. But not much. "Holy crap," she says. "Michael, do you know what this is?"

"It doesn't really matter what it is," I shout. "The cops are here!" They weren't actually here yet. But I could hear them coming up the street. "We need to go... NOW!"

32

Crystal jumped on the back of the motorbike and jammed the key into Michael's hand. The bike started with an almost bumblebee-like buzz and her heart sank. And as Michael twisted the handle, she was immediately terrified by just how slow the thing was moving.

"We're toast," Michael shouted. "There's no way we're going to outrun anyone on this piece of crap!"

But then, Crystal felt something. Something was vibrating in her hands. She glanced down and watched as a small pointer started spinning around in circles on the sphere. Upon closer examination, the sphere almost looked like some sort of complex golden compass.

As Michael pulled out of the cemetery parking lot, heading east onto Crispin Street—away from the sound of approaching sirens—the needle on the Liahona suddenly shot straight ahead, pointing in the direction they were riding. A few seconds later the needle quickly pointed left.

"Take a left!" she shouted.

"What?"

"NOW!"

He did. "I can't get this thing to go faster than 45 miles-an-hour!" Michael's knuckles were white, trying to twist every last drop of power out of the accelerator. She worried about him. It was easy to tell just how bad his anxiety was getting.

The needle shot to the right. "Turn here!" She shouted.

"Here, Michael!" She said, panicked. "Now!"

At the very last second, he managed to make the turn. "What are you doing?" he questioned. "We're never going to outrun them. In fact, we're just making things worse. We're going to get ourselves deeper into trouble by running away."

"I think it's trying to help us!"

"What are you talking about?" he asked, unable to turn his head to see what she was doing behind his back.

"The Liahona," she said quietly, almost whispering in his ear. "It's as if—

"Turn right!" she shouted in his ear, interrupting herself.

He did, but this time the turn was extremely sharp and the bike slid on some sand and fell on its side. Both Crystal and Michael slid several feet on the sandy pavement before quickly getting back on their feet. "What the hell are you doing?" he shouted, brushing sand off his backside. The sound of sirens was creeping up fast. They were right around the corner now. "I'm done," he said, putting his hand on his head in anticipation. "It's over, Crystal."

But she wasn't ready to quit. She ran over to him, the Liahona grasped tightly in both hands. "Look at this, Michael." She pointed at the compass needle. "It's telling us to go that way." She then spun around in circles to demonstrate that it always pointed in that same direction.

"So," he said snidely. Clearly giving up. "Big deal. It's a compass." The police vehicles were visible now. Just a couple blocks away and coming fast. "It's all over, babe."

"Sorry," she said. "You may be ready to quit, but I am not!" She grabbed the motor bike and took the controls. "You can stay here and face whatever's coming—" She perched the Liahona between her knees and started rolling the bike forward.

"—or you can get your butt on this bike!"

He watched the police cars get another block closer and then turned and jumped on the back of the bike. "I love you, but you're freaking crazy!"

"Perhaps a little." Her tone was somewhat joking, however, equally serious. "The Liahona keeps pointing in different directions as we ride," she continued. "It's not just a compass." She twisted the handle as much as it would go and they took off down a side street. "I know it's crazy, but I think this thing is trying to help us get away."

"You're right, it is crazy," Michael confirmed.

But she wasn't listening anymore. Her eyes were fixed on the needle at the top of the Liahona. She took a sharp right, then a quick left down a dirt path. It wasn't a road, and it didn't go on very far. Suddenly the needle spun in circles and then pointed backwards. "What the heck?"

"What is it?" Michael asked, concern marking his voice.

She didn't answer she just carefully turned the bike around on the very narrow walking path, and as she did they see three police cars, sirens a blarin', speeding by them on the main road. The cops never stopped. They just keep going.

Slowly, Crystal took the motor bike back to the main road. She could still hear the sirens, but could no longer tell where they were coming from. But they were no longer visible so she pushed the bike back on the road. Immediately the needle shot in a new direction. Back the way they had come. She pinned that throttle and let the Liahona guide her.

Two blocks.

Left turn.

One block.

Right turn.

Three blocks.

Left turn.

But there was a problem. "There's no left turn!"

"What?" Michael asked.

"The Liahona was pointing left, but there's no road!" Suddenly, the needle started going crazy. It spun circles for several seconds before finally stopping. This time, pointing backwards again. She turned the bike around quickly and started back. "What the heck?"

"What about this?" Michael asked. It wasn't a road, but rather a driveway the wrapped around the back of someone's private residence. "If you're right about this thing..."

She knew that he was right. She pulled off the road down the long driveway, around the back of a large bungalow, then stopped next to an elderly gentleman, who was loading a couple small suitcases into the back of a brand new jet-black Ford E-Series passenger van.

"Ah, jist in tyme," the strange old man said, as he tossed in the second bag. "Git in."

33

"Excuse me?" I say, confused.

"Put the motabyke under the ca'port and git in the van," the old man repeats, sternly. "We haven't much tyme."

"Do it," Crystal demands. It's almost a whisper. "The Liahona led us here. Just go with it... please."

I get it. We have little choice. However, something about this feels wrong. Batnaz is missing and could very well be the next person to end up dead.

And now we're being pursued by the police!

Just fantastic.

Crystal jumps off the bike, hides the Liahona under her shirt, and crawls into the back of the large van as I quickly park the bike under the carport.

The sirens are getting louder.

They're close. Very close.

I jump into the van and start to close the door behind me, but the old man is already in the driver's seat throwing the van in reverse before the door even latches. I quickly make my way to the backseat and sit. "What the hell's going on?"

"Git in the fa' back," the man says. "Keep ya faces 'way from the glass. The winda's may be da'k but people'll still see ya if ya git too close."

The old man backs out of the driveway and starts down the street. "In fact, jist lie down," he says, peering at us through the rearview. "Keep as fa' 'way from the glass as ya can." But Crystal doesn't listen, keeping her head up, gazing in shock as the old man drives straight toward the cacophony of sirens and flashing lights—right into a heavily guarded police blockade.

"What are you doing?" Crystal shouts, ready to open the van and jump out. *"Stop!"*

Crystal quickly ducks her head as the old man lowers the driver's side window and waves at one of the officers blocking the road. "Hey Bobby," the old man says with a smile, as he slows to a full stop at the road block. "What's goin' on?"

"A couple of real winnas vandalized Pioneer Cemetery," the officer says. "Seen anything s'spicious 'round the house?"

The old man shakes his head. "Just headin' on ova ta see yer Ma. Need anythin' while I'm out?"

"Not today," the officer says. "Just remind her, again, how much I love her—'kay?"

"Ya turned out a'right, kiddo."

"Thank's, Dad." The officer waves the old man through and we drive on without a single officer taking a second look.

The old man takes a left and then another immediate left and quickly accelerates to highway speed and takes in a long, deep breath. "Not much excitement happens 'round these pa'ts," he says. "But road blocks... for a couple vandals? Well, even that one's a stretch."

Crystal and I move toward the front of the van, sitting in the captain's chairs just behind the front cab.

"So," the old man says, giving me a strange look through the rearview. "What exactly have ya gone and done?"

How the heck do I answer that?

I'm still trying to make sense out of what happened back there. The Liahona, taking us on a crisscross trek through a tiny neighborhood, leading us to this old man's house—a man we had never met before—where he was not only waiting for us, but was ready to sneak us out of town.

I mean, seriously… What the hell just happened?

"I'm jist playin'," the old man says, breaking the silence. "Batnaz called me." The old man stares at Crystal now through the mirror. "Said he was in some sorta trouble; said I needed to git ya back to the airfield wit'out delay. His instructions were cleah and quite direct."

"Batnaz contacted you?" I ask.

"Yeah," he says with a bit of concern in his voice. "Said he was hidin' in da men's room or some'tin. Didn't quite understand what he was try'n ta say 'xactly, he was whisperin'. Sounded desperate. Said he had little tyme; that he needed me to remain sylent and follah his ordas p'cisely."

"What orders?" Crystal asks.

What could he have been hiding from? I think. Batnaz was only in the terminal for a few minutes before Crystal and I entered. The terminal was empty.

The old man turns down State Highway F, back towards the airfield and continues talking. "He explained in fine detail what I was ta do, "Leave the motabike in the cemet'ry parkin' lot with the key and a note readin': It takes a weary female. Race home, load the van wit the suitcases I packed the nyght befoah." The old man pauses a second. "Two of the items I packed have been in the family for generations, so I know that whateva ya doin', it's gotta be da'n impo'ant." He pauses again, perhaps hoping we might let him in on what was going on back in the cemetery.

Truth is, I'll be damned if I even know the answer to that.

The old man continues, "He told me to git ya outta town and back to the airpo't, immediately."

Crystal gazes at me with concern, "And what are we supposed to do when we get there?" she asks.

"That's all he said," the old man explains, pulling down Curtis Street. "Ya wanna know what's truly amazin'?"

Crystal perks up.

"Never even met da guy," he says. "It's just some'tin we've always done, since I was little. When one of them Disciples call, ya don't question... ya don't hesitate... ya jist do."

Disciples? I think, gawking at Crystal.

"But seriously," the old man continues, "whatta ya up ta?"

After another moment of awkward silence, I gaze at the old man in the mirror. "Why are you so willing to drop everything on a whim and follow orders—break the law, in fact—for some guy you have never even met?"

"And why did you refer to Batnaz as a disciple?" Crystal pauses and thinks about that a moment. "Well, I mean... I suppose he is a disciple, but—"

"I'm sorra," the old man says. "I've sid too much. The wyfe use'ta wa'n me 'bout runnin' my mouth like that."

The old man pulls into the airfield parking lot and squeals the van to a stop at the curbside, outside the door of the terminal. "This is wha we pa't ways," he says, suddenly sounding a bit cold in his tone. "Don't fo'get to take them bags I packed ya. The back dowa's 'ready open."

I step out of the van and help Crystal out. We grab the suitcases, and I'm just about to close the rear doors when they start closing on their own. "See ya 'round," the old man says, waving at us as the van starts inching forward. "Gotta check on the wife—poor soul. Hope she remembahs me t'day." He looks sad for a moment, then smiles as he puts his foot down and speeds off.

Poor guy, I think.

"Alzheimer's sucks," Crystal says, slipping the Liahona into one of the bags and then heading off for the terminal entrance ahead of me, where a nice gentleman stands waiting.

The man opens the door, and I watch her slip inside.

I rush up the walkway toward the entrance, but the man lets the door slam closed behind Crystal. I'm just about to grab the handle when the door swings back open.

"Sorry about that," the man says, "The lady dropped her bag." His face is sincere. "Forgive me, sir."

34

I need to remind myself that this is an airport and not a deserted shopping mall, which is exactly what it looks like.

There are shops all around the large open-concept terminal, but everything is closed. There are metal gates, pulled part way down in front of all the shops, just enough for employees to creep underneath.

I glance at my watch.

"Last flight out," the man says.

I hadn't noticed that the man was following us.

"Last flight?" I say, looking at my watch, again. "It's only 8:36 p.m." I glance out the front entrance to the tarmac outside. There are still a few moments of daylight remaining.

"This is a private airfield, sir," the man explains. "We closed nearly two hours ago. We were given special orders to wait for your arrival before locking up."

My head starts to throb.

What the hell…

"Who gave those orders?" Crystal demands.

But the man doesn't answer, instead he hastens his step, moving ahead and opening the door going out to the tarmac.

"Your plane is waiting," the man says. "Straight ahead."

It's Darlene.

Batnaz? I think.

I glance at Crystal, who doesn't look back, but just runs.

I quickly gain on her, but she makes it to Darlene first,

climbing those dozen steps in stride.

But I'm right behind her.

"Batnaz?" Crystal calls out. But the jet's fuselage is silent.

Empty.

A familiar voice sounds over the speaker system as the doorway begins to slide closed. "Take your seats. We'll be in the air momentarily," the pilot says.

There's a slight shake and subtle hum as the staircase retracts.

Crystal puts the Liahona in her bag, then places both our bags in the overhead compartment.

This is strange, I think.

We take our seats and buckle the restraints as Darlene begins to taxi the runway. Suddenly, the thrust of her jets pulls me back. It's a violent takeoff. I'm reminded of the violent landing.

The shorter than desirable runway.

Moments later we're leveling out. As Darlene settles into a comfortable cruise speed, I expect the pilot to announce that we're now free to roam the aircraft. Instead I'm startled by a sound behind me, and before I can ask what it is, the look on Crystal's face sends a spike of terror down my spine.

"Did you retrieve it for me?" It's Lilith.

35

There was something about Lilith. Something that drew people in and created puppets out of them. She was beautiful beyond compare and seductive. Even women found it difficult not to gaze upon her with desire. She just had it, and she abused the hell out of it.

"I'm here to help you," Lilith explained. "You don't need to believe me. However, it is true."

Crystal and Michael had strong reservations about trusting Lilith. After all, she had misled them back in Kirtland, and then violently threw them out of her SUV at the Monument to the Three Witnesses. What was there to trust about her? However, something about Lilith compelled them to trust her. It forced them, almost as if she had some sort of mystical power. For reasons that were beginning to give Crystal a migraine, they found themselves believing and trusting every word she said. And, though they knew something wasn't right, they were powerless against it.

It was Lilith who made the suggestion that they should explore the bags the old man packed for them. They pulled them out of the overhead compartments and opened them up on the table that Lilith pulled down from the wall.

Ordinary.

Nothing but items you might bring on a long trip. Crystal placed the Liahona on the table beside her and started pulling stuff out of her suitcase. A few changes of clothes––Crystal was curious how the old man could have known her size, let alone her style.

There were also hygienic supplies packed in a clear storage container and tucked inside a pocket was a bank deposit bag.

Michael found the same bank bag in his case. He carefully shook the bag. It was heavy and felt as if full of coins.

He unzipped the bag and was shocked to see wads of cash—but not any currency he had ever seen before.

He took one out and examined it close. "Is this... Mormon money," he questioned.

The beehive at the center and the word DESERET arched across the top may have been enough confirmation in itself, but the signature along the bottom sealed it—

Brigham Young.

"I had no idea Mormons had their own currency," he said, putting the bill back in the bag.

Crystal looked intrigued. "Me either."

Out of the corner of his eye, Michael noticed Lilith moving about the cabin. She was almost nervously pacing the area between the seats. *What the heck is she doing?* He thought. Returning his attention to the bank bag, he spotted, mixed in with the cash, several torn pieces of paper with strange symbols written thereon. "What's this?" he said, holding them up for Crystal to see. The pieces were clearly part of a much larger page that had been ripped to shreds.

Crystal noticed the same fragments of paper in her bank bag and immediately laid out the contents of both bank bags on the table and began to piece together the torn page.

The symbols were strange. Certainly nothing Michael had ever seen before, and based on the expression on Crystal's face, she was equally lost. But having an expert understanding of symbolism she quickly fit the dozen or so pieces together into what she determined had to be the next clue in Brigham Young's Roadmap. There was just one problem—

"I've never seen anything like it," Crystal says, and that makes me nervous. After all, how are we going to have any chance of cracking this, if one of the top cryptologists in the world is baffled by it?

"Do you have cell service, Michael?" she asks.

"Sorry, no," I respond. "I have nothing."

"We may need to wait until we land to look this stuff up."

"I'm not sure about that." I spot something peeking out from beneath a pair of slacks in my suitcase. It's a small wooden box, about the size of a large bible. It's adorned with intricate engravings of floral motifs surrounding a near perfect representation of the Salt Lake Temple. Along the top is a beehive and just below that is a line of text. It's clearly written in the same strange symbols as the page that we had just reconstructed.

ⴲ

ᗺꟼᎸᗰ ᴎᗷ ꙅᎾꟸꙅᗝᴦꚔ

"My God," I say. "Look at this." I ease the delicate lid off the box. Inside lays what appears to be the remains of a book, its pages barely bound together, some separated from the binding altogether. There's no cover and the pages have very visible signs of age and damage from moisture and insects.

"What is it?" Lilith asks. She's still pacing about, which would normally make me quite nervous. I hate when people pace. Strangely, however, her pacing has no effect on me. I laugh to myself. *The simple fact that I can say that it has no effect on me, is, ironically, it having an effect on me.*

And how exactly is she *"helping us?"*

I lift the pages out of the box and replace the lid. Then I carefully place the pages on top. There are hundreds of them, and each has the same symbols as the box and the reconstructed page printed all over them.

"Are you sure you've never seen this writing before?" I ask, handing Crystal what clearly looks to me like the cover page of the book. "It can't be that obscure." I grab a few coins off the table. "Everything is plastered with it." And then I notice it. "These coins. They're not all minted using the same strange symbols." I hold up a couple of the coins for closer examination. "This one here," I say, handing it to Crystal. "It's in English."

Crystal grabs the coin and reads it aloud.

"Holiness to the Lord."

She then swaps the coin for another and a light instantly flickers on. "These coins say the same thing," she says, quite enthusiastically. "I'm certain of it. See how most of the words have a strong similarity to each other?"

That's nice, I think. *But honestly, I don't see it.*

Crystal holds the two coins side by side so I can see more clearly. "Look closer," she says.

"Wait... I *do* see it," I say. She's right, looking at them side by side makes all the difference. "In fact '*to*' and '*Lord*' look almost identical."

look almost identical."

```
Holiness to the Lord
```

ᎮᎾᏞᏫᎥᎾ ᎴᏫ Ꭹ ᏞᎾᎮᎥ

"But then the rest doesn't look right at all," I say, looking out of one of Darlene's small windows—that now familiar black arch stretching out across a deep blue horizon. Even though it's late, there's a surprising amount of light way up in the stratosphere.

Crystal doesn't respond. She immediately turns to the cover page, still in her hand and within seconds declares—

"I know what the book is!"

For decades Crystal had studied the art of translation. Understanding symbology was only the beginning. She knew one must also be incredibly keen on noticing patterns. The basics of language are the same no matter where in the world you are. It uses a set number of symbols, which are then combined in some way to form sounds, words, and phrases.

Understanding the time period when the language was created also plays a big role in understanding the context of the symbology.

She attempted to explain how she came to her conclusions; however, it was not at all easy to learn the art—taking countless years of intense study, trial and error to master—let alone explain the art to the unexperienced.

But she gave it her best.

"It's immediately clear," she said, pointing at the ⴘ , "that this symbol means *the*."

Michael was nodding, but she could tell he was barely following.

She steered his attention to the coins. "There is no question in my mind," she said, "in my experience, that these two coins say the same thing."

```
Holiness to the Lord
```

ⴘ0Ⴑ⊬ⴙ8 ⚋0 Ⴘ Ⴑ0Ⴔ⚑

"So if you trust my experience, then you can know that from this we learn a few things," she continued. "We know that ⴘ means *the*, and ꓷO means *to*, and ꓡOꟼꓯ means *Lord*."

Michael was looking as though the lights were coming on. But he still wasn't saying anything.

"We can take this knowledge a step further by breaking down each word." She grabbed a pad and pen from a pocket in the side of her chair and wrote out the symbols, along with what she believed were the corresponding latin characters:

ꡙ = L		ꓶ = T	
O = O		ꓧ = N	
ꟼ = R		ꟼ = H	
ꓷ = D		ꓱ = E	
ꝸ = S		ꓨ = The	

"It doesn't look like much," she said, "but believe me, it is a huge leap forward for me. Knowing these characters helps me find the patterns that are consistent in languages throughout the world. Knowing that this text is on all these Mormon related items helps me put this language into clear perspective." She looked at Michael as her husband, for the first time in many hours. She smiled, warmly. "You should understand this," she said. "Think about that show you watch all the time."

"What show?" he questioned.

"The one with that Sajak guy," she said. "There is little difference between word games and what we're doing here. You are looking for patterns in the text to help you figure out the words. With that Wheel of Fortune game show you know the words are in English, so you can figure the answers out easily."

Michael agreed. He usually got the answers long before the contestants ever did. He often thought he should sign up to be on the show, but he was always too busy.

"Imagine now," she continued, "that the puzzle is not in English, but rather it's in a language you don't recognize." She lifted up the cover page of the book. "That is what we're dealing with here. We're trying to figure out a word puzzle in a different language." She realized that the analogy probably wasn't the best, but it was all she could come up with. "But what really matters," she continued, "is that we work towards figuring out the other symbols and we do that by figuring out small sections of text at a time." She wrote out the text from the cover page of the dilapidated book.

She let Michael and Lilith look at the text a long moment, hoping that one of them—her husband, she hoped—would add in the characters they already figured out and then search for patterns. But neither of them were saying anything, nor were they looking like they were on the brink of revelation, and the clock was ticking and she could not just let them—

"The *Book of Mormon*," Michael said.

Crystal smiled.

"Is it?" he said, looking for confirmation. "It's the *Book of Mormon*, isn't it?"

"How did you figure it out?" Lilith asked.

Michael explained that he replaced the characters he knew

from figuring out the symbols on the coin. He then tried to put the message into context—the cash, the coins, the etchings of the beehive, the Mormon temple on the box.

Crystal, having already figured out the text, proceeded to write the translation of it as she saw it, explaining that it was becoming evident to her that this was someone's attempt at making a language that was more phonetic than English. "Unlike English," she said, "where you have several characters coming together to create a different sound, or a single character sounding different depending on what characters surround it, with *this* language you have a single character representing each sound. For instance, the word '*of*' is represented by two characters, one symbolizing *awe* and the other, the sound of *v*."

the   b   oo   k   awe   v   m   aw   ur   m   u   n

Seeing it written out helped it make more sense to Michael. He had really, simply taken a guess. Just like he did most time when playing Wheel of Fortune. He used reason and context to make the best guess possible. But it was really just that—a guess. With it written out he could see and better understand how Crystal was figuring this thing out, and he knew she was right. "You really impress me," he said.

"Don't be impressed yet," Lilith said. "She still needs to decipher the roadmap."

Of course she had to be right.

Crystal goes to work translating the message from the torn piece of paper, writing it down as it's written and then making her translations in the margins as she figures each letter and word out. Some of it comes quickly, but much of the message remains obscure. I pray that things become clear to her soon. Time is not on our side. Batnaz is missing, and there's no way in hell we can just sit here and let him die.

The pilot enters the cabin and swaggers to the bar. He's an older gentleman. White hair. Old military flight jacket. Not at all what I imagined. "So," he says, grabbing a 2-liter bottle of Coke from the fridge. "Where are we headed?" He stands there a long moment, waiting for an answer that doesn't come. "We only have so much fuel and this baby guzzles it like iced tea in Arizona." He waits a bit longer, then pours himself a glass. "I need to know pretty soon."

I gaze at Crystal, praying she can figure it out. The pilot empties the glass in one pull and stands there.

Waiting.

Lilith is still pacing the cabin. She's staring at something next to Crystal. I think it's the Liahona, but I'm not sure. With each pace, back and forth across the cabin, she gets closer and closer to the table. *What is she doing?*

"I've got it," Crystal shouts, jumping to her feet. "I know what it says!"

"Was it something I said?" the pilot says with a grin.

Crystal quickly writes out the deciphered message. It always impresses me how quickly she can figure things out.

> *the lords hand is young*
> *blessed by eternal power*
> *it is he who holds the key*
> *and awaits the final hour*

Crystal starts reading the message out loud as Lilith grabs the Liahona from the table. In an instant, the lights blow out with a thunderous crash and the windows go black, as Darlene's engines whistle a high-pitch squeal and wind down to a halt.

"What the..." The pilot drops the bottle of cola on the floor and sprints to the cockpit, sliding the door closed behind him. As he does, the cabin goes pitch black, like when we cut power and went stealth to unlock the Skytale cipher.

Darlene shakes violently and I'm thrown to the floor with a force that steals the wind from my lungs. "Crystal!" I try to shout, but I can't make a sound. I try to collect myself and consider what to do. However, a feeling takes over my body and soul. It's a familiar feeling that cannot be ignored.

We're going down!

36

I fumble around in the blackness for my iPhone, praying like mad that the flashlight works. It doesn't! My phone won't even wake up. It's completely dead.

I feel around for Crystal, who had been sitting right next to me. "Crystal." I reach to my left, patting around the headrest of her seat. "Where are you?" But there's no answer.

I'm really getting worried. I feel my pulse rise. Sweat is already dripping down the small of my back. "Crystal," I say louder. I kneel on the floor and pat around.

Nothing.

"Where the hell are you?"

I return to my feet and, holding on to the headrest of my chair, I reach over to the chair in front of me and carefully make my way toward the cockpit. "Hey," I shout as I find the door and place my ear against it. "Open the door!"

For a long moment there is nothing. Not a sound. No movement inside. No light. Nothing. I slam both fists on the door. "I said, open this damn door!"

Another moment passes. But there's still nothing.

Then, I hear a click from inside.

The door slides open ever so slightly. Light from inside bleeds into the cabin, blinding me. The light appears to be coming in from the windshield. I hear the pilot scurry back to his seat and mumble something under his breath.

I take advantage of the flood of light and look toward where

Crystal was sitting. I still can't see her. I crane my neck, hoping to find her. But there's no sign.

Oh, dear God!

"The whole damn thing is dead," the pilot shouts. "What the hell happened back there?"

I turn and face the old man sitting in the pilot's chair, gripping the controls like a rookie cadet. The terror in his eyes is palatable. Here sits a man—decades of commercial, private, and military flight experience—pinching goose eggs.

Through the windshield I can see that familiar black arch bending across the deep blue horizon. I breathe a sigh of relief knowing that, though it had felt like we were free falling, in actuality, we are still flying strong at 60,000 feet. But the relief fades fast, as the pilot looks me, dead in the eyes—his entire control panel, dark—and says, with a lump choking his throat, "Do you believe in God?"

The chanting in Crystal's head grew deafening as the cloaked figures circled around her, getting closer and closer with each sweeping sidestep. It was suffocating. But it wasn't mere claustrophobia she was feeling. No, this was something quite different. Pure terror overwhelmed her as she began to feel something moving around inside her head. The chanting continued on and on as they grew closer and closer...

I run like a bullet back into the cabin and take advantage of the light from the cockpit to look for Crystal. As I make my way back to where we were sitting I spot her. She's curled up in the fetal position on the floor, propped up against the wall about a foot away from her chair. Totally still, silent. "Crystal," I shout. No response. I move toward her and as I do something rushes by me. It's like a violent gust of air. Almost knocks me over. I grab the headrest of my seat, stabilizing myself. Then, suddenly, the cabin goes black.

Lilith! I think. Actually, I know. She's up to something, and whatever it is, it cannot be good.

Instinctively, I reach for Crystal, quickly finding her in the pitch blackness, and pull her close. She feels strange. A deep feeling of dread fills my soul as I kiss her on the face. "Oh, Crystal." I place my ear to her mouth and listen closely. I can feel her breathing. "I love you." I cradle her a moment longer, then rest her back on the floor and move as quickly as I can through the darkness toward the cockpit.

"Open this door, Lilith!"

The door doesn't open.

"Michael." It is Crystal. She's calling me, but it's just a faint whisper. I can barely hear it. "Please, come back."

You have no idea how badly I want to run back to her. But, whatever Lilith is doing is dire. I must get inside this cockpit, and fast. "Open this damn door, Lilith," I scream, thrusting my body against the door and kicking it with enough force that I thought I might just break it down.

"Open the door... NOW!"

Finally, the door slides open. As my eyes adjust to the blinding light I am stricken with terror as I see the pilot's body, slumped over the controls. "What have you done?"

But Lilith doesn't answer. Then I realize, she's sitting in the co-pilot's chair yanking on the other set of controls, very clearly fighting to keep Darlene from falling out of the sky. She glances at me with cold eyes, "I did nothing!"

I gaze out the windshield. The black arch is gone—nothing but blue sky, with patches of cloud and rain that chop by with alarming speed. Suddenly, Darlene hits a pocket of heavy air and it nearly tosses me out the cockpit door.

"Stop standing there like a damn idiot," Lilith shouts. "Move him to the floor and grab the controls!"

I gather my wits and quickly wrap my arms around the pilot's chest. I've never moved a dead body before, but it's obvious. The pilot has left the building—or rather, the aircraft. It's a Herculean task, like lifting a small VW. As I lock my fingers together across his breastbone and spin him around, I feel something hard sticking up from the left side of his upper chest.

A pacemaker, I realize. *This man had a heart attack.* Whatever killed the power to Darlene, as well as our phones and electronics, also killed the pilot by killing his pacemaker.

Son of a bitch!

I place the pilot on the floor out of the way and take his seat. My heart is racing like the Indie 500, as is my spiraling out of control mind. I haven't the slightest clue what I'm doing, but for the love of all that is good and for Crystal, I'm going to do it.

I place my hands on the controls and pull with all my might. Immediately, I can tell that it's futile. Without power, the most we're doing is limiting the aircraft's vibrations; we're not stopping Darlene from falling. I have no idea how much altitude we have left. However, I can see the ground, and it's coming up fast.

We're over a forest. The trees and mountains are, at best, just a few miles below. There's no more rain. No clouds. Just clear blue skies and green green ground, approaching like any man would pray to never have to witness.

I have no idea how long it took for Darlene to fall all this way; it feels like it took an eternity. Gazing out the windshield at the trees growing larger and larger by the second, a flood of memories flashes through my tumultuous mind.

Crystal. Her strikingly beautiful blue eyes. Our meeting in my class at Harvard Divinity back in Cambridge was no accident. As crazy as it sounds, even to me, I know we were preordained to be together. If I were cursed to live a thousand lives, I'd never love another as much as I love her.

Savanna Campbell. Even though she turned on me and became a mystery even unto herself, she ultimately gave herself to me in a way no one else ever has. I shall never forget that moment—in a tunnel just outside the Holy Sistine Chapel, after causing so much pain and confusion for me, finding out that she was working with the enemy, in a split second decision that I am sure will be rewarded, Savanna threw herself in front of a bullet to save my life. I miss her dearly. We had countless wonderful times together.

Something tells me we shall meet again... soon.

I feel a breeze on the back of my neck and a soft touch on my shoulder. "I love you." Crystal says.

I clench the controls tighter and pull them even harder. It fights me like a shark being reeled in off the side of a deep sea fishing rig, but I muscle that thing like nothing I've ever experienced before.

Crystal wraps her arms around me from behind and puts her face to my right ear. "It's okay, Michael." She's crying. "None of this is your fault. I love you so much."

"Touching," Lilith says. I forgot she was even here, my mind, lost in the moment that was about to take everything away. "But I'm not dying on this godforsaken thing." Suddenly, the controls lift in my hands. How can she be so strong? She's nearly half my size. Lilith pulls her controls, and I feel Darlene's nose lift. But it's too late. It's impossible to know exactly how fast we are going, but if I had to guess, based on the speed we were going at the time we lost power, and the fact that all we've done is fall ever since—not to mention, the closer we get to the ground the harder it is to focus on any one point on its surface—I'd say we're going well over a thousand miles per hour. Darlene's nose lifting at this point is only stalling the inevitable. I release my hands from the controls and stand tall.

"What are you doing!" Lilith shouts.

But I don't answer. I take Crystal by the hand and leave the cockpit.

Darlene is flying surprisingly smooth right now. From the cabin—with all the windows blacked out from loss of power—it could be easy to forget that we're falling to our ultimate demise.

I sit in the first chair we come to and pull Crystal into my lap. She lays down across my legs and curls up to my chest. She has the Liahona in her hands, tucked in between us. For a moment it looks like she's praying—something I've never seen her do before. But then she opens her eyes and smiles. "It's okay."

"No... no it's not." The words crack as they escape my mouth. My chin starts to quiver uncontrollably as tears stream down my face. "I'm so sorry."

"It's okay," she stresses, acting as if nothing is wrong—as if everything is going to be just fine. "I love you, Michael, and nothing will ever change that."

37

I gasp for air as my eyes open. At first it hurts—like pins being stuck in the back of my neck and in my eyes. I struggle to breathe. My chest is heavy. The room, barely lit, cold. The table I'm laying on is freezing, hard, like metal. The smell, it's strange yet somehow familiar. Like bleach, but there's also something else. The stench turns my stomach.

Am I naked?

I sit up on the table and place my feet on the floor.

I am naked.

The floor is like ice.

Suddenly there's a commotion behind me and in a mad rush a group of men run up and lie me back down. I feel a pinch in the right side of my neck and immediately a wave of heat envelopes my body and I drift asleep.

"Mr. DiBianco?" a woman says softly in my ear. My eyes open slightly. The light in the room is blinding, immediately triggering a headache. "How are you feeling?"

"Like I've been hit by a truck." As my eyes adjust it becomes clear where I am. But just in case I was not able to make the connection on my own—

"You're in the hospital," the woman says, rather loudly, apparently trying to call attention to our location. She lowers her voice and says, "My name is Mary. I'm a nurse and I'll be taking care of you while you're with us."

"Why am I here?" I ask. My mind is blank. I have no recollection whatsoever of what brought me to this place.

The nurse circles around from the right of my bed to my left and grabs a blood pressure cuff off the rollaway cart. "I'm going to take your vitals. Is that okay?"

"Nurse," I say, as she lifts my arm and wraps the cuff tightly. "Mary, is it?" She looks at me. "Why am I here?"

Just then a group of men and women in white lab coats enter the room. One is carrying a clipboard with a small electronic device attached to it. She stands back, taking note of everything that's happening in the room, while the other four stand around my bed and gawk, waiting for Nurse Mary to finish taking my vitals.

"120 over 80," Nurse Mary says as she sticks a thermometer under my tongue. She feels for my pulse and then waits a moment. "Pulse is 68." There's a beeping coming from a small device on the rollaway cart, and she pulls the thermometer from my mouth. "Everything's perfect."

A little too perfect, I think, as memories finally start surfacing. *Oh God...* "Crystal!" I say, however even I could barely hear her name escape my lips. "We crashed." Under the circumstances, with all I've been through, how can I feel calm? How can my vitals be normal? I haven't taken any anxiety medication for at least 24 hours. I should be a wreck.

Two male doctors approach my bed, one on either side, each grabbing his stethoscope from around his neck. "Do you mind if we take a listen to your heart?" the man on my left asks, as he presses a button on the bed and I lay back.

Both doctors take turns listening. "Impressive," one says, the one on my right. "Hard to believe you were—"

"In a accident," the other finishes.

"Right." The doctor on my right reluctantly agrees, as he presses another button on the bed and my upper body is lifted into a seating position. "Please lean forward for us. We're going to have a listen to your lungs."

These doctors are hiding something, and it's as obvious as the feeling I have that something just isn't right. Something inside me is different—very different.

"I've never seen such an incredible recovery," the doctor on my left says. "Your vitals: heart, lungs... everything. You're completely sound." The look on the man's face is not one of a doctor happy for his patient, rather, it's the look of awe and discovery.

What the hell happened to me?

Something is amiss and with all my soul, I need to know. 'What exactly happened to me, doc... and where's Crystal?"

"You were in an accident."

"Yes, I know. However, something's wrong, and you're not telling me the truth." I bend over and feel my legs. "Did I lose a limb? Am I paralyzed?"

"No," one of the women doctors declares as she takes the man's place on my left. "That's the miracle, Mr. DiBianco; there is literally nothing medically wrong with you."

A cold look comes upon the face of a fourth doctor as she places her hand on her cheek and says in a questioning tone, "It's almost as if you weren't in the accident at all."

"Well, Mr DiBianco," Nurse Mary says as the group of doctors back away suddenly, gather around the woman with the clipboard briefly, then leave the room. "You should get some rest. I'll be back in a couple hours to check on you." While

Nurse Mary's smile is truly genuine and caring, I simply cannot shake the feeling that something is deeply wrong, and these people are hiding it from me.

"Nurse!" I say, perhaps a bit too loudly as she's about to leave the room. She pauses in the doorway and turns to face me. "My wife," I can feel the tears welling in my eyes as the thought approaches my lips. "Is she okay?"

A look takes over her face. She tries to hide it, but it's there. "Give me just one second." The look is fear.

It's a strange feeling, being alone after all we've been through. It feels like ages ago that we encountered President Batnaz in our hotel room in Paris. Yet, this feeling goes far beyond momentary solitude. Something deep inside of me feels like it's been stolen away, lost forever. I know what it is, though I refuse to admit it.

The cold sterile nature of the hospital does little to ease the feeling of loss. I sit up in bed and place my feet on the cool, hard floor. The curtains are wide open, exposing the natural light from outside, along with what little scenery wherever this is has to offer. I stand up and adjust my IV tubing and wheel the IV pump and drip bag over to the window so I can have a better look.

The sun is shining, the sky is clear, and there is nothing but green trees and mountains for as far as my eyes can take me. In that instant I am struck by a vision of free falling—green trees and mountains growing closer by the second.

I'm startled back from the vision just before I hit the ground. *What the hell?* I think as I quickly close my eyes. For the first time since waking up, I can feel my heart racing again. But only for a moment.

I take a deep breath and return my gaze outside, only this

time I look down. My room is easily four, perhaps five stories up. Below me is a parking lot, a few smaller buildings, and what looks like a tiny restaurant. However, everything is quiet. The lots are empty.

Where the hell am I?

I turn and examine the room. There's not much to it: a typical hospital bed, a rolling nightstand, a tiny television, privacy curtain which is pulled all the way open and is tucked behind the tv—clearly that doesn't get much use. Then there's the typical medical equipment attached to the walls, and... wait. *How did that get here?*

In the corner of the room, resting on top of the small kitchenette countertop, just a few feet from a single basin stainless steel sink, is a small brass sphere. It's tucked away just enough so that, from the bed I couldn't see it, and even now, I can just barely make it out. But, there it is...

The Liahona!

I grab the IV pump and drip bag and start wheeling it toward the kitchenette—just on the other side of the bed, by the entrance. As I make my way around the bed, the Liahona comes into perfect view. Suddenly, The room goes pitch black and I feel something rush by me, nearly knocking me over. A moment later I feel an unmistakable feeling.

I'm falling, and fast!

"Mister DiBianco," Nurse Mary shouts with concern as she catches my fall, snapping me out of the terrifying vision. "You should be resting." She puts her arm around my shoulders and helps me back to my bed.

There's a stocky gentleman accompanying her. He's wearing a while lab coat. However, he does not look like a typical doctor. Based on the look on his face, he's not here to listen to my heart

—more like break it. "Doctor Roberts and I would like to have a word with you."

I follow her lead and return to the bed. I sit on the edge and motion for them to pull the chairs from the wall around to my side and sit with me. "What's this about?"

"It's about your wife, Michael," she says solemnly. "It's about Crystal." Nurse Mary turns and faces Doctor Roberts with uncertainty and sadness in her eyes.

Doctor Roberts crosses one leg over his other and adjusts his lab coat, then thinks about it for a moment and readjusts his posture. He plants his feet on the floor and leans in closer to me. I can see what looks like a tweed jacket beneath his lab coat, and I catch the subtle, yet noticeable scent of cherry pipe tobacco on his clothing. Whoever this man is, he is not a medical doctor. My guess, he's a shrink—a psychologist hired by the hospital to handle difficult situations, such as the one that I feel in my heart is coming.

"I'm afraid there is no easy way to say this, Michael." Doctor Roberts voice is soft and soothing. "However, your wife, most sadly, did not survive the accident."

And there it is. The proof of what it was I already knew yet refused to admit. But, now that it's been said—now that my ears have actually heard the words spoken—I can no longer deny it, and the feeling hits me like the avalanche that robbed me of my parents when I was just twelve.

"Move your damn asses!" DiBianco's father shouted.

They tucked in close to their knees and rode the monstrous wave of snow and ice down the mountainside. It roared like a mighty beast longing to devour them in one solemn gulp. The sound was deafening. The ground shifted and quaked.

Time seemed to stop, and DiBianco felt something grab him from behind, pulling him to safety. Though he wasn't safe. Not even close. He watched his mother and father tumble head over foot through the raging avalanche; skis twirling through the air, poles spearing the sky like deadly javelins.

After the avalanche settled and the ground hardened over in a solid white blinding wasteland, young Michael ran down the mountainside, tears flooding his eyes, heart racing a mile a second; he ran toward the spot where he last saw his father get devoured by the snowy beast.

Plopping down on the calm, ice-encrusted surface, he franticly heaved fistfuls of the heavy ice and snow, knowing all along that every second he fought to save his father was another second his mother had to suffer.

He followed them the best he could, but somewhere along the way he lost sight of his mother.

Michael heaved massive chunks of snow from the hole with his arms—scraping, digging, pulling with all his might. The hole grew larger and larger. Then he felt something. A hand! Rejuvenated, the young Michael dug faster, harder. Thoughts of his mother filled his mind and his heart, and he burst into tears.

"I'm sorry mom," he wailed. "I love you." He dug and dug. His father's hair stuck up out of the snow. He wasn't moving, he wasn't making any noise. "God, I'm too late!" Tears poured from his eyes. "God help me. I'm so sorry!"

Just as the avalanche buried my parents alive, suffocating my mother to death before my eyes, then taking my father mere days later, now it has returned to claim my soul.

The world around me vanishes as I break into sobs. I see Crystal. She's laying across my lap, curled up to my chest. Her soft vanilla scent fills my senses. There's nothing about this woman that isn't perfect in my eyes. I hug and kiss her, holding her tighter than ever before. I lay her down on the bed and she giggles. We cuddle and caress each other; her eyes so full of life—her spirit, powerfully addictive.

I close my eyes and let her warmth fill my soul. It permeates every recess of my world, filling my heart with more joy than any man should be allowed to treasure.

I open my eyes.

The room is empty.

A dimly lit prison.

The bright sunny day outside my window has faded to a deep purple twilight, and now I lay in this sterile white hospital bed, a hollowed-out corpse of a man.

38

"What we're about to tell you can never leave this plane; do you understand?" Savanna said, leaning in closer to DiBianco, who was sitting nervously in the jet plane's upscale leather seating.

"Yes," he said. "Perfectly."

"Good." Savanna rose from her seat and topped off her glass with another pour of scotch, squeezed a lime wedge inside, then dropped in the peel. She grinned, then turned to gaze at Crystal. "She is beautiful, isn't she?"

DiBianco's face went flush.

He tried to hide it, but he could not.

"I think it's time we just spit it out," she said, plainly. "Don't you think so, Crystal?"

Crystal nodded.

"Smile, Michael," Savanna cooed. "This is good."

Nothing about this sounded very good at all.

"When you were a boy," Savanna continued, "you were adopted by a priest, yes?"

"Yeah?"

"Do you know why?"

"Because my parents were killed in an avalanche." DiBianco was positive. "I watched it happen. That man was kind enough to take me in."

Savanna fished a small device from her coat and fumbled it in her fingers. "Your parents were told of the prophecy, but they refused to listen—refused to obey."

"*What are you talking about?*"

Crystal was stern. "Your parents were important—"

"*Very important,*" *Savanna interrupted. "And yet the moment their power was taken away, they fell, along with the rest of them.*"

DiBianco gazed at the device in Savanna's hands.

"*Tell me,*" *Savanna taunted. "Can you recall anything at all from before your parents died on that mountain?*"

That's odd, Michael thought. He couldn't really remember a single thing from before that day.

"*Shortly after your parents died,*" *she continued, "do you remember where you were brought?*"

To his dismay, he could not remember that either.

"*They planted something in your brain, Michael. A nano-processor. It reprogrammed you—it changed you!*"

"*Bull!*" *he shouted. "I watched them die!" Tears welled in his eyes. "I dug my father out of that mountainside, just to lose him anyways a few hours later. I watched my mother's head get chiseled out of the ice; the rest of her remains weren't found until the following spring—half eaten by wild animals!*"

"*Those memories were planted!*" *Savanna shouted.*

DiBianco's pulse raced, but it wasn't anxiety, it was fury. He struggled to refrain from lashing out.

"*Soon you'll understand,*" *Savanna said. "Soon you'll see the truth. You'll see with such clarity and divine force that your clouded beliefs will no longer blind you." Savanna passed the small remote to Crystal. "It is time.*"

DiBianco gazed at the device with horror. He wanted to lurch out, grab it, but before his mind could send the signal to act, her finger tapped the red button.

"*Mister DiBianco!*" It's a woman's voice. It's quite stern—

adamant even—yet cautiously quiet. I can feel a set of hands on my shoulders, though I can't quite tell if they are trying to hold me down or rattle me awake.

I jerk my arms up in an attempt to shake the hands loose and I'm just about to speak, when—

"Shhh!" The woman places a hand over my mouth, glances at the open door, then speaks under her breath, "I'm President Jon Batnaz's daughter. Please, your life is in grave danger!"

"You're president Batnaz's daughter?" I say, still in shock after that dream, only to be awoken to that grim message.

"Come on," she stresses. "We haven't much time. There'll be more any minute."

"More what?" I question as I carefully pull the IV from my arm and hit the pause button on the pump so as not to flood the floor with whatever it is they were feeding me and to avoid sounding the alarm. "What the hell is going on?"

She tosses my clothing and shoes on the bed, "Here, put these on," then opens a plastic hospital bag that was laying on the counter. "This will do. There will be time to explain once we're out of here." She examines the Liahona, but she doesn't touch it. She grabs a handful of blue rubber gloves from beside the sink and slides several pairs over each hand. She looks like she's about to grab the Liahona but then stops. She looks around, spots a stack of folded white blankets, then takes one, unfolds and wraps it around the small brass sphere, never once letting her gloved fingers touch it. She then carefully lifts it off the counter and places it inside the plastic bag. The entire operation takes several minutes and is like watching someone handle nuclear waste.

I button my pants and secure my belt, then toss my loafers on the floor and slip them on. I don't question why she handled the Liahona in such a delicate manor. After all, I remember what happened to Darlene after Lilith touched it. Though the thought does cross my mind, *is she afraid to touch it because she harbors darkness like Lilith?*

But I'm not given time to consider all the possibilities. I either trust that this woman is speaking the truth and therefore my life is in danger and I must leave, now. Or, I trust the hospital staff, whom I know have not been straight with me, and who have been acting strangely ever since I showed up here. I am liking my odds better with this woman. "Excuse me, Ms Batnaz—"

"Wells," she corrects with a smile as she starts for the doorway, then pauses to peek down the hall. "Pricilla Wells. Now grab the bag—" she points to the hospital bag containing the Liahona "—and follow me."

"Wait, what…"

But she's already gone. I grab the bag and run after her, stumbling on my feet as I go. My head is spinning, but I keep moving, clutching the bag tightly to my chest.

There is a strange smell in the hall, almost like car exhaust, and as I pass each hospital room, I am taken aback by what I see—or should I say, what I don't see.

They're all empty!

And when I say empty I don't just mean that there are no patients in their beds. No, I mean that every room is completely void of absolutely anything and everything.

As I'm running, I hear a loud humming noise emanating

from one of the rooms ahead. I slow my stride and peer into the room, and I stop dead in my tracks, staring at the sight.

There's a small piece of machinery inside, with a single lightbulb flickering softly, shining upon what I can easily tell is a cluttered desk, a few folding chairs, and two motionless bodies laying on the floor. I can't make out who they are, as their faces are turned away from the door. However one of them is wearing a tweed jacket.

What the hell?

"Let's go!" Pricilla shouts, her voice echoing off the barren walls of the building.

I take off running. I run toward Pricilla, but quickly slow myself to a crawl once again as I approach the end of the hall. Sprawled out on the floor in front of me are two large men, dressed in tactical gear, each with an AR-15 slung around his shoulder. "Are they, dead?" I ask. I can only imagine the shock on my face.

Pricilla pushes open the door to the emergency exit and ushers me through, then closes the door tightly behind us. The stairwell is completely dark. She clicks on a flashlight and points it in my eyes. "Quickly," she says. "We must get to the sub-level. There will be more!" She starts running down the stairs, which is a wonder in itself as she's wearing heels.

I follow as quickly as I can. But to be honest, I feel a little sluggish. Whatever it was they had been intravenously feeding me, it was not mere saline. They were keeping me relaxed with something. Even though I am dizzy and disorientated, I keep up, and we quickly hit the sub-level.

"How the heck are we going to get out of the building from the basement?" I ask as we finally pass the plaque on the stairwell wall that reads "Sub-Level."

It sure as hell looks like we're in the basement. However, just as we turn the corner, Pricilla pushes open a large steel door, and a blast of hot, heavy air strikes my face.

The lot is dark. No street lamps to be seen anywhere. I can just barely tell that it's a parking lot. And parked right outside the door is an idling, jet black Mustang GT 5.0 with a tall, blacker-than-black man holding open the passenger door.

Pricilla motions for me to enter, and she slides into the backseat right beside me, then turns to the man who closes the door and runs around to the driver's seat. "We haven't much time," she says. "Step on it!"

The roar of the Mustang's V8 engine is nothing less than beast-like as the driver throws the shifter into first gear and we rocket away. The power reminds me of Darlene.

As we drive away from the hospital I turn in my seat and gaze in shock at the place we just were. It's a massive, abandoned warehouse. The entire building is dark, plastered with graffiti, the vast majority of the windows are boarded up, except a few along the top floor, where one stands out from the rest—a lone, flickering light backdropping the silhouette of a woman with long hair, staring at us as we race out of the parking lot and down a dark street.

Lilith felt her jaw clench tight as she watched the black Mustang—its headlights and classic triple-lit taillights striking in contrast with the blackness surrounding it—disappear into the night.

She stepped away from the window. The constant hum of

the generator was quickly growing on her nerves. She swung her right arm out at her side and flicked her hand, and the flickering light blew out with a crack, and the roaring voice of the generator choked and died.

In the darkness, Lilith's stunning olive green eyes took on a more oil-like appearance. They almost looked black. And as the glow of the moon slowly permeated the room, bringing the cluttered desk and office chairs back into view, so too did it illuminate the bodies, which lay motionless across the floor.

Lilith crouched down on bent knee and placed her right hand upon the forehead of one of them. He was a tall, middle-aged man. He reeked of cherry-flavored tobacco and wore a tweed jacket. She placed three fingers on the side of his neck and grinned as the body began to stir.

39

"Did you kill those people?" I ask Pricilla, as the Mustang drifts around a sharp curve and then speeds down a narrow backroad packed with multi-family apartment buildings.

"Of course not," Pricilla declares with a chuckle. "We're Mormons... not murderers."

As we approach the end of the road the driver downshifts the Mustang, causing the tires to chirp and squeal as he quickly turns down another, even narrower alleyway. There is nearly no leg room in the back seat of this car. My legs are pinned behind the driver's seat, and I can barely move.

"Michael," Pricilla says reaching over and placing her left hand on the drivers right shoulder, "meet Samuel."

The driver looks at me in the rearview—his head touching the roof—and nods. "I prefer Sammy," he says in a thick Nigerian accent. His eyes, a strange combination of gentle giant and major badass.

"Sammy is my driver, my pilot, and partner. If I may say so, he is the best thing to ever happen to this organization."

By the way they're looking at each other in rearview, I'd wager that their partnership goes a little beyond business.

"How did you do that back there?" I ask, scratching my head, attempting to make sense of the events that just transpired. "What exactly happened back there, and who are those people? They're clearly not really doctors."

"Actually, they are." Pricilla adjusted herself in the cramped confines of the Mustang's backseat and turned to better face me. "You were being held at a makeshift black ops government facility," she explains. "After the crash, which completely annihilated Daddy's SonicStar, you and Crystal were taken to a local hospital." All of a sudden she looks uncomfortable, shifting in the Mustang's stiff leather seat. "Michael. I'm not exactly sure how to say this to you." She looks as if she wishes she hadn't sat in the back seat with me. "Crystal wasn't the only person to die in that crash."

"I know," I affirmed. "The pilot had a heart attack caused by a failure of his pacemaker. "Whatever happened to Darlene also took out the poor guy's heart."

"No, Michael." She pauses. "I mean, yes, the pilot did die. You're right about that. However..." she pauses once more.

What the heck is she trying to say?

"Michael, no one survived that flight."

She's lost her marbles. I mean, clearly she's off her rocker. "I'm afraid I'm quite alive and well," I point out. "Perhaps I should leave? You could just let me out at the next corner."

"I know how it sounds," she says. "But think about it. Don't you remember waking up in the hospital morgue?"

"No... I'm pretty sure I'd remember something like that!"

"You don't remember waking up in a cold dark place, naked on a metal table, only to be drugged back to sleep by the technicians who found you—a dead man—about to get up and walk out of their morgue?"

It's a little foggy. However, I do remember. "How could you know about that?"

"We have eyes and ears everywhere," she explains. "There really isn't much we don't know. Except for..." she pauses.

"Except for what?"

"There have always been secrets that even we are not privy. It drives me nuts, but Father has his ways."

"Batnaz. He's behind all of this?"

"For the most part," she confirms. "But now he's missing and we haven't been able to reach him or the others."

"The others?"

"He has partners. However, we've never been allowed to speak with them."

"This all sounds rather shady... wouldn't you agree?"

"I assure you, Michael, we're the good guys here. Once we get to the safe house I'll explain more."

"Safe house?" *What the hell have I gotten myself into?* As we pull down yet another narrow side street I begin to notice the sun rising. *Was I really out all night long?* The dream seemed to go by so quickly. Then I was being woken up by this strange woman. *A woman who single-handedly knocked out an entire black ops team,* I realize. "You never did explain how you knocked out those people back in the black ops facility."

"We took advantage of the nano-processor still wired in your brain," she said proudly.

"What?" I say as I instinctively rub my head in the area where I was told the chip was implanted—

I look at the small device in Crystal's hands in horror as she smiles at me and presses the red button.

"I momentarily shut down your brain's ability to register sound generated by your eardrums. During that narrow window we protected our own ears with specialized noice cancellation earplugs and then fired a high-pitched resonator cannon which completely knocks out anyone not wearing protection within a 500 yard radius. Once I knew everyone was out, I made my way through the dark building to extract you. You having that chip in your head made that job remarkably easy."

The Mustang finally pulls into a tiny rundown garage, adjacent to an old three-story apartment building, and the door closes behind us and the lights come on.

Sammy kills the ignition and steps out of the car, then flips the lever moving the driver's seat forward, allowing for me to get out.

I grab the hospital bag containing the Liahona from between my legs and exit the car.

Pricilla quickly walks around the car and rushes me out the side door into the tight space between the two structures.

Sammy locks the garage and catches up just as we duck into a side entrance of the apartment building and make haste up several flights of stairs. By the time we reach the top floor I'm struggling to catch my breath.

Pricilla enters a code into a keypad and opens the door. Inside is everything you would expect to see in any ordinary apartment. We walk into the kitchen, and Pricilla pulls a chair out from the table and motions for me to sit.

I do. I place the bag with the Liahona on the floor between my legs.

"We should be safe here," she claims as she takes the seat next to me and crosses her legs. "At least for awhile."

Sammy walks into the family room and stands by a window, keeping watch.

"So, what do we do?" I ask. "And why are we here?"

Pricilla grabs her iPhone from her back pocket and opens up an app. "Are you familiar with the Light of Christ?"

"What do you mean?"

She never removes her eyes from her phone as she flips through what looks like pages of a book. "I quite literally mean what I said. The Light of Christ. It's not a trick question, nor a rhetorical one." She finally looks like she found what she's looking for, then starts to read out loud.

> *Who alone possesses immortality and dwells in unapproachable light... To Him be honor and eternal dominion!* ~ *1 Timothy 6:16*

> *This is the message which we have heard of Him, and declare unto you, that God is light, and in Him is no darkness at all.* ~ *1 John 1:5*

"These verses share something more in common than just mentioning God and Light in the same sentence. Both writers had visions of the glorified body of God." She taps her iPhone's screen and is instantly brought to another Bible verse. "In Acts, Paul, who wrote the Letters to Timothy, had his life-changing experience on Damascus Road where he saw the transfigured Christ." She clicks another link. "And in Corinthians, Paul speaks of his vision of the transfigured Christ entering into the third heaven—or Celestial Kingdom as Mormons understand it. The Book of Revelation speaks of John the Beloved having visions while on Patmos. John also witnessed the transfigured Christ on the mountain." She puts her phone on the table and looks at me. "Both men had a personal knowledge of the energy that exists in Heaven.

"Light is only a small portion of the energy that belongs to the family of radiation known as the electromagnetic spectrum. These energy waves—which are actually photons... small bundles of energy—range from radio waves to gamma rays." She points up to the light in the ceiling overhead. "For light to be "unapproachable" besides being pure, as with a laser maybe, it would need to consist of a ton of energy—more energy than we can even fathom. The most powerful part of the light family that we're aware of is gamma rays, which we know can damage cells, even kill us. The closer we get to a light source the more powerful the energy is.

"Science divides the electromagnetic spectrum into three parts, yet they are indeed one spectrum. And light is overwhelmingly acknowledged in the world of science to have a dual nature, consisting of both energy and particle." She smiles in a prideful manner that would appear to stake claim to some newly discovered knowledge. "Perhaps, this is how Jesus could be both God and man.

"The Liahona is an artifact that was prepared by the Lord." She picks up her iPhone and swipes a finger across the screen. "Alma from *The Book of Mormon* states—

> ***And now, my son, I have somewhat to say concerning the thing which our fathers call a ball, or director—or our fathers called it Liahona, which is, being interpreted, a compass; and the Lord prepared it.***

"In the hands of the righteous—like the prophet Lehi, who first discovered the Liahona outside the door to his tent while guiding his people through the wilderness to the promised land—the Liahona helps guide your way."

I think about Crystal and our escape from the Monument to

the Three Witnesses. The Liahona, in Crystal's hands, guided us out of an impossible situation, to a stranger who was prepared and waiting to help us. Remembering Crystal brings a painful sadness to my heart. It's all I can think about.

"However," Pricilla continues, "that is but one small aspect of the power within the Liahona. You see, that tiny brass ball, hiding away in that cheap plastic bag of yours, contains a core of Divine energy." She smiles and places her hand on my shoulder. "Michael, do you understand? The Liahona contains an actual piece of God. It contains a small trace of His Divine Energy. It's how God was—and apparently still is—capable of communicating with us."

"How is that dangerous?" I ask, as I reach down between my legs, reach into the plastic hospital bag, manipulate the blanket, and remove the Liahona with my bare hands.

The look on Pricilla's face is one of absolute terror.

"I mean, being able to commune with God can only be good, right?" I place the Liahona on the table in front of us.

"There's a darker side, Michael," she explains, staring nervously at the Liahona. "It's the reason for all this unruly madness that's taken place over these last few days—all these dire means that Father has taken to recover the Liahona and put it back in its proper place, where no evil can ever find it."

"What darker side?" As I examine the Liahona closely for the first time, I am stricken by a strange feeling. It's a feeling I've never felt before, and it's frightening. It almost feels as if it is reaching into my body and touching my very soul.

"In the days of Lehi, there were no electronic devices of any sort, anywhere in the entire world. In the hands of the righteous, the Liahona would open a sort of portal between Heaven and Earth. But in the hands of the wicked—the truly evil—the Liahona would do absolutely nothing."

"Okay," I say, questioning where this could be going. "But I saw what it did in the hands of Lilith. When she touched the Liahona..." As the words exited my month, suddenly everything become clear. "Electromagnetism!"

"Exactly," she confirms. "Have you heard of an EMP?"

"Of course," I say. "Some believe the entire world could eventually be destroyed by Electromagnetic Pulses." I smirk. I've never given the theory any serious weight. "Don't get me wrong," I continue. "I understand the disruptive power of an EMP. However, it's not possible to destroy the world's—or even a small country's—entire power grid with a simple EMP. If it were, someone would do it. Don't you think?"

"You're not wrong, Michael. However, we're not talking about an ordinary EMP. In the hands of evil, the Divine energy within the Liahona becomes unstable, lashing out against the darkness that has come in contact with it. This battle of pure Divine light and darkness—two things that simply cannot occupy the same space—causes an EMP more powerful than anything we can remotely comprehend, let alone ever become capable of producing."

Suddenly, the Liahona starts to glow, startling us as we both sit back, away from the table—away from the Liahona. The needle quickly spins several times and then stops. It appears to be pointing at the wall. "What the heck is it doing?" I ask as I stand and stare at the glowing Liahona.

It is okay, my son. It's a warm voice that speaks, not to my ears or to my mind, but it radiates throughout my soul.

Pricilla must be able to see something happening in my eyes, because her faces goes pale with fear.

I cup my hands around the Liahona and lift it from the table, and as I do, the needle changes direction. I follow it, and it leads me through the kitchen, into the family room, and to a wall, just feet away from where Sammy is standing, keeping watch out the window. There are no pictures on this wall. Nothing that could be a message, or anything of significance whatsoever. "I think this thing is broken."

"I don't think so," Pricilla says, suddenly looking alarmed. She is standing behind me, gazing at the Liahona and the wall where it's pointing.

"We have company," Sammy says. His Nigerian accent is so full of might. It's striking, yet in a way, humble.

I glance out the window and see a barrage of black SUVs surrounding the safe house. As they come to an abrupt stop I can see a woman—*Lilith,* I realize in horror—step out of one of the SUVs, along with a man in a tweed jacket—the same man who shrinked me back in the makeshift hospital. She waves her hand and over a dozen men in black tactical gear quickly approach the building.

Pricilla grabs the hospital bag from the kitchen and runs back to me. "Here, put that thing away, quickly!" She looks out the window at the woman as she enters the lower level. "It's even worse than you think. We have to leave, now!"

Pricilla waves a hand over the wall—the same wall the Liahona was just pointing at—and suddenly a split opens up in a seam within the wallpaper. She presses on the seam and a doorway opens. "Let's go!"

40

The passageway is dark, lit only by the light from Pricilla's flashlight. It's a narrow passage that goes on forever. The smell in here is somewhat nauseating—a strange musty blend of hundred-year-old dust and mold. As we turn a corner the passage opens up into a small room with a single light overhead and a shiny set of stainless steel doors.

Another elevator, I realize.

Sammy presses the button and the door opens, revealing a high-tech, state-of-the-art elevator. Nothing like what I imagined would be hidden in this dark, filthy passageway.

I am ushered inside the bright space and stand in the rear corner, watching as Pricilla and Sammy insert their index fingers into the tiny slots within the panel on either side of the open door. The door slides closed, and a green arrow appears above the door, pointing down. There are no buttons. No way to select which floor to stop on. We're on a one-way trip someplace.

But where?

"That woman works for my father," Pricilla says, breaking the silence. "But she went rogue. She has tasted the power of the Liahona and will now stop at nothing to get it back!"

"You know Lilith?" I question. Even more appalling, "Lilith works for Batnaz!"

"We've been following your progress every step of the way," Pricilla explains. "Things were going perfectly, until Lilith got involved in ways she was never intended to and ultimately got her hands on the Liahona."

"Wait… what did you say?"

The elevator door opens and Sammy, followed by Pricilla, guides me into a small chamber, where, again, they insert their index fingers into slots in the wall and suddenly a massive, thick door lifts up into the ceiling, exposing a large bunker. The elevator ride was much longer than expected, and it felt as if we dropped fast.

How far have we gone into the ground?

"Please," she says, holding out her hand toward the bunker. "Enter." She then follows me into the brightly lit military-like space. "I hope you understand," she continues, "with Batnaz missing and Crystal, regrettably, no longer with us, I had no choice but to intervene. You need my help."

But I'm still stuck on what she said back in the elevator. "Lilith works for the Church?" I can feel my pulse rise. This is unimaginable. "Batnaz knew who she was all this time!"

"Please, Michael, let me explain. It's not how it looks."

Just then a massive blast rumbles the foundations of the bunker, rattling my eardrums. Light clouds of dust billow in from between the cracks around the massive door.

"My God!" she cries. "They found a way in!" After a brief moment of panic she yanks my hand. "Come on, let's go!"

I clench onto the plastic bag containing the Liahona and allow her to pull me along.

Sammy runs ahead and waves a hand across a blank section of wall and a large crack appears. He pushes it, and another doorway opens.

Moments later we're climbing out of a grate somewhere deep in the woods. It's thick. Dense. Not a path or trail to be seen anywhere. However, I can hear a familiar sound somewhere off in the distance.

Pricilla pulls me along and, like magic, I can feel welts appear on my face as we run through thick brush and tree branches, the tromping of militant feet marking a fresh trail behind us. They're gaining fast. We enter a clearing in the wood where a large fancy black helicopter sits, idling. There's a large Mercedes Benz logo on the tail.

This thing is sharp!

Sammy clicks a button on a tiny remote in his hand and the passenger door slides open.

As we climb into the surprisingly quiet machine—its whirling blades slicing the air overhead with a soft shuttering hum—Pricilla glares at Sammy, "Ready your weapon, Sam!" She looks frightened. "I see no way to avoid it this time."

Sammy nods, then reaches under his suit coat, just as the men in tactical gear enter the clearing and start firing.

Sammy slams the passenger door shut and returns fire with a large caliber pistol, as he dives behind the chopper shouting something about needing a raise.

Pricilla digs two pistols out of compartments inside the cab and hands one to me. "I'm sorry that you've been dragged into all this, but it's time to get our hands a little dirty."

Suddenly, the defining smash as glass fills the cabin. The small window to the side of the passenger door, shot out by gunfire.

Pricilla returns fire through the broken window as Sammy muscles his way into the cockpit, grabs the controls, and swiftly takes the chopper to the sky.

The men on the ground are relentless. *How can they have so much ammunition?* I think. The only people not firing at us are Lilith and the man in the tweed jacket, who's standing by her side staring up at us as her henchmen unload magazine after magazine of AR-15 rounds into the air.

Pricilla and I quickly empty two, 12-round, 9-millimeter magazines at Lilith and her crowd of men. Clearly we are outmatched. But as we lift away from the clearing, I watch in awe as Lilith falls into the arms of the man in the tweed jacket. Immediately, the rest of her men cease fire and turn their undivided attention toward her.

"It's over," I say, gazing at the clearing as Lilith's men lower her body to the ground. "She's dead!"

But Pricilla doesn't look too sure. "You don't understand," she starts, but then stops, allowing me a moment to feel the victory. After all, it is a win, even if just a momentary one.

Just then, Sammy begins to lose control of the helicopter. It's twirling in circles. "Damn it," he shouts. "I think they shot out the rotor!" He casts a glare at Pricilla who quickly jumps up front into the cockpit and grabs the controls, while Sammy jumps back, slides open the door, and leans out to see the damage. "Son of a..." He stops, takes a deep breath, then calmly says, "Damn."

Sammy steps out onto the the skids and shimmies his way toward the tail, holding tight to the handles welded onto the body of the chopper. The wind is incredible, and even though Pricilla is doing her damnedest to keep the chopper flying straight, it just keeps spinning around and around.

Sammy, holding on for dear life, reaches back and high over his head, and grabs the small piece of what looks like the tail and breaks it off. Immediately the chopper stops spinning, and then starts spinning the other way. But Pricilla quickly corrects the spin, and Sammy jumps back in the chopper. "Damn thing was rubbing the rotor." His accent may be thick, but his English is perfect. He tosses the broken tail fin on the floor and says,

"Don't worry, there is plenty left." He jumps back into the cockpit and laughs. "I really should get a raise!"

Pricilla casts him a glare and climbs back into the cabin, brushes some broken glass off the seat, and sits beside me. She has a piece of paper in her hand. "Let's talk about the riddle," she says as she unfolds the paper and sets it in her lap.

"What riddle?" I ask.

"The riddle Crystal was working on before the crash."

"Oh." I glance at the paper, and I'm suddenly struck by the strangeness of everything. The irony of how Crystal died in the exact same manner as her father, as well as the shocking reality that absolutely nothing is what it seems. That absolutely everything we had gone through with Batnaz has been closely monitored and scrutinized by this woman. It all feels wrong. I mean, I feel like I've been horribly played and so far, I have lost the game in every imaginable way.

"I know this is hard, Michael," Pricilla says, handing me the paper. "But my father is still out there somewhere. I cannot allow myself to believe that he's dead. As difficult as it may be to accept, we have to complete this mission."

"Do I?" I say, softly, as I take the paper in my hand and study the riddle printed thereon.

> *the lords hand is young*
> *blessed by eternal power*
> *it is he who holds the key*
> *and awaits the final hour*

"I've already lost everything, Pricilla. Why would I choose to continue this losing battle?"

"You were chosen for this, Michael," she says with a solemn smile. She places a hand on my knee and then steers my gaze toward the hospital bag on the floor between my legs. "The Liahona has chosen you, which means that God has chosen you." She pauses for a moment, waiting for me to react. But I don't. "Michael, if we don't find my father and get the Liahona to him before it falls into the wrong hands, the entire *world* could be next in line to lose the battle."

I lift the wrinkled paper and read it to myself. I then glare at Pricilla with perhaps a bit of spite in my eyes. "The message is clearly speaking of the Lord, Jesus Christ—the Lord's hand. I believe it's Christ who holds the key to finding The Secret."

Pricilla nods in agreement, "But the message doesn't seem all that clear. Christ holds the key and awaits the final hour?"

What does it mean? My head starts to throb thinking about it. "I can't make heads nor tails out of it."

The final hour of what?

I imagine Christ nailed to the cross. *Is that the final hour?* I then envision Christ coming out of the heavens—*the Second Coming.* I scratch my head. *Is that the final hour?*

"What if we're on the wrong track?" Pricilla says. "What if the message isn't referring to *Jesus Christ*, but rather, an individual... a regular man?"

Suddenly it sparks in my mind and I know it to be true. "Not just *any* man," I agree. "But a man who sacrificed everything for his faith. A man who left everything behind, leading over 70,000 men, women, and children 1,300 miles over desolate terrain, into a western wilderness?"

The lords hand is YOUNG, I considered again, knowing with

absolutely certainty that it was right.

"Brigham Young!" We both say together. And like that, the once cryptic message becomes clear.

the lords hand is young
blessed by eternal power
it is he who holds the key
and awaits the final hour

Fifteen minutes later the chopper lands beside a small hangar at a tiny airstrip where a private Cessna Citation awaits. It's a far cry from Darlene. However, Sammy swears it will get us to Salt Lake City in under an hour.

41

The Cessna Citation touches ground at Salt Lake City International at 8:36 am. Pricilla and Michael make their way down the mobile ladder and hop into an airport shuttle that was ready and waiting for their arrival.

Sammy follows close behind, nodding at another gentleman as he runs up the steps into the plane. "Make sure you don't hit anything this time," Sammy says in a sarcastic tone as he steps away from the mobile ladder and watches his baby get taxied away toward a small private hangar.

Sammy takes the front passenger seat in the shuttle, and without hesitation the driver gets them on their way. "Where?" the driver asks. It's a good question. Sammy pulls down his sun visor and looks at Pricilla and Michael through the attached lighted mirror.

Pricilla meets his gaze. "I might have some ideas," she says. "But I don't know for sure. Not yet." She thinks about it a moment. "Temple Square might be a good place to start."

As the shuttle pulls out onto the main drive from the airport's parking lot—amidst dozens of cars, busses, and shuttles—a small, silver sedan with Utah plates cruises up behind them. In the driver's seat is a man wearing a tweed jacket and smoking a Swisher Sweets cigar.

Pricilla and I compile a list of the locations most likely to hold clues to solving this damn riddle. Actually, it's Pricilla compiling the list. Admittedly, I know very little about Salt Lake City, having only briefly looked into the area while researching my book on Freemasonry; and frankly, without Crystal, this is beginning to feel like a futile mission. But the places Pricilla is jotting down make sense.

✓ *The Beehive House*
✓ *The Brigham Young Family Cemetery*
✓ *The Church History Museum*

I glance up at Sammy. His eyes are split between us in the back seat and the ever-changing surroundings out there. The highway is packed with traffic—all three lanes for as far as the eye can see. And we're driving east, making it worse, because the sun is absolutely blinding.

I spot the driver's eyes in the rearview. He's not looking at me, he's looking puzzled at something behind me.

"What is it?" Sammy says, obviously noticing the same thing I did. Sammy turns and looks out the rear window.

"I don't know for sure," the driver says under his breath. "But I think we're being followed." Seeing that Sammy is now looking out the rear window, he says, "Silver Lexus, three cars back in the center lane."

Sammy turns his head back around and returns his gaze to the visor mirror.

"What's going on?" Pricilla asks, noticing the commotion.

"Don't turn around," Sammy explains, locking eyes with her in the mirror. "Act the way you have been."

"We're being followed, aren't we?" she surmises.

Sammy only nods, as he scopes the area for a remedy to the situation.

"The Salt Lake Police are just ahead," the driver says.

"Yes," Pricilla says. "Pull in there."

The driver pulls into the police station. A small group of officers are gathered outside the front entrance. It appears as though they are having some sort of drill.

The driver stops the shuttle in a tow away zone by the entrance and I immediately jump out. I approach the officers, a bit too aggressively and, of course, they take notice and motion for me to stop.

"Can we help you, sir?" one of them asks as they all take on a defensive posture. "Speak your business." A couple of the officers rest their firing hands on their weapons.

"Sorry, officers." I stop and put my hand up in front of me. "Someone is following us." I point in the direction of the silver Lexus, parked on the side of the road—the driver clearly looking our way. "He's been tailing us for miles," I explain. "We pulled in here hoping to lose the guy. However…" I wave my finger at the man in the Lexus, still staring at us.

Two of the officers start toward the car and the man immediately drives off. However, he quickly turns into the lot and drives straight toward the officers, who immediately draw their weapons, shout a few words, then open fire.

The car careens into a series of reinforced concrete barricades along the side of the building, completely smashing the front of the car beyond recognition. Any ordinary man likely wouldn't survive such a crash. However, this man steps out of the car and stares directly at me.

What the hell? I think, as I stare in disbelief. It's the man in the tweed jacket. The man who stood by Lilith and caught her fall as she fell dead in the gun fight.

The man in the tweed jacket grins at me, glares at the hospital bag still grasped in my hands, and then charges, full speed at the group of armed police officers.

"Freeze!" the officers shout, almost in perfect unison, as they draw their weapons. "We will shoot you!"

But the man in the tweed jacket doesn't stop. He reaches his right hand under his jacket at breast level, and without hesitation the police fire. The man sprints—faster than I've ever seen any human run—toward one of the officers, grabs him by the arm, then falls limp to the ground. A shocked expression crosses the officer's face and his eyes flicker—changing from a chocolate brown to solid black, then back to brown.

The officer looks at me and smiles.

42

The perfect, grid-lined streets of downtown Salt Lake City are thickly woven with deafening traffic. This once simple Mormon settlement, at the heart of a desert wasteland, today is a thriving metropolis for the entire Salt Lake region.

As the taxi sits idle, waiting for the painfully long traffic light to change—Sammy and Pricilla sitting on either side of me in the backseat, the hospital bag containing the Liahona pinned between my legs—I admire the eclectic array of inspiring and somewhat curious architecture.

To our left is a building that looks remarkably similar to the former World Trade Center in New York City. Standing at least four-hundred-feet tall, this single building has the appearance of being three separate towers, standing abreast, with the center tower being several floors taller than those flanking it. Across from that concrete monstrosity is an elegantly designed, modernist complex from the eighties, complete with dozens of wrought-iron balconies, overlooking Temple Square and the mountainous skyline backdropping the domed state capitol building off in the distance.

But it's the green monster stalking us that arrests my immediate attention. Spanning across all six lanes of this gridlocked highway, the bronze, four-legged spider stands tall over the road. Perched upon a giant beehive on the monster's back is a bronze eagle—its wings spread wide. Below the eagle and beehive is an upside-down five-pointed star.

The Morning Star, I realize. While many look at the upside-down five-pointed star as a sign of the devil, it is actually, in most cases—such as this, with the elongated bottom point—symbolic of Jesus Christ.

"It's called The Eagle's Gate," the cabby says, noticing the look on my face. It's the look of awe and wonder, mixed with a splash of, *what in the bloody hell is that?* "The Eagle's Gate is nearly eighty feet wide," he explains. "And the four-thousand-pound bronze eagle has a wingspan of twenty feet."

The light turns green, and the taxi takes a left turn onto South Temple Street. "Brigham Young had the gate built as the main entrance to his property." The cabby pulls over into the right lane. "It's gone through many repairs and upgrades over the years, but it still has that same old charm."

Charm? I chuckle at the thought. *Is that what it's called?*

"It looks like some sort of science fiction monster," Pricilla says, stealing the thoughts right out of my head.

The taxi pulls to the side of the road in front of an eighteenth-century Greek Revival mansion. Its towering Greek columns make it look like a temple. However, there is something else—something that really stands out to me. At the center of the roof is a single stately tower. On top is yet another massive beehive. "This is it," the cabby says with a smile. "The Beehive House." He holds out his hand, waiting for payment. "If you're quick you might make the next tour."

43

"The Beehive House is one of the twenty-five most visited national landmarks," the tour guide says as she walks us through the strikingly beautiful home. As we enter the main living area, I can see how much care and attention to detail the curators of this museum give to this amazing space. While the home is clearly very antique, all the Victorian era furniture, handcrafted millwork, luxurious draperies are pristine. And the air is fresh. Nothing here smells old.

"About five years after the Latter-day Saints arrived in the valley, they built this The Beehive House as an official home for Brigham Young, president of The Church of Jesus Christ of Latter-Day Saints and later, Governor of Utah." The guide walks us from the family room into the dining room, where a large table is ready to seat a dozen guests, complete with the finest china, gold eating utensils, and crystal stemware.

"You'll notice that nearly every room has its very own fireplace," the guide points out. "Brigham lived in this house from 1855 until his death on August 29, 1877. The house sits one block east of Temple Square, on the southeast corner."

The guide walks us up a set of stairs and down a hall, stopping briefly at each room, staged in period furnishings. "Mary Ann Angel, wife of Brigham Young, was the first of his families to live here. Later, Lucy Ann Decker and her three children moved here. Lucy would often entertain company while Brigham took care of official church duties."

I study each room carefully. They are quite cozy spaces. Warm, inviting. Meticulously made beds, a thoughtful blend of both hand-hewn and porcelain knick-knacks, and neatly placed clothing. Everything is made to look as if the Young family has just stepped out for a bit and would be returning at any moment. But I can see nothing that can help answer the second half of the deciphered clue—

> ***it is he who holds the key***
> ***and awaits the final hour***

The tour guide continues as she starts back down the stairs, "Like the activities of a beehive, this home reveals the industry and cooperation exhibited by family members and Brigham Young's strong work ethic. In 1852, an annex connecting the Beehive House to the Lion House was constructed. The annex housed Brigham's office, which he used as the executive office for the territory of Utah. It was later used as the official church offices until the Administrative Building was completed in 1917." The guide pauses. "That's the granite building with the giant fluted Greek columns to the west of here, just past the Lion House," she explains.

"In 1855 Brigham Young had another, larger home built to accommodate his growing family. Brigham was known as the Lion of the Lord, and therefore this home was called The Lion House. Today, the Lion House remains a social center for wedding receptions, group meetings, and birthday parties. Its entire lower floor is a tremendously popular eatery." The guide points in the direction of the Lion House. "There are no tours of the Lion House," she explains. "But I'll give you some of the highlights if you desire."

I nod in agreement. "Yes, please do," I say.

"Well, one of the most important rooms in the Lion House was the old parlor on the main floor. Brigham would ring a bell to call his family for prayer. Since his children were homeschooled, they did most of their lessons in there." She walks us back toward the main entrance of the Beehive House, still talking, "Truman O. Angell, architect for the Salt Lake Temple, also designed the Lion House. It has a sandstone foundation, and the upper floors are coated in sun-dried adobe brick. Each floor has a long hallway running the length of the building." Feigned surprise sweeps her face, clearly she's been working this tour far too long. "There are *forty* rooms, and the walls are *twenty-three* inches thick; many of the rooms have fireplaces, all have windows. Some of the small wavy panes of glass are original."

She opens the front door to the Beehive House, steps onto the porch and smiles, holding the door for her guests. She glances at her watch. "It's 11:30. Perfect time to stop in at the Lion House Pantry for some world famous rolls and a lunch that you can truly write home about."

The front windows of the Lion House are lit ablaze, a bright amber glow emanating from elegant glass chandeliers, shimmering through delicate white draperies. Even at this early hour the glow is dramatic. The green wrought-iron gate leading to the front entrance is closed. The flower garden filling the space between the iron fence and the stucco and stone facade of the Lion House is beyond comprehension. It reminds me of Crystal. Her beauty was beyond measure. Frankly, this is the most beautiful flower garden I have ever seen. *I wish Crystal were here to see it.*

A sign on the corner points toward another entrance in an alleyway between the Lion House and the Administration Building. But this is not an alleyway in the way you may think. It is more like a parkway, with lush trees and shrubs, decorative lampposts with flowering plants hanging off each one, and elegant wrought-iron benches lining the building two-by-two. For a moment I feel like I'm back in Paris, walking the *Rue de l'Abreuvoir*, hand-in-hand with Crystal. My heart bleeds with the sudden recollection. I grab my face in my hands and squeeze the memory from my consciousness.

I open my watery eyes. Pricilla is holding Sammy's hand. They both are studying my face. "Is everything okay?" she says in a soft voice. To our right is the eighteenth century stucco and stone Lion House, with its charming bright copper flashings, wavy windowpanes, and wooden green shutters. "You're thinking about your wife, aren't you?"

I don't answer. I don't really need to. I think it's pretty obvious. On our left, directly across from the Lion House, is a massive, granite structure, wrapped in Greek columns. *The Church Administration Building*, I recall the tour guide saying. Straight ahead, is the newer Church Office Building, soaring well over four-hundred feet into the air. It really is amazing how much it reminds me of the World Trade Center.

At the far end of the Lion House is a sign attached to the building and wrapped in green wrought-iron trim. It reads—

Lion House Pantry

Along the bottom of the sign, an area that looks like a whiteboard, is a hand-written message.

> *Smiling People*
> *and Fabulous Food*
> *all at the Lion*
> *House Pantry!*

Inside, gorgeous solid oak planks—each secured to the floor with what looks like hammered wood dowels—shine a perfect golden glow.

The smell is all-consuming and instantly makes my stomach roar to life. On my left is a stainless steel display packed with decedent pies, cakes, and pastries. *Is that Carrot Cake?* Crystal loved that stuff.

Just beyond the dessert display is a large brick fireplace with iron pots hanging along its inner walls. The wall housing the fireplace is made of mortared stone. *The outer wall,* I realize. It is beautifully kept. All the inner walls are brand new, painted white, with solid oak trim and wainscoting.

The hostess is an attractive young lady with flowing red hair and sparkling blue eyes. I have to stop myself from staring. She has a striking resemblance.

Crystal?

I can feel my pulse rising.

God, how I miss her.

As the young hostess guides us to our table, it becomes apparent why so many people love this place. I hold the hospital bag tightly in my hands as we leave the main foyer into a porcelain titled corridor, lined with an endless array of hot and cold prepared foods. The aroma is, well—

Wow!

And this is not your typical cafeteria food. Everything looks top notch. Fine dining at its best.

The food corral exits into a small dining room, which splits off in all directions into several other, separate dining rooms. All of the furniture is finely crafted oak. Absolutely nothing cheap in this place. Yet, as new and perfectly maintained as everything is, it still feels like the eighteen-hundreds. Nearly every table is full. We finally stop in a corner of a room lined with stone walls and olive green, upholstered oak benches. The lighting is so soft, elegant, giving the illusion that the place is lit by oil lamps.

Pricilla and Sammy take their seats, together, across the table from me. "So," I say as I sit on the bench seat in the corner facing into the restaurant. It's obvious now why they don't offer tours of this place. It has been renovated and cared for to the point that it likely holds no, or very little, actual historical value anymore, aside from the outer shell of the building that is. The Lion House is still very much an active member of society, and from what I can tell, it holds no further assistance for us. "What do we do now?"

Suddenly, a light turns on in Pricilla's eyes, and she jumps out of her chair.

"What is it?" I ask but she doesn't say anything, she just grabs Sammy by the hand and stares me straight in the eyes. Whatever it is, it has her lost for words.

"For crying out loud... what is it?" I say again.

She finally regroups her bearings and says in the most matter of fact tone, "I know where to go." She looks at Sammy, who gazes back inquisitively. "Come!" She says, then pulls Sammy toward the exit.

"Wait!" I shout, causing heads in the crowded restaurant to turn. I make a bashful gesture—a silent apology. "Where are you going?" I say, lowering my voice.

But she's already out of the dining room. She's back in the foyer by the exit before I can even get out of my seat.

Damn it! I think, the smell of prime rib, vegetables, and fresh-baked cinnamon rolls enveloping me like a fleece blanket. To the chagrin of my protesting stomach, I run after them.

44

Pricilla takes us around the back of the Lion House, along the backside of the Beehive House, to the main road. "There's no doubt in my mind," she says, as we cross State Street—the massive green spider-monster to our right and the capital building in the distance to our left—and make haste down 1st Ave. "This is where we're going to find the answer we're looking for."

"Where?" I ask, for the third time, noticing my tone getting frustrated.

"The Brigham Young Family Cemetery," she says. "You'll understand when we get there."

I suppose, given our lack of success at finding anything of interest at any of the museums and historic sites, it's only logical to check. *But a cemetery?*

"What exactly do you expect we'll find there?"

"Just follow me," she says, picking up her pace. "Come on!"

As we approach the knee-high fieldstone wall, topped with classic wrought-iron fencing, I can see the luscious trees, flowerbeds, and monuments beyond and realize; this is anything but the typical cemetery. I suppose I should have expected as much, seeing as how the Richmond Cemetery, where Crystal and I dug up the Liahona, was no more a cemetery than this is. This place is more like a memorial park.

God, I feel so lost without her, I think as I enter the gate into a lush green park full of strategically placed trees, pristinely manicured patches of grass, and tall flowerbeds. A stone pathway circles a bronze monument of a man embracing a woman and child. Pricilla and Sammy walk one way around the monument, and I the other. There's something else, too. He's holding a hat. I consider the clue.

it is he who holds the key
and awaits the final hour

"Could the clue be referring to family?" I say as we meet again on the backside of the monument. "The thing Brigham Young holds onto until the final hour?"

Pricilla looks intrigued. "If that's what it is, what are we supposed to do with that knowledge? I don't think that's it."

Sammy continues deeper into the park. "We should keep looking," he says, in his deep, thick accent.

"There's also the hat," I point out. "It's not the easiest to make out, but he is holding a hat in this monument."

Pricilla looks closely. "You're right!" She climbs up, into the flowerbed, then lifts herself up onto the granite platform and examines the bronze sculpture closely. "There's nothing here," she says. "No message. No clues. It's just a hat."

"What the hell are we supposed to be looking for?" I express. "How will we even know if we find it?"

"Hold on a moment," she says. "There's a plaque here." She pauses a moment, reading. "This likely isn't Brigham Young. The plaque reads that this is a sculpture by Edward J. Fraughton honoring the six thousand pioneers who lost their lives crossing the plains between 1847 and 1869." Pricilla jumps down from the platform and crawls through the flowers back to the stone path. "Let's catch up with Sammy. There has to be something else here."

We step down a few brick steps to a lower section of the park that opens into a large grassy area with a large stone paved circle, at least thirty feet across, ringed with forest-green iron benches. At the center of this circle is another flower garden, with a bust of Brigham Young sitting on a granite pedestal. Just beyond the circle, to the left, is a small iron-fenced area no more than a hundred feet squared. A bronze placard, with an ox skull at the top, reads—

GRAVE OF BRIGHAM YOUNG
Prophet - Pioneer - Statesman
Born June 1, 1801, at Whitingham, Vermont.
Died August 29, 1877, at Salt Lake City, Utah.

I step back and explore the entire park with my eyes, every statue, every monument, the grave, anywhere Brigham Young could be seen holding something—anything.

Then I see it. How I missed it is beyond me. But it's sitting right on a park bench at the heart of the cemetery—right in plain sight—a life-sized bronze statue of Brigham Young, holding a copy of the *Book of Mormon*, reading to his son, who stands over his right shoulder, and to his small daughter who is sitting on his lap, staring starry-eyed up at her father as he reads.

The exposed pages are plastered in the most intricate etchings of text that I have ever seen made in bronze. It is as clear as if it had been laser-printed to paper.

"There's no way this was done by hand," Pricilla says, admiring the craftsmanship. Then, upon closer examination, "Hey! Someone added something here."

I move in for a closer look and can feel the excitement flood my veins and my face. "You're right! There are masonic symbols scattered all throughout this text." I grab my iPhone and enter the seemingly random symbols and immediately know what we're looking at.

⌐⌐⌐⊑⊏⌐⊏⊏⌐∪⌐⊏⌡∨∪⌐⌐ ⌐⊏⌐⌐⌐∨〈^⌐⊑∨∪⌐⌐∪

⌐⌐⌐⌐∪〈∨∪⌐ ⌐⌐⌐∪⌐ ⌐〈⌐⌐^∨∪⌐⌐⌐^⌐⊑⌐⌐⌐⌐

∨ ⌐⊏⌐⌐∪⊏⊏〈⊡ ⌐∨⊑∨⌐⊑⌐⌐⌐⊑⌐ ⌐⌡⌐⌐∨⌐⌐∪⌐ 〈

"This is it," I declare. "We found our next clue!" But it doesn't take long for the excitement to die as I realize that something is wrong. "Damn it!" Suddenly, I long for Crystal's companionship and her expert help. "We need a key."

I try every possible word we can come up with relating to the *Book of Mormon* to use as the key—

Remembering to drop the repeated letters:
Mormon *(morn)*
Book *(bok)*
Moroni *(morni)*
Lehi *(lehi)*
Nephi *(nephi)*

—Hell, we even try **hat** and *family*.

it is he who holds the key

I think back to the Beehive House—the bedrooms. The family rooms. *It's been right in front of our eyes this whole time.* "One thing I've learned, while researching my last book," I explain, "is that Brigham Young was known for many great things. But there is one that became so commonplace, so ordinary and dominant in his personality and his daily being, that I completely overlooked it." I pause, hoping that Pricilla and Sammy are reading me. Now that I see it, it's so blatantly obvious. "As Brigham Young got older he became almost entirely dependent on it. He could barely walk without it. It's been in virtually every monument, every statue, and every portrait we've seen of him today."

"His cane," Pricilla realizes.

I nod as a grin fills my face and I use my phone's sketch pad to draw out the Pigpen cipher codex—

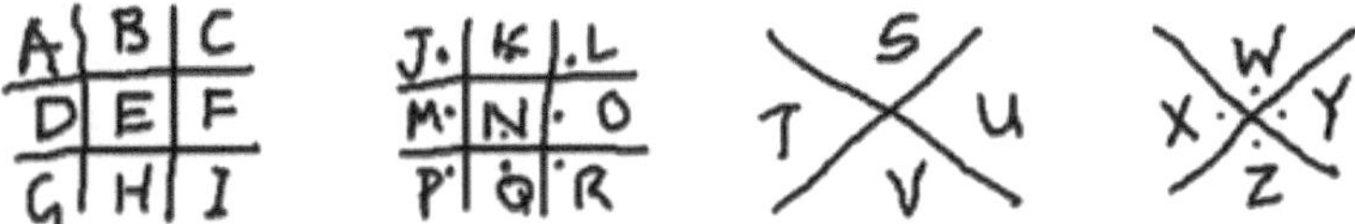

I then enter the KEY in the first boxes, shifting the rest of the letters into their appropriate corresponding positions—

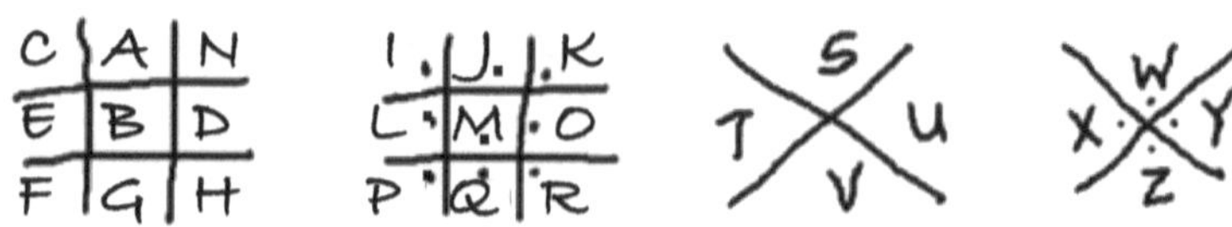

I write out the decoded letters, and it doesn't take very long at all to figure out where the word breaks belong—

THELORDSHANDISAPEXDEEPSUBROSACHA

RNELLAYWAITFRACTUREDSACREDCORNER

STONEANNUMTWOSCOREFORTIFIESPLAIT

Only the emerging message is again, anything but clear—

the lords hand is apex
deep sub rosa charnel lay wait
fractured sacred cornerstone
annum twoscore fortifies plait

45

The hood of the Salt Lake City police cruiser was still warm, after all, he'd been trailing them all morning. This was the first time he'd had the chance to actually get out of his car and stretch his legs a little. Officer Matthews stood, hip to his fender, right hand resting on the air intake on the hood of one of the department's brand new supercharged Dodge Charger.

All of his life Matthews had considered Police work to be a thing of utmost importance. He watched his father grow in the force and treasured the many stories his father told about his grandfather, who also climbed high in the department, eventually becoming the Sergeant for the Salt Lake City CIU.

Matthews wanted the very same for himself. He longed to get off patrol and join the Community Intelligence Unit. That's where all the action was. But ever since his run-in with the stranger in the tweed jacket—the man who almost ran him down before crashing his Lexus into the Police Station, then running at him and grabbing his arm before falling dead in the station parking lot—something inside of him changed. It was like he no longer had control over his life—his mind.

Matthews watched carefully as the tall black man moved toward Brigham Young's grave. The other man, the one clutching the plastic hospital bag, was sitting on a park bench, talking with the woman. He fixated on the hospital bag. The Liahona was in that bag. But as strongly as it was calling out to him, he knew that following Michael to the conclusion of

Brigham Young's secret roadmap, would pay off in spades.

He couldn't quite hear what they were saying. However, to his surprise, he could read their lips as well as he could read a book. *Strange,* he thought. *I could never do that before.* Nonetheless, he watched, and he read every word.

46

Sitting on the park bench beside Pricilla, staring at the newly decoded message in my hands, I am stricken with a sense of hopelessness—the harsh reality that Crystal was the one who really knew what she was doing. I... well, I was just her student. A follower. I loved her dearly and she impressed me with her knowledge and her endless wealth of skills.

I look up at Pricilla and the look on her face is a testament to the fear and uncertainty on mine. "Don't worry so much," she says. "You can do this—we can do this."

I glance over at Sammy, who is making his way back toward us from Brigham Young's grave. He smiles at me. It's a subtle smile, but it's there. Sammy is clearly a man with a past. He is rock solid, physically, and the emotion on his face is that of a military man. If I didn't already have a good idea of what makes up this man's heart, I am quite certain that he would scare the crap out of me.

I return my gaze to the message and consider the lines—

the lords hand is apex
fractured sacred cornerstone

"All of these clues have been written using a consistent formula," I explain. "If we group the first and third lines together, we should be able to figure out where the message is trying to lead us."

"Apex means peak," Pricilla says. "The top of something."

"Yes," Sammy agrees. "But what?"

Pricilla then reads the third line—

fractured sacred cornerstone

"A cornerstone is part of a foundation," she says.

"That's right, it's literally the corner stone of a foundation and is used to hold all the other stones in place. But what would make a cornerstone sacred?"

"The first cornerstone that is laid for a temple is blessed by the Prophet of the Church," Sammy says. "This would make that stone sacred, would it not?"

Pricilla nods in agreement. "And it just so happens, the original cornerstone of the Salt Lake Temple broke after being buried to hide it from Federal troops during the Utah War, causing the Mormons, who had been slaving for years— ox-carting those massive sandstone blocks weighing nearly five tons each, from a quarry twenty miles away to the temple grounds—to completely start over from scratch, this time using quartz monzonite—a much harder stone."

"If that's not enough evidence," Sammy says, with a knowing smirk, "my ward Bishop once taught me that Utah— the name given to the state by a U.S. Senator bent on denying the Mormons their request to name their state Deseret—is actually derived from the language of the local Ute Indians. It literally means Top of the Mountain."

"Apex," I realize, recalling scripture from Isaiah that states the mountain of the Lord's house—the Lord's temple—shall be established in the top of the mountains. "I'd say it's pretty clear that we need to get over to the Salt Lake Temple."

47

Racing on foot, making our way toward the Salt Lake Temple, I consider the rest of the decoded message. *The rest of the verse doesn't seem so simple to figure out,* I think.

deep sub rosa charnel lay wait
annum twoscore fortifies plait

We pick up our pace, running down 1st Ave, back toward Temple Square. We have to stop briefly on State Street to wait for traffic to clear. As we're waiting a Salt Lake City police cruiser with its lights flashing races down the side of the street and turns right toward the temple. I can't explain why, exactly, but I swear there's something familiar about the officer inside that car.

Pricilla stares at the massive Salt Lake Temple poking out from behind some trees, just beyond the reflective pool.

Standing between us and the temple is that magnificent four-hundred foot Church Office Building on the right and the Lion House and Joseph Smith Memorial Building on the left.

Sure, we may have been a full block away, but the temple stands so proud. The afternoon sun playing on the golden angel Moroni atop the temple's highest spire and shimmering off the reflective pools and fountains is nothing less than magical.

Pricilla finds a break in the traffic and runs across the road.

Sammy and I follow close behind, and we quickly make our way across the courtyard between the Business Offices and the Lion House. The shimmering image of the temple off the reflection pool water takes my breath away, and from the look on Pricilla's face, I'd say she was just as awestruck.

"I've been thinking about it," I say. "And I just can't make any sense of those other two lines."

Pricilla stops for a moment and thinks about it. "Let me see that again." She takes the sheet of paper and says, "Sub rosa is a Latin phrase. It means Under the Rose, which is a phrase used to denote secrecy or confidentiality." She pauses a moment, really taking in the stunning beauty of the reflective pool and the temple rippling in its sun-glistening water.

"Yes," Sammy agrees. "Even the U.S. military has started using the phrase to denote covert operations."

"Alright, so we have another reference to a secret," I say.

"Not just any secret," she clarifies. "A charnel is a vault." She grins. "A secret vault lay wait."

"Where?" I ask. "In the temple?"

She clearly doesn't have a solid answer yet. However, I think it's obvious to both of us that the last line—

annum twoscore fortifies plait

—at least the first part of it—refers to the building of the Salt Lake Temple. "It took forty years to complete the Salt Lake Temple," she says. "Annum twoscore."

I nod in agreement. "But plait? What the heck does that mean, at least in this context?"

She thinks long and hard about the word.
Plait.

Pricilla considered the word for a moment and tried to think of other words that she had studied in the military that were similar or that were derived from the same root.

But she just could not think of any.

So she pulled out her smartphone and did a quick search for the word plait in the dictionary.

The definition was almost verbatim what she had been thinking. However, scrolling down to the bottom of the page, she found exactly what she had hoped to find—

ORIGIN, late Middle English: from Old French pleit, meaning 'a fold'

That's it! she thought.

"The saints are a fold unto Christ," she declared, then read the origin of the word aloud. "The long, arduous process of building the most grandiose temple of the Lord had to have been beyond grueling," she said. "If anything was going to fortify the saints, it would have been that."

forty years fortifies a fold.

But a secret vault, hidden in the temple?

Pricilla recalled a memory from her childhood.

She recalled her father reading a story in The Ensign—a church magazine—that spoke of a time capsule, buried in the foundation of the Salt Lake Temple.

The Record Stone, she recalled.

deep sub rosa charnel lay wait

A secret vault lay wait in the foundation of the Salt Lake Temple, she thought. She wished she could recall more of the story, but it would have to do. *That has to be it!*

She had no doubt in her mind.

They were after the Record Stone.

The only question… How in the world were they going to get to it? It was buried deep inside the temple foundation, finding it was not going to be an easy feat. They could not enter the temple. Sammy and Pricilla were not endowed members and Michael wasn't even a member at all. And the last thing any of them wanted was to raise suspicions by snooping about the grounds all cloak-and-dagger-like.

Besides, where would they even start? The temple was massive; the largest the Mormons ever built. She knew that if they were going to have any success of finding the Record Stone they were going to need help. And, as painful as it was, she knew exactly where to go.

48

Pricilla had not seen or heard from her grandmother since she was a child. Last she knew, she was living in Salt Lake City—just a mile or so from where they now stood. It had been so long, and she had no idea if she could still be reached, or if she would even recognize her. She was only twelve when they last spoke. However, she knew if there was anyone in this city who could—and would—help them, it was her. She knew things—private things. She always had answers.

Pricilla takes Sammy and me on a short trek northward, away from Temple Square, to the neighborhood she claims she grown up in. Needless to say, I'm quite surprised by this.

As is Sammy. "What are we doing, Pricilla?"

"My grandmother knows things. She can help."

We walk—more like *speed* walk. It's hot, the sun is beating down on my sweaty forehead through a light canopy of rustling treetops. Incredible how out of shape I've become. And it doesn't help that I can't get my mind off Crystal. "Can't we just go to the temple and look around?" I ask. "I mean, something as meaningful as the Record Stone must be documented somewhere." I think about it a moment. "What about the Church History Library?"

She doesn't answer. We walk another block and then turn

right onto a short dead-end street, where a small grouping of quaint ranch-style homes lay perched around a cul-de-sac.

Sammy stands back on the sidewalk beside me as Pricilla walks up to one of the houses and knocks on the door. The house is a soft salmon color—almost pink—with white shutters. There's a mailbox on the street, attached to a signpost that reads—

Wells Residence

The woman who answers the door is old, perhaps in her late seventies. Her eyes light ablaze, and she grabs Pricilla in her arms and starts to cry. "Come in!" she says, waving to us all.

"I thought I would never see you again," the old woman cried in a soft, yet clear voice. "Please, come in!" She smiled. "Have a seat." She motioned toward a small rickety table at the center of a cozy, cream-colored kitchen. "Who are these fine young gentlemen?" She pulled two delicate-looking white chairs out from the table, and Michael carefully sat in one of them.

Pricilla turned and smiled at Sammy who was standing just inside the doorway, looking at a picture hanging on the wall beside the refrigerator. It was an old black and white photo. Sammy was looking strangely at it when Pricilla finally said, "Grandma, meet my husband, Samuel."

Her grandmother smiles in a slightly reluctant manner. Pricilla couldn't tell if she was intimidated by his size and demeanor or his color. Either way, she tried to put it aside. "And this is Professor Michael DiBianco. He's a friend of—"

"*The* Michael DiBianco?" The old woman's face instantly transformed from reluctant host to dearly delighted. "I know exactly who you are! You're the young lad who saved my Catholic Church from being destroyed by satanic terrorists?"

Michael looked somewhat embarrassed, but nodded. "Aren't you Mormon?" he asked. "Like your granddaughter?"

"Yes dear," she replied. "I am today, but it wasn't always that way." She grabbed her granddaughter by the cheeks and lured her into another suffocating hug. "Oh, my darling princess, it's so wonderful to see you again!"

Sammy, still standing by the door, pointed at that old black and white photo on the wall and said, "This woman." He studied the photo carefully. "She looks exactly like you."

The old woman nodded, thought about it a moment, then responded, "That is my mother."

But Sammy didn't take her answer very seriously, because there was someone else he recognized in the photo. "Then who is that man who looks exactly like Pricilla's father?"

"Grandma," Pricilla said, clearly not paying any attention to Sammy's comment, "Father is in danger."

"Oh my," she replied, almost in a patronizing tone. "I assure you, your father is in no danger." She paused, fiddling with her wedding ring for a moment before returning her attention toward Pricilla. "Your father is a very special man." She considered her next words carefully. "He told me once, long ago, that your mother was the most special woman he had ever met, and that's saying a lot." She smiled warmly, momentarily lost in a memory. "Good Lord, is that saying a lot, coming from such an amazing man."

"Grandma," Pricilla interrupted. "That's really quite cute and all, but seriously, we have to find the Record Stone."

"The Record Stone?" she questioned. "You mean the Salt Lake Temple Record Stone?"

"Yes, Grandma."

Her grandmother broke out in laughter. "Of all the things I could tell you, of all the lessons I could teach, you want to know about that silly Record Stone?"

Pricilla sat there, shocked and confused by her laughter. "Yes," she said. "We feel it holds a clue to how we can find the next location on Brigham Young's roadmap."

"Wait, what did you say?" she snapped. "Stop right there," she demanded. "The roadmap is nothing to be spoken of." She stood from the table and began nervously pacing the tiny kitchen. "How did you hear about the roadmap?"

"Father—"

"He told you about the roadmap!"

Pricilla nodded. "He explained that a critical piece of the secret has been lost and that we must restore it, bring it back to its rightful place before The Revealer returns."

"He told you *that?*" She paused, looking quite confused, and deeply concerned. "No one is supposed to know about the roadmap or the secret that it protects, let alone find it." Grandma looked pissed, but then she thought about it. "If he told you, there must be a damn good reason." She was still pacing. "I mean, he would never speak of the roadmap," she said under her breath. "Unless..." She shuddered at the thought.

"Grandma," Pricilla paused, briefly, staring at the hospital bag clutched in Michael's hands, considering carefully what it was she was about to say. "We have it. We have the Liahona."

"It's time for you to go," her grandmother ordered.

"Go?" Pricilla said. "But where?"

"No questions," she said. "You cannot be here!" She hustled

them out the front door, then tore a piece of paper from a small pad on the fridge and scribbled something as they were leaving. "It was quite nice to see you, Pricilla," she said. "And an honor to meet both of you fine gentlemen."

"Likewise," Sammy said with a subtle nod and a smile.

"Especially you, Mr. DiBianco." She smiled, taking his hand into hers, secretly placing the message she had written into his palm. She then led them down the steps, onto the walkway, and turned back toward the house.

"But Grandma—"

"The Record Stone is no longer in the foundation," she said. "It was removed many years ago. The contents are now stored at the Church History Library at Temple Square."

Pricilla turned to say thank you, but the door was closed.

I take the piece of paper the old woman placed in my hand and unfurl it, careful not to let anyone see. Why was she so secretive? Why were we so abruptly thrown out of her house? What if she was trying to warn me about something—or someone?

As Pricilla and Sammy start walking back toward Temple Square, I take the opportunity to sneak a peek.

You have a far greater
purpose than you know

TRUST NO ONE

49

The Record Stone had been excavated in 1993. After months of research and hard work locating where the Record Stone rested inside the massive Salt Lake Temple's endless foundation, and after countless hours of careful excavation, the heart heavy team of excavators reached inside and pulled out what would later be described as being like Papier-mâché.

Everything in the 136-year-old time capsule, buried in the foundation by Brigham Young in 1857, had been all but destroyed—except for a small treasure trove of pristine gold coins—due to a crack in the foundation that allowed water and condensation to seep and creep inside. What remained was gathered, photographed, analyzed, and placed in a protective vault inside the Church History Library.

They walked the half-dozen blocks to the Church History Library, just diagonally across the street from Temple Square, and were greeted by an extremely friendly middle-aged woman, The Church History Library director, who informed them that the vault that they wished to access was restricted.

"You must either be a member of the first presidency," she explained, "or at least have written consent. I'm sorry."

"Can you at least tell us what's inside the vault?"

"I'm very sorry," she reiterated. "I cannot help without written consent from someone in the first presidency."

They were left with no other choice. Without Batnaz there to help them, they would have to find some other way.

"Do you have a restroom that I could use?" Michael asked, subtly shaking his right knee.

"We do," the Director said, pointing deep into the heart of the library. "All the way in the back, to the right."

"Thank you."

The Director's pulse was racing, but she was trying to hold it together—trying hard not to break a sweat or show her fear in any way. They hadn't told her all that much. Nothing, really. They had simply said to alert them if someone came asking to see The Record Stone today.

The three strangers hadn't noticed—their eyes fixated on the back of the library, where she had just directed them to go—but as soon as they turned around, the young Director carefully reached under the counter and pressed the red button, exactly as she had been instructed to do.

She was a bundle of nerves.

She could feel the sweat dripping down the small of her back, and her knees were getting weaker by the second.

This was not the type of thing she ever dreamt she would have to confront, not with this calling.

All she could do now was wait. Wait and pray that her life and the lives of all her library patrons—she guessed, close to one hundred people—were not in any serious danger.

As she watched the three strangers walk away from her toward the back of the building, the library phone rang.

"Yes?" she said, still shaken, quickly realizing she had answered the phone incorrectly. "I'm sorry. Church History

Library. Director Sheryl speaking. How may I assist you?"

The voice on the phone surprised her.

"Yes sir," she said, nervously. "Two men, perhaps in their forties—one is very tall and very black—and a woman, long brunette hair with brown eyes. Really pretty."

She nodded as the voice spoke in her ear.

"Yes sir," she said again. "Understood. No questions."

She nodded more, a look of profound relief suddenly sweeping over her face. Then she smiled. "I love you, too."

50

"Anything yet?" Sammy said, looking back and forth down the rear aisle of the library. It was clear. Most everyone was toward the front of the building, except for a couple, who Sammy saw walk down to the far end, opposite of them, as they approached the restrooms. "There is no way we're going to get into that vault without permission."

"I'm well aware of that," Pricilla said as she exited one dark room—a plaque on the door read, *private*—and quickly ducked into another, just a few feet further down the aisle.

"What exactly are you trying to do?" Sammy said.

Michael exited the restroom and ducked into the dark room with Pricilla.

"Oh, lovely," Sammy said under his breath. "You are going to get us arrested. Then how will we fix this problem?"

"I'm looking for something," Pricilla said. "Keys, notes, anything at all that might point us in the right direction—"

"What are you doing?" the Director of the Library said, as she came flying out from around the corner and spotted Pricilla hunched over, looking inside one of the dark rooms.

Pricilla stood straight up and attempted not to look exactly how she imagined she must have looked. "I'm just waiting for my friend to get out of the restroom." She was sure to say it loud and clear, so Michael would not come barreling out of the other room.

"Well," the Director said. "You'll be happy to know that I've been given clearance to aid in your request." The woman smiled—but it was odd. A smile Pricilla couldn't quite read. "You can tell your friend to come on out of my office now."

The Church History Library Director takes us into a small climate controlled vault in the basement and removes a box that resembles a large safe deposit box from a wall mounted storage unit. Inside are the remains of The Record Stone. We examine what's left of the items: an original, hardbound copy of the Book of Mormon, historical books, pamphlets, periodicals. Sadly, all that remains of the paper is truly beyond salvage.

"It's like someone tried to make papier-mâché out of it," Sammy says. He's absolutely right. There's no way we were going to handle or read any of it.

The small treasure of gold coins, however, are as beautiful today as the day they were minted. Much nicer than the coins Crystal and I found in the bags we were given by the old man back in Richmond. But they are the same coins.

"There's nothing here," Pricilla says, sounding defeated.

How can this be?

"After all that," Pricilla says, shaking her head in disbelief. "We're at another damn dead end!"

"We need to explore the basement," I say. "Whatever it is we're after, it's gotta be hidden inside the temple itself."

"There is no 'basement' in the temple," the library director explains. "What you might think is a basement is actually the first floor. There is, however," she lowers her voice, as if about to say something she shouldn't be talking about, "a network of tunnels under Temple Square. Many have been sealed off, too dangerous. But there are some still in use. The prophet gets to work each day using a secured network of tunnels that stretch from the basement of his apartment building, to the church offices, to the temple itself. Some of the tunnels are open to temple patrons, too," she explained. "Many have walked the tunnels en route to baptisms and weddings and things of that nature."

"How can we access these tunnels?" Sammy asks, very matter-of-fact.

"There are entrances scattered all over the city. However, the closest one is located just beneath the security office within the temple itself. No visitors are allowed, though."

"Thank you for your help," Pricilla says, grabbing me and Sammy by the hand and yanking us toward the door.

"What are you doing?" I ask, and I grab the hospital bag and follow her lead.

"I think I know how we can get into that tunnel."

"How exactly?" Sammy asks.

"The head of security, Timothy Rutland, is a good friend of my father's. We've been in his office countless times."

"Good luck," the director says, waving. "I must say, you have some pretty powerful friends out there."

I don't have a clue what she is going on about, and I don't much care, either. This is the biggest lead we've had since leaving Richmond and we are not about to waste another second standing around chit-chatting about it.

51

Pricilla always felt small standing next to the Salt Lake Temple—one of the most amazing structures she had ever seen. The three of them walked right up to one of the two identical twelve-foot tall, oak doors—six massive panels adorned with several motifs and symbols, with exposed brass hinges that had the appearance of golden flowing vines—each set into its own massive stone tower, which flanked the 223 foot center tower of the Salt Lake Temple. Her hand clasped onto one of the two brass doorknobs, each engraved with the iconic image of a beehive and the words, Holiness to the Lord. Behind each knob was an elaborately carved brass escutcheon, filled with as many motifs and symbols as the incredible doors themselves.

But she also felt something else.

It wasn't that she felt small, she realized. But rather, she felt the mighty power of God encompassing her.

This is a very special place, she knew in her soul. And even though she no longer had a current recommend, she and Sammy were actively working their way back. She still harbored a trace of hard feelings due to the way and the reason she lost her recommend. However, in her soul, she really did understand, and she was sorry. Sorry to God for falling into temptation, and sorry for tarnishing her father's name—or at least that's how she felt about it. She still felt the guilt.

Marriage always comes first.

They enter the lobby—the only area of the temple visitors

are allowed to enter. To their left was an entrance to a massive spiral staircase that looked as though it might go all the way up to the top of the left tower of the temple, and to the right was a long hallway leading to another spiral staircase.

The other tower, Pricilla knew, having climbed them before.

They stepped through an archway, and under a low-hanging golden chandelier, into a room with a large counter, where an elderly gentleman dressed in a pure white suit greeted them.

"Good afternoon." The attendant held out his hand.

"I am sorry," Pricilla said, "We don't have recommends."

The attendant looked confused. "How can I help you?"

"I need to speak with Timothy Rutland," she explained. "It's a very important matter."

The attendant left the counter, disappearing around back for a moment, and almost immediately an older lady dressed in a white flowing dress came to the counter and directed them to take a seat, then proceeded to check in other patrons.

When the elderly man finally returned, he came with a petite, young, blond-haired woman, also dressed in white.

Obviously not Timothy Rutland.

She approached with an outreached hand.

"Pricilla," she said with a smile. "I've been expecting you."

I am immediately stricken by the young lady's stunning blue eyes. Reminds me so much of Crystal. "My name is Mallory Portman," she says, as she leads us deeper into the temple—into a restricted area, beyond the counter, where no one is allowed to go without a temple recommend. This doesn't appear to matter to her—not one bit. "I am the assistant director of security for the Salt Lake Temple."

"My father sent us," Pricilla says. "We need to—"

"I am well aware of why you are here," she interrupts. She swiftly and quietly leads us through a stunningly decorated, well lit hallway, adorned with the fine art depicting Christ and prophets of the church, then down a flight of stairs, into a concrete corridor, and into a large room, labeled simply—

Temple Security

Inside, my eyes witness the most elaborate, most sophisticated security system I have ever seen, rivaling what most banks use to protect their vaults.

Clearly, Mormons take protecting their leaders and their sacred property with extreme urgency.

The woman brings us into a tiny room with no windows and a half dozen chairs lining the wall. "Have a seat," she says, then pulls out a retractable table from the wall and reaches for my plastic hospital bag.

I instinctively pull away, hugging the bag tight against my chest. There's no way I'm letting anyone touch this bag. Even Pricilla looks terrified at the very thought of it.

"Please forgive me," she says. "However, we must inspect any bag that is brought into our security offices."

I cannot let her touch the Liahona. I know it sounds crazy, considering who she is and where we are, but what if this woman isn't worthy? What if her touch causes a massive EMP that destroys everything across the entire City? I'm reminded of the message Pricilla's grandmother wrote me.

TRUST NO ONE

"Please, don't," I plead.

Sammy places his mighty hand between Ms Portman and the bag clutched tightly in my arms. "I believe it is safe to leave this poor man's personal effects... personal." It wasn't a question. Sammy made his point loud and clear. "If the head of security wishes to inspect the bag, so be it."

She thinks about it a moment, then slides the table back into the wall. "Have a seat. President Rutland will be with you shortly. Oh, and he *will* want to inspect that bag." She exits the room, closing the door behind her.

52

Thomas R. Rutland was a kind, welcoming man with a somewhat stubborn streak. He has been the head of security for nearly a decade, and there was a damn good reason why that was. Nothing bothered him, and nothing slipped past him either. Absolutely nothing happened within the temple or its network of tunnels without Timothy Rutland watching.

While en-route to the temple security detention room to see his guests, Rutland suddenly became dizzy. He placed his hands on the wall to stabilize himself.

"Are you okay?" his assistant, Ms Portman asked, reaching out to help.

"Yes, I'm fine, Mallory. Thank you. I'm just feeling a little under the weather." But the fact was, he was perfectly fine when he woke up this morning. He was in good spirits and feeling wonderful at the diner where he grabbed breakfast. He didn't have a clue why he was suddenly ill.

He gathered himself and continued on down the corridor, toward temple security, still trying to place the moment when he started feeling sick. It wasn't like him to be so fixated on something like this. However, he was off his game, and it drove him nuts. Then it occurred to him. He started feeling a little strange after his good friend, Officer Matthews from the Salt Lake City Police Department, showed up to meet with him. He stopped dead in his tracks, standing in the middle of the hall, head in his palms, trying to remember that visit.

What did we talk about?

He could not remember.

President Rutland shook the nagging thought from his head and continued on down the hall, picking up his pace. He knew exactly who was waiting for him in the detention room. There was no way they were slipping away this time.

"The door is locked," Sammy says, clearly annoyed. "This room feels like a prison."

He's right. Something feels very wrong about this. Pricilla is sitting in the seat beside me, her legs crossed—how she can cross her legs—how she can do anything—in jeans that tight is beyond me. She is clearly nervous. "I thought you were friends with this guy," I say. "If this is how the Church treats friends, I'd hate to be an enemy."

"I don't understand," she says. "Mallory is usually more understanding. I've never seen this room before."

"Well, it certainly would appear that things aren't going the way you hoped," Sammy states, pacing about the room. It's the first time I've seen him look nervous. "Do you have any other great ideas?"

I look around the room. It's very small. Perhaps ten feet by ten feet. The walls are solid concrete. No windows, not even in the solid steel door. The only defining feature in the claustrophobic space is a single black dome in the ceiling— clearly a camera, watching our every move. No doubt there's a microphone, too.

My hands start to tingle and a low, rumbling hum fills my

head. "Do you hear that?" I ask.

"What?' Pricilla questions.

"You can't hear that?" I say louder, trying to talk over the sound building in my head.

Pricilla and Sammy look oddly at me—concerned. "Are you okay?" Sammy says. He places his hand on my shoulder and quickly pulls back. "What was that?" he shouts.

"I don't know." But I felt it too. It was like a massive static electric shock. Suddenly, I can feel my chest start to constrict. I can barely breathe.

My God, I'm having a heart attack!

I press my right hand into my chest and when I do, I feel the weight of the hospital bag lift off my lap.

What the...

I take slow deep breaths through my nose and turn my attention to the bag. My heart doesn't hurt, I realize. My entire body feels like it's being energized. I reach into the bag, remove the white hospital blanket, and squint my eyes as a bright gold glow fires up out of the bag into my face.

There are letters glowing across the side of the Liahona. I reach inside and lift the brass globe out into the open. Pricilla and Sammy look on with awe.

There are just two simple words—

Leave Now!

There's a loud click at the door, and we all jump—even Sammy. Pricilla and I stand from our seats and stare at the door. It never opens. I look over at Sammy who reaches for the knob and gives it a twist.

The door opens all the way, exposing an empty corridor. The

Liahona starts to glow again, and I can feel the needle spinning. It's almost as if I have become part of the compass.

"I don't know what's happening here," Sammy says. "But I do know, with all the cameras around here, we haven't much time. If we're going, we'd better go now!"

Without thinking, I run out the door, the Liahona raised in my hands in front of me, and I follow where it leads.

Pricilla and Sammy don't waste a second of time arguing about where we're going or why, they just try to keep up as the Liahona guides me down a narrow staircase, into a dingy hallway, barely lit by a few dangling lightbulbs.

President Timothy Rutland took a deep breath as he approached the door to the temple security detention room. He wasn't sure what he was going to say, but that didn't matter, did it? He paused at a security monitor showing the traffic in the hallway and looked strangely at himself, turning his head to the left and to the right inquisitively. The image showing in the monitor was definitely not that of President Timothy Rutland, but she already knew that.

Lilith stared at her striking olive green eyes, then watched as they blinked from green to solid black, then back to green again. *This is it,* she thought. She finally had them. Now all she needed was to get them to lead her the rest of the way. The Liahona was no longer enough. *If that single artifact has that much power,* she thought, *imagine the possibilities to be had in the motherlode?* She wanted the ultimate prize—the secret hidden at the end of Brigham Young's roadmap.

She took those last few steps to the detention room with haste and opened the door. To her horror, there was nothing in the room but an empty bag and a wrinkled hospital blanket. She stared up at the camera, then looked out into the corridor.

President Timothy Rutland ran out of the holding room, back down the hall to the security office and ordered his men to send footage of the detention room to his private monitor. It only took a few seconds for the footage to appear on his screen. A look of fury came across his face—his eyes flickering from green to pure black, back to green—as he watched the events unfold. He watched as they left the room and headed down stairs toward an abandoned series of tunnels.

She smirked internally. "I've got you now."

It smells old and dirty, like an old service tunnel. I have to duck in areas to avoid hitting my head on beams and pipes. I can only imagine what Sammy's going through back there. But I'm not about to stop and take a look. I'm not sure the Liahona would let me, if I tried—that's how it feels, at least.

I can see the end coming. Up ahead, a single lightbulb hangs from a wire in front of what looks like a sealed doorway. The Liahona is guiding me in this direction. I'm physically compelled to follow. I step under the light. There's a small palm reader on the side of the door. I think about it a moment. There's no way we can get through this. Why is the Liahona taking me here?

"What is it?" Pricilla asks, as the two of them move in closer.

"We're stuck," I say. "It's a dead end."

"Why would the Liahona bring us here if it were a dead

end?" Sammy made a good point, but still.

"Stop thinking about it and try," Pricilla says.

I cradle the Liahona in my left arm like a football and place my right palm on the reader. Instantly, the door pops. But just a little. I grab the Liahona again with both hands and Sammy pushes the door open. It takes considerable effort.

The tunnel beyond is narrow, dingy, barely lit by a single lightbulb over the doorway. In the distance, perhaps ten yards away, is another archway. A single bulb shines light on another small stretch of tunnel—barely enough light to keep from walking into walls. However, the Liahona's compass and soft golden glow illuminates the path better than any light can.

"You know," Pricilla says, sounding a little nervous, "my father once told me that Ted Bundy walked these tunnels."

"Now, why would you say a thing like that?" Sammy actually looks bothered. His hard shell is breaking.

As we walk past the next lighted archway and continue to follow the tunnel which turns to the right. I hear something. "Did you guys hear that?" I ask, stopping abruptly.

"I didn't hear anything," Sammy says, then sticks his ear out to investigate. "But admittedly, I was listening to Pricilla's failed attempt at scaring us."

I listen for a moment longer. "It sounded like footsteps," I say. "But I don't hear it anymore. Keep your ears peeled." I start back up, picking up the pace a little. The Liahona leads us past a few more lighted archways, turning right at each junction. It's a surprising distance.

And the constant downhill grade is taking its toll on my back, and now it's getting steeper. But I can see something glowing up ahead—something beneath the next archway.

A door.

President Timothy Rutland stood quietly, just out of sight and watched the soft glow of the Liahona gracefully shine a path directly to his treasure. He watched the group make their way down yet another stretch of tunnel and then stop at what clearly—even from several yards away—looked to be a doorway. It had a light blue aura around it. Indeed, this doorway was special.

This is it!

A black vapor slithered out from the shadows, slithering through the dank subterminal air with unnatural swiftness. President Rutland stood there in the darkness, motionless, staring an empty gaze, then fell with a muffled thud to the dirty tunnel floor. The serpent-like mist crept up behind Pricilla, as if stalking prey, and then vanished into thin air.

Pricilla gasped.

"Is something wrong," Sammy said, looking concerned, as he reached his left arm around her shoulder.

"Sorry. I just got a chill, is all," she said pulling away from him. "I'm good."

Sammy touched the back of her neck, and she pulled away again. She felt cold to the touch and was acting very strange.

"Let's just get this over with," she said in a demanding tone.

Michael planted his hand on the palm reader, and once again the door slid open. Only this time it opened quickly and fully, and let out a gust of chilly air from inside.

53

Pricilla felt her hair and blouse pull away from her skin, as if sucked into a vacuum. It was like walking into a wind-tunnel. They entered. It was dark. A small bluish light flickered on as the door closed behind them.

She could feel—could taste—the change in the air. The dinginess from the tunnel faded, and that old musty odor was replaced with clean, nearly pure, oxogen.

Pleasant.

Comfortable.

She suddenly felt the filth on her skin.

The blue light faded as another door opened, and all three of them instinctively threw their arms up over their faces—Michael using only one arm as the other cradled the Liahona—protecting their eyes from the intensity of the light.

After a few moments their eyes adjusted, and they found themselves in a massive climate-controlled space.

A granite and stainless steel cavern, with a sea of black and white checkerboard tile stretching out in all directions. Greek columns, as tall as the eye could see, filled the space. Row after row, aisle after aisle, wall to wall, floor to ceiling, the chamber was packed like the vaults of the Smithsonian Institute.

As they entered deeper into the space they realized that they were looking at some of the most incredible religious artifacts they had ever set eyes upon.

"Few souls know of this place," a voice spoke from within.

"Far fewer have ever entered."

With all the reverberation caused by the stone and steel, it was hard to make out who it was, but something about the voice was familiar. A tall man, dressed in a long white robe, stepped out from behind a pillar, and without thought Pricilla fell to her knees, gazing in wonder at the sight before her.

Michael and Sammy stood by her side, speechless.

Daddy?

"Spare us the theatrics," Batnaz orders, motioning for Pricilla to return to her feet. "You have no power here, Lilith!"

"NO!" she screams, her voice screeching. "We had a deal!"

"Our deal was void the moment you decided that getting your hands on the powers housed in this tomb was more important than following orders." Batnaz raises his hand.

"You can't do this!"

With a snap of his fingers Pricilla vomits up black vapor. It shoots from her mouth like an erupting volcano, spiraling above her head like a snake, before vanishing into the air.

Pricilla collapses into Sammy's arms, but quickly regains consciousness. "What happened? Where are we?" Then she sees him—her father—and runs into his arms.

"What the *hell* was that?" I shout.

"She is referred to in the *King James Bible* as the screech owl," Batnaz explains. "Other, more closely matched translations of the Hebrew text, refer to her as a lamia, or Lilith."

"Lilith was a demon?" Pricilla says in shock.

"I enlisted her to execute a simple plan. She would perform

tasks for us that could never be asked of a human." He pauses for a moment, making sure that thought was able to sink in. "In exchange, she would receive something demons are forbidden to have—a permanent body of her own."

"What tasks?" Sammy questions. "What exactly could you ask a demon to do that you won't ask *me* to do?"

"Do you really have to ask?" Pricilla says. "Seems obvious."

Batnaz makes a quick circling motion with his hand, and three other figures cloaked in white robes emerge from the shadows. "There is much to explain," he says. "However, I feel it to be most advantageous to start from the beginning—the beginning of an era, that is."

"We're listening," I say.

"Shortly before the martyrdom of Joseph Smith, Joseph had constructed a tomb," Batnaz starts. "It was a place where he had wanted to be buried along with his family. Yet after his death, his wife, Emma, would have no part in it, afraid that the tomb would be raided and Joseph's body mutilated. To this day no one knows exactly where that tomb is. But Brigham changed that. After settling in the Salt Lake Valley, he had a new tomb constructed. He was determined to fulfill Joseph's wishes, no matter the cost.

"Remember David Hyrum Smith?" he says to me.

I nod my head.

"Remember the task he was given? Until that time, no one knew where Joseph was buried. His remains were feared lost forever. But with David's help Brigham had the remains of Joseph, Hyrum, Emma, and their parents transported to the new tomb." He spreads his arms wide at the vast space before us. "Right here!"

"So, that's it?" I ask. "This is the secret?"

"Part of it," Batnaz replies. "A rather small part, actually." Batnaz opens an old book and carefully flips through its brittle pages. "We made every possible effort to protect The Secret. Joseph Smith suggested that we create a secret organization, he coined it the Kingdom of God. It became known to the general population of the church as the Council of Fifty. However, to the members of the organization, it was simply, The Order. The Order served one principle purpose: to build up the Kingdom of God on Earth in preparation of the second coming. However, there was a second, even more important purpose—one that few people knew about. To protect the secret."

He finds what he's looking for, places a bookmark ribbon between the pages, and continues speaking. "Joseph Smith and Brigham Young worked in secret to create a roadmap that would lead only a truly worthy soul to the secret, should knowledge of its existence ever become lost. Joseph died shortly after work on the map started. Brigham worked on it for decades before hiding it away.

"The tradition of keeping The Secret secure continued for generations, until, seeing that corruption had deeply infested The Order, President Heber J. Grant—The Order's last remaining rightful leader—secretly dug out Brigham Young's roadmap and spent years following it. He located the secret and scattered it in an effort to ensure its safekeeping. Grant never told a soul what he had done. He died leaving not so much as a clue as to where the secret now hid, or that it had ever existed."

Batnaz returns his attention to the book and reads aloud, *"Dico autem vobis vere sunt aliqui hic stantes qui non gustabunt mortem donec videant regnum Dei."* He then looks up at Pricilla and continues from memory, *"Filius enim hominis venturus est in gloria Patris sui cum angelis suis et tunc reddet unicuique secundum opera sua. Dicit ei Iesus si sic eum volo manere donec veniam quid ad te? tu me sequere. Exiit sermo inter fratres quod discipulus ille non moritur et non dixit ei Iesus—"*

Pricilla's face floods with emotion. "He shall not die," she interrupts softly, almost childlike. "But if I will that he tarry till I return, what is it to thee?" She smiles, tears streaming her cheeks. "I remember you reading that to me as a child."

Batnaz returns the smile and continues, "The quote is actually a compilation of scripture. Regardless of the controversy these verses have generated over the centuries, the reality is, they are undeniably fact."

"That's ridiculous!" Sammy declares. "How can you possibly believe that there's a man living on the earth today, who stood heel to heel with Jesus, the living Christ?" Sammy is disgustedly skeptical. "A man who has lived for over two-thousand years!"

"Not one," Batnaz clarifies. "There are four."

That's about as much as I can take of this nonsense. "My wife died to get us here!" My heart breaks just saying the words. "She is gone. And for what?" I am certain the look on my face is one of madness, but I don't care. "I feel like I've been played. You haven't come close to explaining the dishonesty, the conniving, the trickery. Clearly you were never in any kind of danger." I think about it a moment, and the more I do the more I seethe. "Why couldn't you have brought us here in the first place?" My anger only grows more intense the more I think about all that has happened. "My wife wasn't the only one killed in all this insanity. The Prophet of your church was murdered! Does that not matter? Then an apostle l, and you went missing. We thought you were dead! I haven't a clue what's true and what's not anymore!"

"We had no choice," Batnaz explains. "We had to test you—had to get you to come, no matter what the cost."

"No matter the cost?" I shout. "My wife is *dead!*"

"Please, hear me out," he pleads in the most sincere tone. "Everything will make sense. I promise." He looks at me with eyes that calm the soul, at least for the moment. He makes a hand gesture and the three cloaked figures standing behind him step forward and lower their hoods, exposing their faces.

Pricilla and Sammy gasp in unison.

What the hell is going on here? "You're dead," I shout, gazing at the first man as his face enters the light. He is the Prophet—a man whom I saw strung cruciform from a tree in the Sacred Grove, tortured beyond all comprehension. Then comes the second man. Jacob. His body was ripped to pieces in the Kirtland Cemetery. "I saw your mutilated bodies."

"If it's proof you want," Batnaz says with hands extended at his sides, welcoming his guests. "Proof you shall have."

It takes a moment for the reality of what I see to sink in.

What is this?

When it suddenly does—

"My name," he says with honor, "is John of Patmos."

—my heart explodes with climatic joy, and tears burst from my eyes, streaming down my face like rivers.

How can this be?

"You may wish to call me, John the Beloved."

This isn't possible!

I fall to my knees, the Liahona still in my hands.

"And these are my dear friends, Peter, James, and Mary."

The third cloaked figure is Crystal.

54

There were four granted the honor to remain on earth, ministering to the Lord's sheep until the day of the Second Coming. "But I tell you of a truth," Batnaz said, in a manner of reciting scripture. "There be some standing here, which shall not taste of death, till they see the kingdom of God."

The man, who, until now, had been known around the world as President Simeon Petros, then spoke, "And Peter, seeing him saith to Jesus, Lord, and what shall this man do? And Jesus saith, He shall not die; but, if I will that he tarry till I come, what is that to thee? Follow thou me."

"Life has not been easy for any of us," Batnaz explained. "We have been forced to live excruciatingly careful lives. No one can ever know our secret. It's the reason I couldn't tell you. It is also the reason things had to be the way they were." He looked sad. "I'm sorry for the game play—as you put it."

But all Michael could do was stare in awe at his wife, standing before him draped in a long white robe. It was clearly her, and yet she was somehow different. "Crystal?"

"No," she said in a soft voice. "I am not the woman you think you know. That woman died in the plane crash." Even though her words said no, there was something in her voice that spoke volumes. There was an emotion there that he recognized. It was her, and he knew it. "That woman will always love you, Michael. And she treasures the time you had together. However, you must understand, that woman was but a tiny fraction of something far greater—something that simply cannot be." Her voice cracked, and a tear fell from her eye.

"Michael," Batnaz said. "This is Mary of Magdala, one of Jesus's closest disciples. Perhaps *the* closest."

"Mary of Magdala?" Pricilla questioned. "You mean... Mary Magdalene?"

"The very same," Batnaz clarified, then went on to explain that in order to fulfill the Revealer's desire to restore the secret, they had to resort to rather extreme measures. "Mary agreed to participate in a ritual that would wipe her memories."

Michael recalled the strange dream-like visions Crystal would often have. She had described being in a place like this—*exactly like this,* he realized.

"We placed her in a home where her adoptive parents, over time, planted childhood memories that would set her on a path to completing her mission. She needed to create a new life. She would work her way into your world and train you—prepare you for this mission. I know it's difficult. However, the life and mission of any Prophet is a difficult one."

"Prophet?" Michael laughed. "What on earth are you talking about? I'm no prophet!"

"But you are," explained Peter. "In the same way that Moses and Lehi were Prophets. You have the power to commune with God in ways that no mere mortal can."

"It's true," Batnaz explained. "Even we cannot speak with God in the same manner as you. Your silence right now tells me that you know it's true. You have felt the power running through you. The Liahona is a powerful instrument. In the hands of the righteous, it works miracles. It allows you to do things no mere man can do."

Michael could feel it running through his body, even now.

"But Crystal," he started. Then realized, "That's why it worked for her? ... She's Mary."

"Yes," Batnaz said. "But even she can't use it in the same way that you can. Your connection is unlike any we've ever witnessed. But you had to be prepared for this day. It is why things had to happen the way they did."

"I don't understand," Pricilla said. "If you guys can't die, then how the hell did you... die?" Her attitude was well noted.

"While we may be immortal, we indeed can die, and *have* many times," Batnaz explained. "The promise the Lord made was that we would never experience the pain of death. But should we ever actually meet our demise, we would rise again."

"And we rise in perfect form," Peter said. "Which is the reason why Mary is back to her old self."

Michael's heart sank. He thought it just may be worse losing her, knowing that she was alive and well, standing right there in front of him, than had she really been dead.

Over the years, Batnaz had come to consider it more of a curse than a blessing. He had been married over a hundred times, had fathered eight-hundred-and-ninety-four children, had lived to see all but a few pass on, and had met with his own death twenty-four times in his 2,056 years on this earth.

Sure, he had never experienced the physical pain of death. However, the emotional pain—the relentless torment of losing love after love, friend after friend, child after child—had driven him to desire real death on more occasions than he might want to confess.

"So I was right," Pricilla said. "That is what you needed that Lilith demon for. To stage your deaths so Crystal and Michael would be lured into your game."

"The restoration of the secret takes precedence over

everything," Batnaz said. "I assure you, this has been no masquerade. We discovered not long ago that Grant left a clue. It was so subtle that we hadn't noticed it until we tried following the roadmap ourselves. He had modified Brigham's map, taking it a leap further than Brigham ever considered. Grant was not in the dark as much as we suspected. Grant wanted to be positive that there could be no chance of the wrong person learning the whereabouts of The Secret. So he fragmented several key elements. Then designed the new roadmap to lead, not to the secret itself—as Brigham's map did—but to the ultimate map decoder."

"The Liahona," Pricilla said, knowing that only God's chosen could use it. It was the perfect way to hide The Secret.

"Yes," Peter said, "and now we have it."

The Disciples take them deeper into the Tomb of Joseph, their eyes in awe at every turn. Some of the church's—some of the world's—most amazing artifacts, many of which thought lost forever, have been preserved in this magnificent space, kept secret for over a hundred years.

Peter explains that, while most of the secret has been restored, there are critical elements still missing. "Now that we have the Liahona, there is only one piece left—" Batnaz finishes his thought, "and it is the most critical."

The Disciples left The Order many years before Heber J. Grant took the high office. They had to become obscured to the upper levels of church leadership. So they vanished for nearly fifty years. When they finally returned, they did so with caution, working their way up the ranks of the church. And at the turn of the millennium, almost 2,000 years after the crucifixion of the Christ, they once again regained their places within the Quorum of the Twelve.

Today, they made up the First Presidency of the church. They had climbed to the top. But much to their chagrin, they lost sight of the secret. Restoring it was going to take a special individual. This person would have to be more than just worthy. They would have to be chosen. Batnaz knew that this chosen person would be in the bloodline of Christ.

"DiBianco," he said.

"Son of White, I know," Michael acknowledged.

"Yes. However, we were never going to capture your attention, or Crystal's, without a spectacle. Crystal would never have come merely to solve a puzzle.

I would have, Michael thought.

"There had to be more. A gruesome murder. A major threat to mankind. Something grandiose. So we used our unique blessing, or curse as it may, to create such a scenario. Was it unorthodox? Yes. Convincing The Revealer that it was worth the deception was pointless. It went against everyone's best judgment. We did this on our own."

"Look, we have made countless mistakes over our long, long lives," Peter says, "however, when we lost sight of The Secret and allowed it to fall into unrighteous hands, we lost favor with The Revealer—with God."

"The only thing The Revealer instructed me to do was find you," Batnaz said, looking at Michael. "It's the only thing He's said to me in decades. He said it would be you who would restore The Secret, Michael. God said it was you."

55

I feel the tightening of my chest again. The energy of the Liahona reverberates my mind, body, and soul. I raise the glowing compass high above my head. It almost feels like it lifts itself. Then, without warning, prayers flood my mind. I'm not consciously praying. I'm not thinking about the words. They just simply flow out of my mind on their own.

The Liahona is taking full control, and it's... *okay.*

An overwhelming feeling, impossible to ignore, consumes me. I am in the presence of something great—something truly powerful. Something incredible.

Who am I? I say, but I don't feel the words escape my lips. The words emanate from my spirit.

Show me, Lord.

I feel a sinking in my heart that rips away at my soul. Intense sadness sucks the life from me, and in that instant, I feel as though there is no God. Only pain and sorrow.

I am alone.

Empty.

Void of all spirit.

A chill grabs deep inside, and every cell of my body is sucked through a rift. Fear grips me like never before as numbness overtakes me.

Then there's nothing…

Blackness.

Silence.

I open my eyes.

I'm kneeling on the cavern floor, arms reaching skyward, the Liahona tight in my grasp.

Am I dead?

I start lifting.

Ascending.

Higher and higher, farther away from my body, still kneeling on the ground below. Getting farther and farther away.

But I'm not dead? I say, panic setting in.

What's going on?

The sky opens and a bright white sun caresses me with warmth and all the fear and sadness melts away.

I squint my eyes as a flash of light envelops me and suddenly I'm flying over a cemetery.

I swoop down, zooming in, like a bird flying free. I see names and dates on the many tombstones. Women, children. It's obvious, these are mothers and their children. I see no husbands––no fathers. Dozens and dozens of stones, each a generation older than the next.

These graves, I realize. *All these people.* They're the wives and children of Jonathan Batnaz—*John the Beloved*. My heart fills with the sadness and loss that I can only imagine he feels.

There's a blinding light.

I'm over the Salt Lake Temple.

All the different symbols and shapes that make up the famous temple's Façade fill my vision as I soar high above.

I don't hear anything, no big God voice, nothing like that. It's like, I just suddenly know. Deep down inside my soul, it's all suddenly clear. The meaning behind every symbol, every marking, every mystery. The answers fill my head.

I swoop in over the twelve foot-tall golden angel Moroni who depicts both a messenger of the Restoration and herald of the Second Coming.

For the Son of Man shall come, and he shall send his angels before him with the great sound of a trumpet, and they shall gather together the remainder of his elect from the four winds.

How can I have remembered that? I think. *I've only read the Book of Mormon once, and it was just research.* Wait, how do I even know it's from the *Book of Mormon*?

I just know.

The three towers on the east side represent the first presidency of the Church and the Melchizedek Priesthood; the twelve pinnacles rising from the towers represent the apostles. The towers on the west side represent the presiding bishopric and the Aaronic priesthood, and the twelve pinnacles rising from those towers represent the high council. Castle-like battlements surround the temple symbolizing separation from the world and protection of the holy ordinances practiced inside the temple.

Six-pointed stars represent the actual stars in the heavens, while upside-down, five-pointed stars represent morning stars, compared to the 'sons of God' in the scriptures.

Each of the center towers feature a pair of clasped right hands—the right hands of fellowship. In the book of Jeremiah the Lord uses this handclasp to denote covenant making—an act at the heart of temple worship.

Located atop each center tower is the all-seeing eye of God. The eye represents God's ability to see all things.

The very things that make non-believers shudder at the thought of church, are so clearly understood, once you clear your mind of all the garbage the world wants you to believe, and you allow your spirit to be filled with understanding.

There's another bright flash of light.

I'm flying over a large hill.

It's twilight.

The full moon paints the grounds in a pale gray hue.

It's a large hill, in the midst of farmland all around. Looks like a dormant volcano, overgrown in grass and trees. There's a boy running up the hill, a lantern burning in his hand. He falls to his knees and starts plowing earth away with his hands. The boy grabs a large stone and heaves it off the ground, revealing something.

Several things are revealed out from the ground. A ring-bound book of solid brass plates, shimmering gold in the soft moonlight. A brass breastplate that looks like it came off a suit of medieval armor, and a sword from the same period.

The boy pulls out a brass orb.

The Liahona, I realize.

There's a light.

Its brightness makes me throw my arms over my face. But it doesn't take long to realize that it doesn't hurt. The warmth is incredible. My eyes adjust, and I see a large palace.

And angels...

They're everywhere.

But as quickly as I see them, they vanish.

There's a throne.

Upon the throne is a man whose skin glows as brilliant as the sun. The man stands, white robes falling gracefully at His feet, draping the man's perfect frame. He looks straight at me, eyes gentle, yet authoritative. He motions to His right. Standing tall on the right hand of God, is another. More beautiful than anything I have ever laid eyes upon.

I fall to the floor, landing hard on my knees. But it doesn't hurt. The floor is warm. I bow and remain still.

"Michael." The voice is pure power.

I can feel it in my soul—reverberating within my body.

"This is my beloved Son." The Father makes a circling motion with His hand and from either side of His throne come into view a concourse of angels. The very same angels I saw when I first entered the palace.

But, they're not angels.

They walk to me.

They surround me.

They touch my face and my hair.

They're physical beings, not spirits.

"This is your family." The voice of God rattles my soul. "Every person who ever lived and all who ever will are my children," God says. "But you, Michael, are different."

Jesus walks with elegance and grace toward me, His hands outstretched in front of Him.

Smiling. So bright is His smile.

It's the way someone might smile when they have found someone they always dreamt they would meet, but never thought they actually would.

I imagine that's the way Jesus smiles at everyone.

"There is a reason you are here, Michael," God says. "You already know the truth. Now you must accept it."

I'm looking down at a large building at the base of a hill. *I've come back to Hill Cumorah.* I look up, hoping to see Jesus, but he's gone. Below me is staging scaling the hillside. High upon the hill, towering proud over the countryside, stands a monument—a golden statue of an angel, rising tall upon a monolithic granite column.

I'm hovering in front of the monument, the sun gleaming off its golden surface hurts my eyes. I shield my face and gaze upon the angel, who is holding the Golden Plates in one arm, and pointing to the heavens with the other.

President Heber J. Grant dedicated this monument a short

time before his death. I don't know how it's possible, but somehow—as if I suddenly have x-ray vision—I see deep within the monument's outer shell. Hidden inside the angel who led Joseph Smith to the Golden Plates—the ancient record that became *The Book of Mormon*—rests those very plates, along with the stones used to translate them.

Millions of people have visited Hill Cumorah. They flood in and out, paying homage to the angel Moroni and the prophet Joseph Smith, never realizing they're standing in the presence of perhaps the most incredible relic ever entrusted to man.

I'm in Darlene.

It's dark. The plane is falling fast—seconds from impact.

Crystal lays across my lap, curled up to my chest.

Crying.

But she's also saying something.

It's soft. Her eyes are closed and her hands are wrapped around my middle. I can just barely hear her words—

Father,

Save this man. He is good. He is more righteous than he knows. Father, I know who I am. I remember now. I know what's coming. Father, I am scared. I'm scared for Michael. Please Father... Lord, bestow upon him the same blessing you bestowed upon me. I would sacrifice anything and everything to have it be so. Lord, hear me. Please, save my husband.

In Jesus' name,
Amen.

I gasp for air as my eyes open. At first it hurts—like pins being stuck in the back of my neck and in my eyes. I struggle to breathe. There's something over my face. A sheet. I pull it off my head and body and drop it on the floor. My chest is heavy. The room, barely lit, cold. The table I'm laying on is freezing, hard, like metal. The smell, it's strange yet somehow familiar. Like bleach, but there's also something else.

The stench turns my stomach.

Am I naked?

I sit up on the table and place my feet on the floor.

I am naked.

The floor is like ice.

Suddenly there's a commotion behind me and in a mad rush a group of men run up and lie me back down. I feel a pinch in the right side of my neck and immediately a wave of heat envelopes my body and I drift away.

My arms drop like bricks at my sides, the Liahona crashing to the hard checkerboard tile floor beneath my knees, too heavy to move, like someone has dumped a truckload of sand on me. I remain still, gazing at the floor of the tomb and the Liahona.

I died in that crash, I realize.

Then I catch the sight of Mary, standing over me in those white robes, and raise my head, tears streaming my cheeks. "I know," I say with a confidence that I have never felt before. "I understand..." I turn to Peter, James, and John and a smile fills my face and my soul. "I understand everything."

Batnaz laughed as the Disciples pulled Michael DiBianco to his feet, knowing that The Revealer had touched him in a way few mortals have ever experienced. Perhaps now they would again find favor with the Lord. "Welcome, to *The Order.*"

AUTHOR NOTES

First and foremost, I feel it is only fair to let you know that I am a devout, temple-worthy member of The Church of Jesus Christ of Latter-day Saints, and while this book is a work of fiction, so much of what I have written in this novel is fact.

There are indeed many incredibly fascinating tie-ins between Freemasonry and early Mormonism. Joseph Smith and Brigham Young were both high-level Masons, and Joseph did, indeed incorporate much of the Masonic ceremonies he had learned in the Masonic temple into the early Mormon temple ceremonies. While I do believe that Joseph Smith was a true Prophet of God, I also acknowledge that he was a man, trying his best to do the Lord's work.

Joseph Smith found a lot of inspiration from Freemasonry, which helped him put into simple to understand terms for his followers, the revelations I believe he was truly receiving from God. Humans are symbolic creatures. We remember symbols and signs easier (and faster) than we remember most anything else. This is the reason why many Masonic-type symbols and signs were adopted in Mormon temple ceremonies. It helped temple-worthy men and women remember what they were being taught, even if the underlying—far deeper—meaning didn't actually become understood, sometimes many decades later.

Joseph Smith understood that every person learns at their own pace. His job, as a Prophet and Teacher, was to guide the process, and make it as simple as possible for the Saints to remember the symbols and signs, which in time, they would one day fully understand, as the Spirit sees fit to reveal.

It is true that Brigham Young created his own version of the Royal Arch cipher, as depicted in this novel.

It is also a true that Brigham Young had commissioned to have a unique Mormon alphabet created, which the church *did* use for a time—publishing many church pamphlets and books, including copies of the Book of Mormon.

And Money.

Yes, Brigham Young founded The Deseret Currency Association, who produced currency in the form of paper money and gold coins, all backed up with livestock.

The story of David Hyrum Smith is also true. Every bit of it—well, except for the one small liberty I took in having him show Brigham Young the location of *The Unknown Grave*. That was simply my imagination at work.

It is true that Joseph Smith had a tomb built for himself somewhere in Nauvoo. Many experts like to speculate, but no one really knows where that tomb is, only that it was built.

And yes, tunnels underneath the Salt Lake Temple and Temple Square really do exist. The stories told are true. They came from www.utahstories.com. The owner of the website was kind enough to grant me permission to reprint those stories in whole or in part in the novel.

Thank you Richard Markosian.

Sadly, the tomb that Brigham Young built for Joseph Smith

under the Salt Lake Temple is purely a work of fiction. But seriously, how cool would it be if it were true?

There are many Christians who believe that Peter, James, and John are still alive and walking the earth as we speak. Mormon doctrine teaches of this and also adds that there are Three Nephites (Book of Mormon Prophets) who are also still alive today. Those three dudes, sadly, didn't make this story. That said, it is often argued that Mary Magdalene was one of Christ's closest disciples—if not *the* closest. Therefore, it goes to reason that she would have been blessed to never feel the pain of death and tarry until the day of the Second Coming.

And no… The Golden Plates are *not* actually hidden inside the statue of the Angel Moroni at Hill Cumorah, so please… I beg you. Do *not* go there and attempt to find them. That *may* not end very well.

And that SuperSonic Jet, Batnaz likes to fly everywhere… While, as of the printing of this novel, it's still under development. However, it is the real deal, McCoy.

Far as I know, there's not a hidden compartment beneath the pulpit in the Kirtland Temple. I made that up.

And, while much of what I wrote in the prologue actually did happen—an angry mob, did in fact murder Joseph Smith and his brother Hyrum at Carthage Jail—the bit about the secret letter Joseph wrote to his wife, Emma, and him giving that letter to his friend Willard Richards—who was actually there, by the way—that was also a figment of my imagination, designed to breath life to the incredibly fun and painstakingly researched work of fiction—

The Liahona Effect

Keith Katsikas is a devoted husband and father to six wonderful children. He resides in Southern New Hampshire with his family, where he works as the Creative Director and Production Manager for a medical diagnostics and pharmaceutical resource company. He loves to spend time with his family and is blessed to be able to sharpen and fulfill his lifelong passion for writing. Keith has sat at the helm of several corporations throughout his three decades of entrepreneurial experience and is currently the CEO of TopShelf Authors & Books, LLC, the parent company of TopShelf Publishing and *TopShelf Magazine.*